WON'T BE DENIED

a novel by

C.F. Jackson

Organized Thoughts Publishing, LLC

FIRST EDITION

Bottles and Cans, written by Gerald Isaac © 2001. All rights reserved for the US on behalf of Hollow Thigh Music (BMI) administered by Careers-BMG Music Publishing, Inc., (BMI).

Umi Says, Words and Music by Dante Smith (c) 1999 EMI BLACKWOOD MUSIC INC., EMPIRE INTERNATIONAL and MEDINA SOUND MUSIC - All Rights Controlled and Administered by EMI BLACKWOOD MUSIC INC. - All Rights Reserved International Copyright Secured Used by Permission.

Crazy, written by Darrell Allamby and Lincoln Browder. © WB Music Corp., Link Browder Pub Designer 2000 Watts Music, EMI APRIL Music Inc. and Cord Kayla Music - All Rights on Behalf of Link Browder - Admiñ istered by WB Music Corp. - All Rights Reserved used by Permission. (21.5 percent)

Crazy,Words and Music by Joel Hailey, Cedric Hailey, Darrell Allamby and Lincoln Browder (c) 2000 EMI APRIL MUSIC INC., CORD KAYLA MUSIC, LBN PUBLISHING, 2000 WATTS MUSIC and LINCOLN BROWDER PUBLISHING DESIGNEE - All Rights for CORD KAYLA MUSIC, LBN PUBLISHING and 2000 WATTS MUSIC Controlled and Administered by EMI APRIL MUSIC INC. - All Rights Reserved International Copyright Secured Used by Permission.

Library of Congress Control Number: 2004097829

ISBN 0-9762230-0-7

Designed by C.F. Jackson
Edited by Karen Gingerich

Printed in the United States of American

ACKNOWLEDGEMENTS

I thank my Heavenly Father, for the gift he has bestowed upon me. May it shine a light of hope, passion, purpose, and strength in others. Thank you to my mother, Veronika Jackson, a friend and a positive source in my life. Thank you to my first reader, Erica, who forced me to walk outside my comfort zone. Most definitely, Karen Gingerich, my editor. Thank you, again for your help. Appreciation goes to my writer's group for the feedback and encouragement. Much love for my cousin, Penny, for showing interest, support, and love in my endeavors.

There have been educators who have made positive impressions in my life. Dr. Florence S. Ferguson, thank you for keeping your door open for me, even if it has been years since our time at Georgia Southern University. Michael C. Robinson taught me more than I can put into words. His work ethics as my high school band teacher was instilled into my character. Ms. Geraldine Fitzgerald, I thank you for your help with my college essay. Also, for my first short story assignment, even if I got an A minus.

Thank you to all my friends and family who have supported me in some form or fashion and who will continue to support me in some form or fashion.

C.F. Jackson

This is book is dedicated to my grandmother,

Maggie Lee Jackson (1921-1992).

I miss you.

Seek
Courage

WON'T BE
DENIED

To Sharon,

Thank you for your support.
I hope you enjoy it as much as I did
writing. Continue support African American
authors.

Peace,
C. F. Recin

CHAPTER ONE

"The life I have known is burning. Let a gust of wind carry the ashes away," I said with conviction in my voice. It felt like an ending to a beginning—I looked forward to.

I looked out my window to see children laughing and playing in the circular fountain rings across the street at Atlanta's Centennial Olympic Park. I quite often glance out of the two-story school building where I teach to see life in progress in downtown Atlanta.

Today was a great day. I received many gifts and cards from my students. I will see many of them next year, just not in my class. Tomorrow I'll begin working with the preschoolers, which will be a nice change of pace.

After a long day with the kids, I made my way down onto Luckie Street and shouted, "Betty, I'll see you in the morning!"

As I strolled down the street, the sky, once pure blue and empty of clouds, began to darken. I looked up to see the clouds roaring in, thick and with a dirty tint. The sky's pure blue had turned somber.

"Great! It's beginning to drizzle," I said to myself, as I continued to walk. The drizzles were coming faster, steadier, and harder.

Spotting a bookstore, I said to myself, "I better go in here, because a sister isn't trying to get her hair messed up."

While standing in the doorway, I decided I'd go inside and check on a few home-improvement books. I like to be creative with my townhouse. There are a few things I have in my home that just stand out and everyone loves them. I try to tell people to check out the show *Trading Spaces*. It's a great home decorating show.

As I thumbed through a book, I sneezed.

"Bless you."

I looked to my right. There stood a stunning African-American man. He looked through the books on the opposite bookshelf, behind me.

"Thank you," I said with pleasure in my voice.

"You're welcome. Make sure to dust the book before you start thumbing through it," he said with a cordial smile.

Like, whoa, what a beautiful brother. He lifted the spirit of my mood.

"Thanks again," I said, as I continued to look through the book. I didn't want to appear overjoyed by him.

In my head, I went through what I just had a glimpse of. A tall brother, who had to be at least six feet, three inches tall, and his gear suited him well. His skin had a smooth, dark caramel tone. His hair was cut low, with a little extra on top.

His voice caught my attention, but his beautiful smile was also inviting. The tone of his voice resonated in my mind: deep, smooth and strong.

As I stared into the book and thought of this man, I casually looked back over to the right to take another look, to make sure I hadn't missed anything.

Guess what? He was gone. "Damn!" I muttered. Some women can be aggressive. That's not me. I like to show interest in a man to provide him an open window. I guess I'm old-fashioned; I like to be pursued.

I grabbed two books and made my way to find a seat. As I walked, I could see through a window the sky falling in a downpour of rain. I looked around the reading area in the bookstore and it was packed. I guessed everyone must have dashed in from the nasty weather.

Beginning to walk away, I noticed a spot next to the brother who blessed me a little while ago.

I walked over to the loveseat and asked, "Is this seat taken?"

He looked up with a genuine smile. "No, please, have a seat."

I thanked him as I settled myself on the right end of the loveseat.

We sat there, each engrossed in our reading. At the same time, I thought of ways to strike up a conversation. I made a quick jerk as I crossed my leg, and one of my books fell to the floor. The gentleman leaned down to pick it up.

"So, you're into home improvement," he said, looking at the book cover.

That's what I was waiting for . . . my window of opportunity to dialogue with this brother.

"Without a doubt. I've had the opportunity to see Ty, Vern, and Frank from *Trading Spaces* live," I stated.

He looked interested and said, "Really? I haven't taken the time to do so myself. How were they?"

"Amazing! I saw them two years ago, at the World Congress

Center. It was at one of their home-improvement expos," I told him, reaching for my book.

"Many people would be amazed at how much home remodeling they can do for themselves," he said. "I'm sure I don't have to tell you." He paused, then said, "I apologize, my name is Travis. Here I am talking as if I know you like that and I hadn't even introduced myself." He extended his right hand.

"Don't worry about it. My name is Maré," I replied, as I reached to shake his hand for the formal introduction.

His hand was big, and he grabbed my hand, firmly, yet gently.

Before we knew it, we hadn't lifted the books we were reading, for we were conversing on the state-flag issue and what we needed to do as African-Americans.

"To even think of voting on a Confederate flag in the year of two-thousand and four is baffling," stressed Travis. "We are going to continue to slide backwards as a people if we don't vote, stand up, and speak up on issues to bring about change." He had a look of concern on his face and in his posture.

"I'll have to totally agree with you and add that we need to fight as a mass, not as individuals. I don't know why Georgia allowed the Confederate flag to be a representation of the state for so long. So many fought to get rid of it. It's only been about two years since the last governor removed it. The new governor used it as one of his platform promises to get elected."

It seemed as if Travis's eyes lit up with the desired interest in people. He pulled out his laptop and began to read, "The unemployment rate is at its record high of the thirty past years." He looked at me, bewildered. "Why are we wasting time and money on a state flag when there are thousands of Georgians out of work? That flag has negative symbolism."

I scrounged up the nerve to jump into relationships and dating. His cell phone rang.

"Hello," he said as he answered it. "No, I haven't forgotten about it and I won't be late," he said firmly, as he mouthed his apologies to me.

"I understand, and I won't be late," he said. He lifted his arm to see the time on his watch.

The joy and the butterflies dissipated quickly as I saw the wedding band on his left hand. Wouldn't you know it; the good ones are taken.

Travis ended his call and again apologized. "My wife knows I enjoy coming to the bookstore every Tuesday and Thursday," he said as he organized his satchel.

He placed his books and laptop into his satchel. He said to me, "On this day, she chooses to schedule a couples' dinner with friends."

I was still baffled that he was married, though I wasn't sure why.

He stood and stretched out his arm for a handshake.

"Maré, I enjoyed our conversation. Maybe I'll see you again. Good luck in your home improvement projects." With a small smile, he turned and walked towards the door.

I looked out the bookstore window to see him hail a taxi. He was more amazing than I would have imagined at first sight.

"That is a lucky woman, Travis's wife," I mumbled to myself as I turned around in the loveseat.

The thought ran through my mind: At my age of thirty-one, where were the men of that quality? Every woman deserves a man who's attentive, who listens, who's a gentleman, who's a conversationalist, who's intelligent, and who's open to change. Travis seemed to have the qualities that I desired at this time in my life.

****

The dreadful rain came to an end. I slowly made it to my side of town: Decatur. Wow, there was a lot of traffic on Flat Shoals Parkway. It had become congested with the heavy growth in the area. God knows the rain didn't help matters.

I walked through the front door and headed straight upstairs to my bedroom. I felt tired, and I looked forward to Friday. As I prepared myself for bed, Travis ran through my mind.

"God, I'm so ready for that special someone to be in my life. And I know I should be patient, for my prayers, wants, and desires shall come to pass."

I began to read through my journal of poetry. I like to write. It allows me to release my inner thoughts to the world, yet they go unheard. I read through one of my favorite poems.

Comfort
The true feeling of comfort I once had
Something I think of deeply on this day
To walk into her home and know I was welcomed
And without a doubt the door was always opened

I was listened to like I had something important to say

Complete uninvited attention
Much treasured time – not to mention

To know where everything goes once I walked thru the door
My treats were right there every week
Vanilla ice cream, chips & the crème soda
Our days just flowed

Heart's desires met and wants – not to forget
Never asked for much, when I did, I received
To be in her presence, I felt nothing but relieved

Can't say what I gave in return
Remember, I was pretty young

Helped in the kitchen, in the yard,
Anything to be at her side

Never felt as if I was an obligation
What was there – true communication

I seek that feeling I once truly had
A sense of peace, joy, and comfort
Something my grandmother and I only had!

Something about Travis took me back to those feelings I shared with my grandmother. A sense of calmness ran through me. That presence . . . I didn't want to lose it.

CHAPTER TWO

"Good morning, Betty!" I said as I walked through the corridor of Lake Vista Elementary. "How are we doing this morning?"

Betty smiled. "All is well. I'm glad you're able to assist us this summer."

"I'm happy to be here—one, because I love the children and two, I'll appreciate the paycheck this summer." We both laughed and nodded as we continued through the hall.

Today was a pretty slow day. Betty informed me that parents like to bring their toddlers and infants in the second week of summer session.

That was cool with me. Being tired, I needed a lazy day. They must have planned the schedule to fit the small number of children for the day. Betty, Jennifer, and I managed the five toddlers and two infants.

Jennifer took charge of the toddlers. I don't know her too well, but we're cordial. She's a recent graduate from Georgia Southern University, my alma mater, as if that made us friends.

I heard crying, so I walked over to the cradle of little Jordan. He's a gorgeous baby, with light brown eyes, a mahogany complexion and soft curly locks that feel like cotton.

"Aren't you a handsome baby," I said as I leaned over to pick him up. I walked over to a rocking chair and slowly sat with Jordan in my arms. I began to rock him and stared into his innocent spirit. Just holding him relaxed my body, my soul, and my spirit.

"You make sure when you grow up to become a quality black man." I took my pinky and allowed him to grab hold of it with his left hand. As I sat there, I thought how we were all once pure and clean, like Jordan. It's amazing how infants can give unconditional love, and we as adults normally have a motive or an issue tied to ours.

Before I knew it, the time had gone and the day had come to an end. Spiritually, I enjoyed the day, more than I ever envisioned.

It was going on four-thirty and most of the kids were gone. Jordan's mother had come and picked him up at three o'clock. His mother seemed to be very loving, nurturing, and attentive. Remaining were two toddlers, Patrick and Laurie.

"Why don't you head on home," said Betty. "Jennifer and I got everything under control."

"Are you sure you'll be okay?" I asked, knowing how ready I was to go. "I don't want to leave any excessive work on you guys." I hoped Betty would continue to insist that I leave.

"Maré, please go on and enjoy your weekend!"

Shoot—no doubt, I was out of there to meet my girls for some after-hours drinks in Sandy Springs.

"Thanks, Betty. You have a good weekend." I walked toward the door, adding, "Jennifer, you have a good one, too."

Man, that was right on time, as I headed northbound to the top of the perimeter. So far, traffic was tolerable, especially for a Friday. I decided to take the surface street route rather than I-85. You never know how backed up that can be.

Cruising up Peachtree Road, I jammed to my joint "Floetry," a hot CD. I made it to Roswell Road where the congestion was expected.

My cell phone chimed. "What's going on?" I said, as I answered the call. It was my girl, Sonya, who I was meeting at Taboo Bistro.

"Girl, where are you at?" She screamed over the loud music in the background.

"I'm about fifteen minutes from the spot," I answered, as I switched lanes. It really amazes me how many of the people in Atlanta lack driving skills, in my opinion. Where I'm from, North Carolina, people are better drivers.

"All right, then I should be there in about twenty minutes," said Sonya. I could hear her finally turning down her music. "Have you heard from Michelle or Erin?"

"I spoke with Michelle a little earlier and she said she'll be there at five-thirty."

"Well, we all know the first to get there is to get a table in the section near the stage, but near the bar," said Sonya. "Let me holler at you later, this is Adrian on the other line."

Adrian is her husband of two years. He and she really compliment each other's character and personality. I respect their relationship. They have ups and downs like all relationships, yet they communicate very well. As we ended the call, I was much closer to the bistro.

Taboo is *the* spot on Fridays for after-hours. Your best bet is to get there straight after work.

I pulled up to allow my car to be valeted and I noticed that I missed a call on my cell phone. As usual, I was the first to arrive, so I grabbed a table in our favorite section.

I began to call Michelle back to see what was going on with her and to check her destination. "Why didn't you answer your cell when I called?" hollered Michelle.

"You may want to simma down," I said, as I looked through the bistro.

She had tried calling to let me know that she wasn't too far from Taboo, which was cool with me because I didn't want to be sitting too long by myself. Just as I ended the call, the waitress made it my way.

"Hi. Is there anything I can get for you?" she asked, as she pulled out her pad.

Not to be sitting there, looking lonely, I decided to order a drink. "Yeah, let me get, um, a watermelon martini."

I began to think about Travis out of the blue. I knew somewhere deep within I was hoping to see him here. I have not ever had a man to leave such a strong imprint on me with his first impression. Well, maybe tonight there would be some quality men up in here.

Not even thirty seconds after the waitress brought my drink, I saw a brother walking in my direction.

"What's up, shorty?" he said.

You see? This is what I'm talking about. I can't stand it when I'm approached with garbage like that.

"Yo, I was checking you out when you came through the spot," he claimed as he took it upon himself to sit down.

"Is that right?" I questioned, taking a sip of my drink.

"Yeah, you caught my eye with your dark chocolate skin, that petite frame, long hair, and your smile took my breath away."

I don't know if I was being hard or what, but that was very cheesy. My skin tone is more of an almond anyway. I just thought: *Dude is trying too hard.*

I looked around for my girlfriends. "Well I appreciate all the compliments," I said.

"Baby Girl, you seem shy. I know you not here alone. Are you waiting for your man?" he asked, as he wiped his brow with confidence.

He wasn't a bad looking brother, but he wasn't at the level I was seeking. He had that nappy hair thing going on, with beautiful dimples. Overall, I wasn't impressed with his approach.

"I'm waiting for my friends, who will be here shortly." I peered at the door.

"I had to let you know how beautiful you were. And that man of yours better treat you right."

A smile appeared on my face from the kind words of the brother. "Thank you. I appreciate it," I said in the most warming voice.

"My name is L.A. and I hope a I get a chance to holla at you later tonight."

Just as I began to answer, "We will see," I saw my girlfriends enter the bistro. "My crew is here now."

L.A. walked off with a little extra pep in his step.

"Mm-Mm, who is your little friend, Maré?" asked Michelle, as she leaned to give me a hug.

"Girl, you know how the brothers are at the clubs." Everyone continued to embrace each other with hugs to say hello.

Taboo Bistro is known as a quaint place to socialize and have after-hours drinks. It is sectioned off into intimate settings. There is an area with red sofa chairs that are arranged in an arc around half the dance floor. Additional yellow chairs compliment them well. Dim lighting allows illumination from the candles on the coffee tables to accent the mood. They also have a phenomenal live band.

Everyone began to order apple martinis. All we know is that on Friday nights, martinis are two dollars.

"The sad thing about it, is that a man can have it all from a woman, if he treats her with respect. Women aren't that hard to please, but the brothers make it out to be like the SAT: overly *complicated*," said Sonya.

"He was all right, just didn't like his approach, with the 'shorty' thing. I'm too old and classy for that," I replied.

"Michelle, what happened to Tony?" I asked suddenly. She had been vibing with this guy for several months and from what we all could see he was on point.

"You all wouldn't believe it. This dude was calling me like he had lost his mind," said Michelle, as the waitress dropped off another round of martinis.

"How did this happen?" asked Erin, as she reached for her drink.

"You were truly feeling dude and all was well," added Sonya.

Sonya is the only one married in the bunch. She tries to feel our pain, but she has been out of the game for over five years, since finding Adrian, the love her life.

As Michelle went into her story, the bistro began to liven up. Many more men began to roll through and, of course, the sisters, too. I could feel my martinis take effect on me. I had hoped I would scout some quality prospects with the intensity of Travis. Man, those martinis were working my mind and body.

"Anyway, we were calling each other on a regular," continued Michelle. She liked to share her stories. How she gets up and goes is something I admire about her. She does many things I want to do and goes to places I want to go. She is a true independent woman. Like me, very strong, educated, well rounded, and beautiful.

"One particular night, I didn't feel like being bothered, so I turned off the cell phone and the ringer on the home phone."

"Girl, you feel that way on some nights," said Sonya.

"Since that night, Tony has called abundantly and it drove me crazy," said Michelle with frustration.

"He was trying to keep tabs on you and you all hadn't even defined the relationship?" asked Erin.

"You know how I work. No stress! Do you feel me?" asked Michelle.

We all raised our glasses to that, "Without a doubt!"

Michelle will dismiss a man if the relationship isn't what and where it should be for her. She feels, at twenty-nine years of age, time is a-wasting.

"Ya'll, I met this brother yesterday at the bookstore, who was out of control," I said, as I ate the cherry from my drink.

Erin looked intuitive. She probed, "Out of control?"

"Yes. He was fine as hell and his voice took over my mind when he spoke." I smiled with delight. I'm sure the martinis added a bit more joy to the memory of the encounter.

"Well damn! I hope you got this brother's number," said Sonya.

"Girl, dude was married," I stated, frowning to express my dismay.

"What?"

"Yeah, we were talking about the flag issue and I was all up in his grill." I laughed at myself. "Then his cell rung, he looked at his watch and, BAM, the ring band!"

"You didn't see it before then?" asked Erin.

"Nah, each time I was next to him, I just so happened to be on his right side."

Sonya still seemed astonished as to what made this man extraordinary. "What was it about him?"

"It's hard to explain, Sonya, but he gave me a feeling that made me glow inside and it was something I wanted to feel over and over."

"Well, we all have experienced that. Most of the good ones are taken and married," said Michelle with a timbre of despair. "Why can't that one be yours, you know? Ya'll know I don't condone cheating with committed men. I'm saying why can't he be mine or why couldn't I have found him first?"

"I feel you on that. Travis is a premiere man." It seemed like, out the blue, the bistro became louder and apparently no one heard what I said. I repeated it and left out his name. Don't know why, but I didn't repeat his name.

The bistro had become filled with many folks on that Friday evening. With the completion of the band's second set, many people began to get their dance on, on the dance floor. I felt the beats of the DJ's mixing of the old school and new school.

Apparently, so did a sister in hip-hugging cargo pants and a light blue, ribbed, button-down shirt. She took freaking to another level. With an attractive man, well dressed, who appeared to be somewhat conservative and intelligent, she wanted to dance as if she was at the infamous Gold Club that used to be off Piedmont Avenue.

The young lady had her butt up in his crotch and he seemed uncomfortable with her dancing. She was working it too hard to gain the man's attention. Lovely sister and she sold herself short for the sake of getting a man. I've seen that often. Is that something we have to do? It's ridiculous to me and it's not that serious.

Most of us desire that quality man to go home to every night. The one who values our strength, our beauty, our intellect, our spirit, our soul, and our capability to nourish a seed.

Once again, I found myself thinking of Travis, with hopes of finding someone in the bistro tonight that could possibly fit his virtues.

As we continued to enjoy the hot bistro band, we skimmed through the spot to see what was there. Nothing or no one had caught our eye. I guess we hadn't caught anyone's eye either.

Before we knew it, it was going on one-forty in the morning. We must've definitely enjoyed our ladies night out.

"Hey, are you all okay to be driving home?" asked Erin as she grabbed her purse.

"Girl, I really don't feel anything from those martinis. I'm telling ya'll, these drinks are watered down." Sonya has a very high tolerance when it comes to alcohol. Sometimes I tease her by calling her 'Alcoholic'.

"Yeah, I'm straight to head down the road," I said, as I stood.

We all made our way to the parking lot and waited for the valet to bring our cars around. While standing there, Erin made eye contact with a cutie.

"Now how did I miss you tonight?" asked the brother, as he walked toward Erin.

You can't tell Erin that she's not Ms. Cool when it comes to getting her mack on. Now, after a brother leave, she flips and loses her coolness with over-joy. I've known Erin since our high school band days and she has always been that way. She's an outstanding woman. The aura that she spouts has nothing but peace and calm. Erin has the most beautiful dreadlocks, which accentuates her lean, toned physique. Her smile burns strength. She exudes confidence, humbleness, beauty, and a soul of tranquility when in her presence.

"Obviously you didn't miss me. You're talking to me now," she said to the man, as she looked out for her car.

"Wow, you are a gorgeous woman and I know you're on your way home. I'd hate to hold you up. Is there a possibility we can exchange numbers, so we can politick at a more convenient time?"

His approach and demeanor impressed us. It wasn't like we were intentionally listening, but they were right next to us.

Erin keyed in his number. "What is your name?"

"Wow, I apologize for not making my acquaintance known to you. My name is Ezekiel Thomas. I wanted to make sure I didn't miss this opportunity."

"I'm Erin and I guess we'll talk soon," she said, placing her cell back into her handbag.

"Most definitely," he replied. He walked away.

"Mm, he is a cutie," I said. He was Erin's flavor when it comes to the visual of a man. He had the Philly-Neo Soul sorta glow going for him. He was hip-hop, but he dressed it neatly, not overdone. He had the body of a football player.

"You know how men do: put their Oscar-winning act on to gain your interest and then flip the script on you, so let's see how he does. I'm not going to lie. He has sparked my taste buds."

CHAPTER THREE

I awakened about eleven-thirty that morning with nothing planned for my weekend. Most important thing to me, when it comes to weekends, is being happy. I get my happiness by being lazy, staying up late, and pretty much doing whatever floats my boat. Not having to work is the extreme joy of it all.

Once I made it downstairs, I grabbed some orange juice out the fridge, turned on the television and lounged on the sofa. Time to cable surf and fit in a nap.

I recently completed redecorating my living room with all the flair I wanted. I love how the room pops with subtleness. I painted my walls lavender, allowing the stoned wall from the fireplace to stand out. To soften the affect of the wall, I found a colorful striped sofa, the same color as the wall, with splashes of red, orange, green, and yellow. I love to walk into a room that's warm and inviting; my desired focus.

I placed a unique eighteenth-century curio trunk I found at an antique shop as an end table. I also added a large blue sitting chair to compliment the sofa. To keep it bright, I placed foliage around the room. The room breathes life and plants do add to the motif.

I decided to keep my entertainment area simple, with the television and stereo located in a deep wooden armoire. The room allows me to set a mood of all sorts, just as long as I get the light right.

I began to surf through the channels and the phone rang. *Now who could that be?* I wondered, as I picked up the phone to look at the Caller ID. It was Erin calling. "What's going on?" I answered.

"Nothing too much. I was calling to see if you were up and percolating."

"Barely. I'm tired as all get out. I'm going to keep my black butt right where it is: at home," I said, as I laughed along with Erin.

"I spoke with the dude from last night and it seems like he may have some business about himself."

"What? When did you two speak? It's not even twelve o'clock," I proclaimed. I reached for my juice.

"Actually, we just hung up. He wanted to talk, so he called. He gave me the run down."

"Okay, let me hear it," I said. I turned down the volume on the television.

"Well, he's thirty years old, originally from Virginia, and he lives in the Peachtree Corners part of town. Where's that?"

"You know where that is. That's up off Peachtree Industrial and the top end of Interstate 285."

"Oh, okay. Anyway, no kids, and he's never been married. He recently opened up his own business—a coffee hut—about six months ago in downtown Decatur. He wants to bring live music and poetry together. That's about it, and we made plans to get together on Tuesday."

I could feel the glimmer of happiness in her voice.

"Sounds like a winner most definitely. No doubt. You may have met someone who could possibly be equally yoked with you. Did you tell him you wrote poetry?"

"No. I don't want to place the blueprint out for him to see everything. I'm going to let him see a little at a time. If he sees too much at once, then he'll know how to maneuver too well without effort. I did let him know that you and Sonya did."

"See, there you go. I don't know why you told him that I did. You know how I am about the penning of my thoughts. As far as his coffee house, it sounds good to me. Maybe he'll have some friends he can hook me up with," I said with a smirk.

"I was calling to fill you in on the Ezekiel situation, but I'll give you a shout later."

As we hung up, the phone rang again. "Unknown number" appeared on the Caller ID. A telemarketer, so I ignored it.

I began to watch a movie that had been on for sometime, and before I knew it, I fell asleep.

I dreamed that everyone I know had met the men of their lives and I remained single. As I looked at them with joy, deep inside I thirsted for the feeling of being deeply in love and married. My soul ached with dreadfulness for the need to be loved.

Oddly, I felt my inner soul weeping. I began to cry uncontrollably in front of everyone. Everyone started to console me and wanted to know what was wrong; hysteria and rage overwhelmed me. Before I knew what had taken place, I went out of control.

I became angry because everyone had something I had yet to obtain at the age of thirty: love and marriage. It seemed as if I was nowhere near. Everyone looked bewildered at my actions and were at a loss for words.

The phone rang and it awakened me; again a telemarketer. I lay there going over my dream because it seemed surreal. The emotions from the dream lingered in my being. I looked over and it was five-ten already. I was more tired than I had realized.

I stretched and yawned to get my blood flowing. It helped remove the feelings I got from the dream. I wasn't sure what was going on with me. Emotionally, physically, and spiritually I yearned for love. Love of that man who could supply those needs and wants I was unable to provide for myself.

Lying there, I allowed my mind to wander to what I could do to attract appealing men. I have high self-esteem, being that I accept myself for who and what I am. People have complimented me on my petite body and my youthful look. I work out when I take the time because my petite size is genetic. I keep myself well groomed from hands and feet to teeth. My style is very casual, more like a J. Crew flavor. But there are times I step out the box to be flashy.

I remember how everyone reacted when I wore a stylish outfit. A cute pair of black hip huggers, topped off with a backless, eggshell-green shirt. The attention I draw like that I want briefly and then I'm content.

I love how attractive it felt when I stepped out like that, but I like to do that in moderation.

Now, the day I met Travis, I sported my standard work gear. I had on a gray, two-toned, half-sleeved light sweater and gray pants.

But it's important for a man to see me within, is my true belief.

I wanted to see Travis again and allow him to fill me up. The brief time we spoke, I overflowed with emotional, physical, and spiritual nutrients. Maybe that's why I thirsted so—I needed to be replenished.

I rolled over and grabbed my drink. The feelings were amazing. It was like the air; I felt it, but I couldn't see it. I wanted to see it and feel it. Hmm, I may have to do a drop-in on Tuesday, to get my vitamin of Travis. He did say Tuesdays and Thursdays . . .

"I'm about to turn into a stalker," I muttered, sitting up and rubbing my eyes. *Nah, I don't think that's it. Someone so amazing has given me a feeling that's extraordinary. I want to experience it again.*

"God knows that I won't mention this to my friends."

I headed upstairs to shower. Being that I had been in my pajamas all day, it would be nice to clean my bottom.

The aroma from scented vanilla candles filled the bathroom. As I stood in front the vanity, I heard the neighbor's twins, Darren and Derrick, playing. I looked out the window and saw the five-year olds playing on their swing set. I drew the curtain to the tub and began the shower.

"Once I get my white pedestal sink and finish painting, I will be happy," I thought. The colors I have chosen for the bathroom are a light pastel green, trimmed in white and with white hardware.

I took my shower and enjoyed the massaging of the water on my body. I could've used a pair of real fingers, those of a man, touching my body to remove any and all the tension. I stood with my back to the showerhead to allow the pulsing of the water to caress my back.

"Ah, this feels good. Better if it was the real thing."

CHAPTER FOUR

Three days later, I left work with high hopes of running into Travis. It was pretty hot. I believe the school thermometer hit ninety-three degrees.

I entered the bookstore, wanting to appear casual and not like a huntress. I walked towards the magazine section in the front portion of the store, near the espresso shop. As I skimmed through the magazines, I heard a voice.

The voice spoke in a different language, but it lifted my body in a way I recognized. I looked around and I saw him. In the espresso line speaking with someone in Spanish, stood Travis.

"Oh, my God, tell me that this man is not bilingual. Tell me he hasn't taken my infatuation to another level."

The man spoke as fluent as a native of South America. He stood there even more attractive than he appeared last week. The more I learned about him, the more I desired him. Or, someone like him.

I picked up a magazine and walked into the aisle. I crossed into his path as he walked from the espresso shop.

"Oops, excuse me."

"Hey, how are you doing? How are your home improvement projects going?"

My heartbeat tripled because he remembered me. I was astonished that he would.

"Ah, pretty good. You remembered—impressive. Excuse me, I almost ran you over. I apologize. What is your name again?"

I had to play it cool. To say his name after five days of our first encounter would be extreme.

"It's Travis."

He tried to recall my name, which was cute. He got the first letter correct, the name itself, far off.

"If my life depended on remembering your name, I'd be dead right now," he admitted with a smile and with a smidge of laughter in his voice. "However, your face—I would've survived."

Just being in his presence made me feel special and unique. I loved how he gave me his full attention and his remarkable his eyes.

For some reason I thought of my grandmother. As a kid, I spent a lot of time with her. She gave me a lot of attention, more than I could've asked for. When I spoke, she listened. I don't remember her responding too much, but her stopping what she was doing to listen meant a lot.

Those were the same feelings I had talking with Travis. That man knew how to give of himself and wasn't selfish about it.

As we stood there, the guy Travis had been speaking with walked by and said something to him in Spanish. Eloquently, Travis acknowledged him and responded. Quickly his attention returned to me.

"Wow, do you speak Spanish fluently?" I asked.

He made a gesture suggesting we walk towards the sitting area with his right hand that contained his espresso.

As we sat, he said, "Yes, I speak it very fluently, as well as German. I have to keep myself above the game, when it comes to journalism."

"You are a journalist? I'm sure being bilingual is very beneficial for your career. To have the capability to speak fluently in German and Spanish must've taken dedication."

Travis looked humble to my compliments. "Thank you. It's something I was determined to achieve when I began this journey. I was given many opportunities that allowed me to accomplish many of my goals. I spent time in Argentina and was able to grasp the culture, more than just the language."

This man had the strength and willpower of a lion taking on his prey. Travis sought out what he wanted and took on all obstacles to get it. As he spoke I could feel his unwavering heart beam with purpose.

"Wow, I'm sure that was an experience you won't soon forget. Are you a writer for the *Atlanta-Journal Constitution*?" I asked, moving the magazine to the side.

"I've been a writer for eight years with the *AJC* and I recently became the editor of 'Be About It', my socially conscientious column. I have my writers find stories that we as African-Americans need to 'be' about and stop 'talking' about. I like to challenge them, as well as myself."

"Okay, I'm feeling that. I haven't heard anything about it. None of the black radio stations have mentioned it."

He nodded in total agreement. "Exactly. That's why I've recently been given the opportunity to air 'Be About It', every Wednesday on

WLAT – 93.9 FM at nine AM."

"Congratulations. That's something our people need to be hearing, instead of all this hip hop and negativity. You're truly an activist."

Right then and there, Travis stole me, the entire me, not just my heart. He is a man on a mission in his life, and so far he has completed each task.

"Thank you. My wife was excited, too, but she doesn't want me to take on too much. Our goal is to be balanced in our lives, not to allow one element of our lives to outweigh another," he replied, as he continued to drink his espresso.

Okay, there he went, mentioning his wife, ugh, like that's a topic I wanted to discuss. I looked as cordial as possible, at least I hoped. The mentioning of his attachment brought a feeling of torture within my being.

I couldn't figure out why I allowed myself to become attached to a man who had no interest in me. I was sure he's truly committed to his wife and an affair wasn't what I desired anyway.

"Enough about me and my career; Maré, tell me about you. What is it that you do?" He looked directly into my soul, as if we were the only two people in the bookstore.

I smiled with joy. "I'm a third-grade teacher at Lake Vista Elementary off of Luckie Street."

"You're the heart of our future. I like that, shaping minds and spirits. Something I admire. How challenging is it to maintain the focus of third graders?"

Quickly, my eyes skimmed the bookstore as I looked for the culprit of an enormous outburst of laughter. Then I said, "Thank you. There're qualities that make up a person where it's part of their nature. That's how I feel about teaching. Many of my friends ask me that and they find it hard to understand. I'm seeking to have my own school, filled with a staff dedicated in the growth, advancement, and well-being of each student."

"I'm impressed with your goal. The youth of today need that, a school that has individualized focus. Have you begun to make this a reality?"

"Not yet," I said, feeling less accomplished than he.

"Why not?" He looked into my eyes for the answer. "You can do anything you put your mind to. It's yours for the taking. What are you waiting for?"

"I don't know. To be honest with you, the fear of it not being a success."

With a stern look, he said, "You'll fail yourself and the children who need you if you don't try. Maré, don't let fear hold you back from trying what's in your heart. You have to go after what you want. Too many black people dream and allow it to slip away through the seams of doubt and fear. Again, what are you waiting for?"

He was right, my being scared and playing it safe. At thirty-one years of age, what was I waiting for?

As I rubbed my left shoulder, I looked up at him and said, "You put it out there Travis. I have to be honest with myself. Fear has been the main factor. I've allowed it to not put this dream in motion."

"Remember this. I've been using it for years: 'The difference between dreams and accomplishments, is purely desire.' It has gotten me through many storms of doubt," he shared, as he smiled with inspiration in his eyes.

I repeated it to show him I'd listened and understood him. Another factor for not starting my own school was I lacked the help and support.

"Thank you for the motivational coaching, Travis. I truly appreciate it. We all need that push in the back and you've opened me to food for thought." I glanced at my watch.

Whoa, it was going on eight o'clock, which surprised us both.

"I hope I didn't interrupt your day here," I said, as I stood.

"No way. I enjoyed our conversation, without a doubt."

We made our way to the entrance, and as I'd expected, Travis opened the door for me. I thanked him. As I stepped onto the sidewalk I began to look for the city's transit system, MARTA.

Travis flagged down a taxi and looked at me. "Maré, it's getting dark out here. Please let me drop you off at your car. Is that okay?"

"Are you sure? I'm heading to the MARTA station at Peachtree Center. I hope I'm not taking you out the way," I said. I jumped into the taxi.

He slid in behind me and slammed the door. Travis directed, "Driver, Peachtree Center please, then *AJC*." Then he turned to me. "I offered and I'm glad to do so. I wouldn't dare allow you to walk down this street as I drove off. That isn't acceptable for me as a man, nor as Travis." He spoke firm on his point. Nice to see chivalry was still alive. "So do you take the train to work?"

"I do both, the train or car, it all depends on my mood. The train allows me to be around others, instead of being solo in the car." I noticed the taxi driver's name tag and read, Shabbir Mohammed. "How about you?"

"Same here. I drive on the days I visit the bookstore. I leave the car at work and take a casual stroll down. I like being among the people, too."

We got to my location and I was definitely not ready for the evening to end. Travis stepped out of the car to allow me to get out at the curb.

"Again, thank you for the ride, Travis."

"You're welcome," he said, as he smiled. "Don't forget to check out the program in the morning on 93.9 at nine and tell your friends."

"I sure will." I waved goodbye as the taxi drove away.

The train ride home was pure nirvana, with a double dosage of ecstasy.

CHAPTER FIVE

With the summer session in full swing, the number of children had flourished to three times what we had my first day. The staff had also increased, with the addition of Andrea, Marcus and Renee. I appreciated having color added to the staff.

I knew I was needed, but I had to find a spot to listen to Travis's show, without any interruptions.

"Excuse me, Betty," I whispered out of earshot of the others. "I have an emergency and need to run to the bathroom." I gave the *universal* look that all women can pick up. Granted my menstrual cycle wasn't on, but it was a good enough excuse to be gone.

Betty's the lead teacher for the summer session. She's a mature white woman who is very giving. I tried not to get into her personal life, but I do know that she's divorced, with two kids. She's always whining about how she's not happy with her weight. Unfortunately, it's not a pretty sight. Her body is shaped like an egg and her face has a weathered look about it. I'm unsure of her age, but I'd guess her mid-forties. Yet her warmth and genuine personality show beyond any external flaws.

I made it down to the first floor bathroom. As I reached into my purse for my Walkman, it turned nine o'clock. I walked around to clear up the static. Right next to the third stall it came in crystal clear.

I heard the DJ say, "This morning we're shooting off a new segment, 'Be About It'. Travis Atkins is our commentator of this weekly editorial."

For the first time I knew his full name and it sounded extraordinary. It was like playing the *Wheel of Fortune*, trying to figure out the puzzle. Once I put my puzzle together, I'd be a winner, for sure.

"Many of you may already know him from his work in the *AJC*. Check him out in the *AJC* and every Wednesday morning at nine o'clock, right here."

I stood in the bathroom with my mouth wide open and my attention totally on Travis's voice. It mesmerized my mind. As I caught myself, I quickly closed my mouth. His entire segment was exceptional. It was filled with as much strength as the conversations we'd had.

I was moved with pure joy from the pleasure of hearing his voice. My mind, spirit, and body had been sprinkled with fruitfulness only he could give. As it had been from the initial meeting, my being was lifted into a hemisphere greater than earth.

When I returned to the classroom, I placed my purse into my locker. "Is everything okay?" asked Betty.

The look of curiosity sat on her face, probably being that my conduct had elevated drastically since my bathroom visit. I hoped she wasn't thinking the worst of me. People are quick to preconceive situations. I really couldn't worry about that; I was filled with Travis.

"Everything is just fine, thanks."

I looked over to see two of the kids shoving each other as Andrea looked on without interjecting herself.

She has been irking me with her funky attitude since she began the summer session. Andrea attends Clayton State College and this job is a requirement to be accepted into the last portion of her degree program.

I walked over to mediate the two toddlers. As they walked off, I said, "Andrea, could you please be of more assistance with the children? We don't accept pushing or fighting!"

She rolled her eyes and released a sigh. You would've thought I spoke in a foreign language because she didn't acknowledge me.

"I'm here. I don't bother nobody; no one should be bothering me," she replied, picking at her fingernails.

This was no surprise, since this is the air she burns off every day in here. Nevertheless, I was shocked by her ignorance.

"Let me bother you this brief moment. I suggest you listen. Betty, Jennifer, and I determine your grade for this job. If you don't want to be bothered, it's all good with us. We will grant you with the grade you deserve. Right now, it's an F."

Looking up with her lips poked out and flipped, she replied, "Whatever. You don't scare me."

"Believe me, it wasn't to scare you. It's a fact. So with this lazy and funky attitude, I suggest that you either straighten it up or move on. There're others who are waiting to replace you. These children need attention, not insensibility."

I'd decided to not cater to people. I agreed with all that Travis stated that morning on his radio show. He said, "Be strong in your conviction for change." He had the best sayings, like that morning: 'Lead, Follow or Get out the way.'

That's it—my motto for this summer. Already I had stepped out of my box by checking Andrea on her juvenile and unprofessional behavior.

"Andrea, I'm here to assist you. This is what you are going to school for. Your lack of interest and participation is trifling. If you're truly feeling this way, you may want to re-evaluate your career goals," I proclaimed, as I walked away.

I hoped I made some sense to her. I could sense an inkling scratching through her surface.

CHAPTER SIX

As I sat in traffic on Peachtree Road, I called Erin to check on her hot date. I searched for my hands-free headset while the phone rang.

"Where were you last night when I called to give you the rundown of my date?" she asked.

She threw me with that question because I couldn't be honest. That wasn't even an option, to let anyone know of my infatuation. That's what I'll label it now, with Travis. I hated lying to her, but it was something I was ashamed to share.

"Ah . . . what time did you call? I was home yesterday, unless you called when I was in the shower."

"It was about nine o'clock. I didn't leave a message."

"You should've left one. Anyway, what's the 4-1-1?" I asked, with hopes that Erin felt my explanation.

Everyone I know is locked on my habits and schedule. I don't like that at all and the questions I get if I'm not home.

"Maré, it was fantastic. We met up after work at Sylvia's off Central Avenue, downtown. I haven't been there before. It was the perfect night. They had this jazz singer there who was accompanied by a pianist."

"That is a very nice restaurant. The food and atmosphere is very ethnic, with a touch of elegance," I said. I had been there before, with a group of friends some years ago.

"Right! We talked the entire evening without a glitch. He's an intelligent brother who appears to be a rarity amongst the worn-and-torn men in this city. Ezekiel writes poetry here and there. Before he branched into his own business he was a graphic designer. The name of his spot is Café Sacrifice because he gave up his comfort zone to step into the unknown. He feels that many of the poets and artists are doing the same when they step onto the stage.

"I see him as that four-leaf clover that sits in the midst of a field of dandelions. When you pick it, you see its perfections, distinctiveness, and why it was strangely in this field all alone," continued Erin, breathing in deeply to sample her feelings all over again.

I wanted to shout with her, how I understood her feelings. I, too, have met someone who fills me up. The feelings are overwhelming and they're similar to those of drug addicts who take a hit of crack and become addicted. Yet, I had to remain secretive about my addiction.

"Sounds fantastic! I hope that this works out because you deserve it," I said, filled with slight envy of her possibilities.

"Don't we all deserve real men who truly want to be in a committed relationship?" asked Erin.

As I made it onto I-20 East, I said in a soft, concurring voice, "Yes, we do—yes, we do."

"You know Sonya got me married to the brother already and with three kids." She chuckled.

I was excited for Erin, but jealous, which I didn't like. I'd better check myself before it became obvious to her or anyone else.

"We know how she is. So what's next on the agenda for you two kids?" I asked.

"I'm unsure. I know my plans are to take it slow. I don't want to jump into this feet-first and not use my head. Develop the friendship first and we are doing pretty good, so far," assured Erin.

"Keep yourself focused and things should be just fine. Hey, when are we going to check out his spot? You know we like poetry."

"I don't know, I haven't made it down there yet myself. It'll probably be a minute before I get there."

"Where are you headed now, Erin?"

"I'm going to the gym. As matter of fact I gotta go, I'm here. I gotta keep myself fine as wine," she said, as she laughed.

I laughed with her. "Yeah, I forgot, you have to work at it. Go and get that sweat on."

I continued to drive home. My mind was filled with nothing but feelings. I've never been as perplexed as I'd been lately. I was having the hardest time stepping outside of myself to see why I was struggling.

Confusion isn't healthy and the feelings I had for Travis weren't tolerable. But I wasn't even trying to fight them.

My insides were discombobulated, like a small town hit by a tornado. Everything in the town that was once grounded was now spinning uncontrollably in the air. Only thing one can do is wait for the tornado to lose its strength. No matter what, the town won't be the same. Everything will be disarrayed when it hits the ground.

To bypass my thoughts and feelings, I turned up the radio. All was fine until I began to sing along and before I knew, I was feeling the words of KC & Jo Jo's song:

> *"I'm just going crazy, crazy, crazy*
> *Just thinking about you lately . . .*
> *I'm going crazy, crazy, crazy*
> *Just thinking about you baby*
> *Now I've finally realized*
> *That you are my true love*
> *And I had a lot of time to think*
> *And you're all I seem to keep think, to keep thinking of, yeah*
> *Now I know I need you*
> *Each and everyday…*
> *I can't live without you . . ."*

Out of nowhere, I began to cry as I sang. They were tears of pure frustration and anguish over Travis and my feelings. More than anything in the world I wanted a resolution to the pain I had come to know.

My tears rolled profusely down my face and the odd thing about it, I wasn't sobbing. It was all the weeping that my spirit had been feeling that burst out. The song ignited my feelings that I had locked up. I couldn't control the tears, and to be honest, I didn't want to. It felt good to my soul.

To be in control is what I'm known to be. I can't say when someone who I know has seen me cry or has seen me in a weakened state, in my eyes. In some form or fashion, I saw not having control over my being, at any given time, as a flaw in my character.

I've always had to be strong. The day my mother walked out, it was like my life never missed a beat. I didn't go through a period of grieving, sadness, or anger. It was like there was never an emotion connected to that moment in time. My brother was nine years old, I was five at the time, and he would often speak of her.

My father never stood as the full man that he used to be. She selfishly took part of him with her.

I, myself, won't acknowledge that I ever had a mother, other than my grandmother. She gave me all the love and affection I needed as a youngster.

Until now, no one had lifted me like my grandmother did. It bewildered me that I craved the love of Travis more than anyone.

This confused me to the point of allowing my mind to take control, allowing it to get what my body, my heart, and my spirit desired, by any means necessary.

CHAPTER SEVEN

Weeks had gone by since my mental outburst and I tried my damnedest to wean myself off that man. I was seeing the turmoil it was causing in my life. However, I wanted him even more than before, because I could see my strength of mind slipping away into a stage of unconsciousness.

I attempted to get myself back on track. I returned calls to my friends speedily.

Michelle harped on my MIA status. There was nothing for me to say other than being caught in something that I am now able to grab a hold of, so it seemed.

My friends mean a great deal to me. They're my extended family. To lie to any of them is a hard thing for me to do.

Wednesday mornings had become as transparent, as Scotch tape. Job or no job, I had to hear Travis's radio show.

"Betty, I need to run down to my car, I think I left some construction paper. I'll be right back," I told her, as I scurried off to the parking lot.

"Good morning, and welcome to the 'Be About It' segment, with our commentator, Travis Atkins," said the DJ.

I sat in my car with the window down. I could feel my body anticipate the sound of his voice. It was like everything in my body paused. It could've been from the heat because it was hot as hell outside.

"Good morning, my people. The key phrase for today is 'Positive Attitude.' I look and listen; I hear an enormous amount of infested negativity from the mouths of black people. We are quick to say what you or someone can't do. Why is that?" stated Travis.

I sat and hung onto every word he spitted, as it fed me.

"It's time, people, to change your attitudes. The mind is a powerful vessel. It's a vessel that can take you anywhere you want to go. Clean it out of all the self-doubt and fear. Yes, you, clean it out and replace it with determination, strength, heart, courage, and desire. You think negatively, then, so shall those thoughts come to pass," he said, as he closed out his segment.

I started to glisten from the heat, but I hadn't quite noticed. If I had, I might have hurried back into the school. Instead, I leaned back in the driver seat to let what Travis said marinate in my mind and my body. I could still hear his voice ringing in my ears.

The sound was something I had missed, like some good freshwater fish.

I realized that I had been away from the classroom as I jumped from my peaceful position. I knew I didn't have any paper in the car and again I had lied to Betty.

As I headed up the stairwell there came Mr. Eugene Walker. He's been the janitor at the school throughout its existence. With a shortcut afro with a few specs of black in it, he stood there with a mop and bucket. As always, he wore his overalls and work boots.

"Good morning," he said, with a look of concern on his face.

"How are you doing, Eugene?" I asked, as I made my way up the second set of stairs.

"Oh, I'm doing just fine. It's you I's worried about. You sitting out there in that car."

I could see the redness in his eyes. I could smell the liquor on him, too, but that's Eugene. No matter what, he's at work and doing his job. He's a tad bit nosy.

"Aw, I'm fine. No need to worry about me. You have good day." I continued up the stairs.

Just as I entered the classroom, Jennifer gave me an odd look and so did Betty.

Jennifer walked over with that same look on her face. "Maré, are you all right? I know we don't talk much, but you have seemed very occupied lately. If there is anything I can do, please let me know."

"All is well. Thank you for wanting to help, but I'm fine," I replied. I smiled to show her.

I was just fine because time had come to stop fighting what I had been hiding inside. Time to let my mind steer me into getting what I wanted.

CHAPTER EIGHT

Thursday, Sonya called regarding plans for a get together at her house in Lawrenceville. She and her husband have a nice home, but it is so far outside metro Atlanta, it has deterred many of my visits.

Adrian was doing a gentlemen's night out, so Sonya wanted company. This would allow for us to get together, chill, have some drinks, eat, and bond.

I was the first to make it over to Sonya's house. As I turned off the ignition, I laid my head back on the headrest and took in a few deep breaths. I prepared myself for the questions that I would be stormed with from the girls. I must keep my composure: answer the questions with the appeal of being real. These women will drill you.

"Yo, what's up?" was the greeting from Sonya as she closed the door.

"Nothing too much. So Adrian is hitting the streets tonight with the boys?" I asked as I removed my shoes in the foyer.

"Girl, yeah!"

We headed into the kitchen where she had started preparing some of the dishes for the night. I jumped in and took over on the chicken fingers.

I got the recipe a few years ago and made it my own. I did a dash of pepper and salt into the flour. In another container I put two eggs scrambled together with milk. I dipped the chicken tenders into the egg mix, then the flour, and then into the hot skillet.

Just as I finished, there came the greedy crew.

"Smells like someone's grandmother in here," said Michelle.

Erin, peeking through the lids on the stove, said, "Ya'll have been throwing down?"

"Damn right," insisted Sonya. "You two need to hop to it and get the drinks rolling up in here."

"You all didn't buy the entire liquor store?" I said, walking over to sit down at the table.

"Well, we figured we could have some options this evening, being that it's all about us tonight," laughed Michelle.

Michelle mixed up some blue martinis, which helped set the

night right. And I was feeling good. I was out with the girls and back to where I should be, on track.

Everyone filled themselves up on the chicken fingers, pasta salad, fries, shrimp, and drinks.

"Hey, next weekend or whenever, we need to make it down to Ezekiel's café. I went down there Thursday and it's very nice. The décor is very calming. He has a lot of earth tones that bring in that mood. You walk in and straight ahead is the cappuccino/bar. He hasn't decided if he'll serve more than cappuccino and wine. Then you have your tables and chairs. Up near the front is the stage," said Erin, gleaming with pride.

Michelle picked up her fourth martini and said, "You know we can do that."

We nodded to concur with Michelle's statement.

"Maré, what's been going on with you lately? You've been on some craziness," said Sonya, looking at me for the biography of my world over the last couple of weeks.

I knew it was going to come and no matter how much I prepared for the oodles of questions and stares, I wasn't ready. If it were a job interview I could sling out perfect answers left and right. Mainly, I don't care about the interviewer, I am trying to get the job and I don't have any personal ties to them.

Trying to look as baffled to the question as possible, "Huh, what?" I said.

"Come on Maré, don't act like you don't know what she is talking about," jumped in Erin.

"Ya'll got me on some okie dope stuff," I retaliated. I tried to perform for the role of best-leading actress.

"We knew you would come off like this, where you don't want to share. If you got a male friend, that's cool, but you don't have to lie to us, your girls, about it," Sonya strongly suggested in her tone.

"Nobody ain't lying about anything. What are you seeing?" I asked, becoming a tad hostile to the interrogation.

"Maré, I've noticed a change in your demeanor. You don't return calls like you normally do. It just seems like you are occupied with another life."

Erin was right! To tell her and the others that they were right wasn't going to happen. Knowing them, they would fade off into tonight, but it wouldn't be the end of it.

"You all make me sick! I've been researching my dream of opening my own school. It has me up late, in the library and on the internet. I'm working on my business plan," I told them, looking around to see their expressions.

Michelle glanced my way with an empty face. "See, you trippin' because you could've said all of that from the beginning."

"No doubt, instead of us going through the twenty-one question game," said Sonya.

Erin looked hurt and puzzled as she leaned forward for her drink.

"I just wanted to do this and keep it to myself. I was going to tell ya'll, but I wanted to get the logistics all mapped out first," I pleaded, as I felt a little relieved.

Erin never said any more about my reason for my change. I was unsure if she expected more of an open line of communication when it came to our friendship. Or could it have been that she didn't believe me?

It concerned me because she knows me better than Michelle and Sonya. I never want to cross the friendship line with her. With my thoughts and feelings of Travis, I knew it wasn't worth my time to discuss them with her or anyone.

CHAPTER NINE

We all slept over at Sonya's house. No one could afford to leave her house after a night of drinking, so that was already in the plan.

The house is beautiful, with four bedrooms, a full basement and a sunroom. Hardwood floors throughout the home accented the vaulted ceilings. Sonya and Adrian are taking their time to add their personal touches to the house. Adrian already changed many of the standard items that the builders used.

It was a bond-filled weekend as we began cooking breakfast. The beautiful grayed Corian countertops complimented the stainless steel appliances in the kitchen.

Michelle did the bulk of the cooking, which was lovely. However, Erin and I got screamed on for not pitching in with the cooking, so we handled our business and cleaned up everything.

"Sonya, that was right on time, this ladies' pajama jam," I said, as I gave her a hug.

"It really was. Even though our old butts fell asleep around twelve," said Sonya, as she burst out laughing.

Michelle looked up as she tied her shoes. "Girl, those martinis will do it to you every time," she added.

Erin still had something about her going on and it was directed toward me.

Opening the front door, Erin said, "We have to do this again."

I headed out to my Honda. As I pulled off, my radio blasted. I didn't quite feel the drive home. Duluth Highway to Decatur is a fifty-minute trip.

It was a beautiful Saturday morning. The sun was bright and there wasn't a cloud in the sky. The morning air sprayed a scent of fresh and new. *With the windows down and the breeze touching me, the ride home shouldn't be that much of a hassle*, I thought, as I noticed I had made the wrong turn.

"Damn it! That's why I hate coming up here. Let me turn around."

I noticed a Sports Authority sign up the street in a shopping plaza.

"Let me check on something, since it's right here," I said to myself.

I recently messed up my favorite pair of Nikes when I washed them. Even though I don't wear them all the time, I couldn't allow myself to go without having a pair available at my beck and call.

"Welcome to The Sports Authority," greeted a redheaded employee, as he smiled.

I smiled cordially and thought how cheerful he appeared. I began looking through the shoes, mainly the prices. What these places want for sneakers has to be a crime. I saw a cute pair, not as cute as my old ones, but they were do-able.

I tried them and they fit pretty well. I liked the gray and navy blue combination. The Nike swoosh was on all four corners of the shoe.

"Hmm, this will do." I flipped it over to check the price. "Ninety-two dollars! I'm not the one. They must've lost their minds."

I decided to look around, since I was there and not buying anything. I enjoy sports, at least the ones with excitement. I played around with a heavy punching bag they had displayed. I didn't go full-force like I would have liked to, being that people were in the store.

I thought about buying a basketball, thinking it would be a good workout to shoot a few hoops. I haven't watched basketball since all the dynasty teams broke up. My favorite was the Chicago Bulls. Shot a few hoops, too.

I strolled through the football section. It's amazing, all the equipment they need to play football. As I began to put on a pair of gloves, I saw a sales rep walk by. I gave a warm nod with a look saying, I don't need any help.

She continued up the aisle, as if knowing that I wasn't a buying customer.

The gloves were amazing, how they have the capability to grab onto stuff, like a suction cup. Right on the label it read, "One hundred percent leather palm to provide superior grip . . ." To put them to a test, I picked up a football, a basketball, and a baseball bat. Nothing slid or slipped.

Many more of the NFL football players need to invest in a pair. Many dropped balls and fumbles could be alleviated. I laughed to myself, knowing if were that easy, everyone in the league would have a pair.

As I exited the door, the same chipper redheaded guy gave me an exit greeting, "Thank you for visiting The Sports Authority."

Again, I gave a cordial nod and smile as the automatic doors glided open.

CHAPTER TEN

There I was, returning to what I had fought so hard to end. Who was I kidding? It had only been two weeks, but I felt it had been an effort.

I decided that I wouldn't seek out Travis today at the bookstore; I would allow myself to be visible. I determined to sit in the reading area in the middle section. The bookstore is airy, yet it can become congested. There are many places to sit throughout, but the seats in this area are more comfortable and they're near the window. It gave me an eye to the outside, as I maintained an eye and ear to the inside.

I hoped my assumptions proved to be right today. I hadn't seen him and I was ready to be engulfed in his presence.

I chose to get a book about starting your own business. I still had self-doubt, but a man like Travis doesn't have time for a woman with flaws, such as fear. Surprisingly, the book caught my attention.

"Hello. Is this seat taken?" he asked in strong tone.

Due to my focused attention, I hadn't heard what was being said. "Excuse me," said the same voice.

Feeling slightly disturbed, I looked up to answer, "N-n-o-o."

"Stranger! I haven't seen you for some time," he said, looking down as he smiled.

My heartbeat pulsated as if it were going to jump out of my chest and begin to break dance. This must mean I made a connection with him and my lack of presence here hadn't gone unnoticed.

"How are you doing? Have a seat, unless you have something to do," I said, organizing my stuff.

"I'm doing well, thank you. What are you reading that is so enticing, where you couldn't hear the room?"

It felt as if I was in high school, with one of those schoolgirl crushes that wouldn't go away. Where the boy poked fun at your name and you still felt as if he was dreamy. Even the one when the boy never truly knew how you felt, but his kindness of speaking was enough to ignite your soul.

With hopes that I wasn't looking stupid and with a huge Kool-aid smile, I said, "I'm reading, 'How to Get Started: Make Your

Dreams a Success'."

"Ah, you jumped on that, I see. I'm impressed. Glad to see that you're working to make your dream a reality. Make sure not to allow the obstacles to end your journey. Keep at it until the end," said Travis.

"You said a lot of things that have been food for thought. Your radio show is outstanding. It just piggybacks you, Travis. I have the opportunity to somewhat know you, unlike many of your listeners; they don't know your genuineness. I'd like to think what I've come to know of you is true."

It was like something had come over me. Like there weren't any obstacles when it came to me wanting this man in my life. I knew what I said was more than an observation of character. These were my feelings and I wanted to make sure he was real.

"You were able to hear the show? That's fantastic! I appreciate your support. Maré, I try to be just me, a man with a purpose. There's enough mayhem in this world. I feel like, why do I need to contribute to it? It's my job to break up as much of the mayhem and be part of the solution. I'm not perfect. I make the perfect effort to be a good black man," he proclaimed, with a look of honor on his face.

This man has taken his life to be a true testimony of faith and purpose. Travis makes his stand on strength, awareness, peace, and knowledge. I wondered why I couldn't get enough; he exudes all these characteristics and more.

I was at a loss for words; he knocked me off my feet. "That's something we all should seek to achieve. Not only as black people, but as a world." I knew that wasn't the greatest response, but I had to say something to end the silence.

"Well, it's something you have to work at, and be determined to swim against the current in the ocean. Too many people would rather float along with the current and complain about everything. Stop conforming and be real to yourself. It's hard to do, believe me," Travis preached, as he smiled to lighten the mood.

"I'm sure it is. We were taught to conform and it actually began in school. It has become a part of our being. To break that mold is a trying task, especially when you have the forces of conformists, like friends and family, lacking the acceptance of your change. Then you're more likely to falter. Why not? It's easier to swim with the current."

Travis listened attentively to every word I said. He appeared awed by my statements, yet I could tell he agreed with me.

"Maré, you're so right. The challenge is to modify our minds as a people." He gave me a look that said, "It sounds impossible, but it has to be done."

I allowed myself time to inhale and exhale to his statement, then replied, "That would be a major movement and a miraculous accomplishment. That would be lovely."

Taking a moment to look away, I saw an old white couple who appeared to be in their eighties. It's hard to tell at times.

They both had pure white hair and skin as wrinkled as crumbled pieces of paper. They slowly sauntered to the exit as their fingers interlocked with each other. I could only imagine how old their love could be. The man seemed a little frail, yet he held the door open for his love.

That's the type of love that never becomes content. The sort of man who values his wife's virtues and does what he has to, to guard them at all times.

Looking back over to Travis as he spoke, I could see that type of conduct from him. His personality is so passionate in all that he does I could only imagine him as a lover.

CHAPTER ELEVEN

Thoughts kept running through my mind that were unacceptable, unlike the moral fiber of my being. Having my thoughts be consumed by one image, of one person, and one feeling, was pure chaos.

I knew it and I had to deal with it. I knew I wanted this man more than life itself. At this time I felt that I wouldn't be denied the love; the relationship; the man; the family; the joy; and the peace, all of it.

These feelings I have inside won't be denied, my inner spirit cried.

I found myself sitting outside of the *AJC*, Thursday evening, waiting for Travis. I decided not to go to the bookstore that day. There were other items on my agenda for the evening.

I felt a tad bit silly sitting there with a dread locked wig on my head and a of pair glasses. I didn't want to appear suspicious to anyone passing by. Fifteen minutes had passed and I was becoming a little anxious. *Could the delay be a sign for me to forget about it and go home?* I thought to myself.

"Lord, is this truly real? Forgive me and please protect me," I begged, as I removed the glasses and rubbed my eyes with my left thumb and index finger.

As I placed the fake eyeglasses back onto my face, I saw a taxi stop in front of the building. I slowly pulled myself up to get a better view of the passenger. Travis stepped out of the car and waved to the driver and began walking to the parking deck.

I set my posture as straight as a ruler; there wasn't any time for sloppiness. I was unsure of what type of car he drove, being that he was financially set. A red convertible Volvo exited with a white man in it.

My eyes remained fixed on the parking garage. I felt a little parched. I feared one unfocused move was unacceptable. I took a deep swallow and a quick roll of my neck.

A winter-green SUV rolled out. It was Travis. I began to drive along behind, staying back at least four car lengths. He was in a Jeep

Cherokee, cruising. We came to a traffic light and it gave me time to take a swig of my water.

We hit I-85. I became somewhat astonished by my actions and by what I had in mind. I drove in complete silence. The only noise I heard was the tires rolling over each break in the highway, and it sounded like a horse galloping. I didn't want anything to break my concentration.

He took the Ashford-Dunwoody exit. As I began to exit, my cell rang. My top lip went up and a sigh released from mouth, but my eyes remained on Travis's SUV.

I was familiar with the area; to the left was the Perimeter Mall and across the street from it was the Crown Ravinia Hotel. The traffic flowed smoothly, but was still a bit busy for the evening hours.

I began to think to myself and wondered what I was doing. The weirdness of my actions had a strong hold on me.

We began riding through a residential area. Two cars were between us as we came to a four-way stop. I quickly examined the neighborhood and I was impressed. The sunset rested parallel to the horizon, which allowed me to get the gist of my surroundings.

Travis turned left and I slowly followed behind him. He turned into a driveway of a beautiful home. I continued to drive, careful not to bring any attention to myself.

"Wow, what am I doing here?" I said to myself, as pulled over at a side street.

I sat there. I relaxed my head on the headrest and my arms slumped in my lap. My eyes were completely closed and I didn't have a care of my surroundings. I should've cared, being that I was a black person with a dreaded wig on in an unknown neighborhood.

I gradually took in several deep breaths through my nose and released them at a snail's pace. It helped to relieve some of the tension that had built up in my shoulders.

"Ruff, ruff—ruff."

I quickly opened my eyes to see a heavyset teenager in cut-off jeans and a tank top, walking her dog. Becoming aware that I needed to head home, I turned around in the cul-de-sac.

I figured my best bet was to take the route that I had taken to get there. I drove past Travis's home again and I felt a bit of a connection. It was like completing a jigsaw puzzle. I was putting something together, not quite sure what the picture would look like, but with high hopes for it to all perfectly coming together.

CHAPTER TWELVE

"Hey, what's going on?" I asked, returning Erin's call. One of many.

We still had a stint between us, but I refused to raise the question. I didn't want to lie any more than I had to.

"I was calling to see what was going on with you," said Erin.

Breathing a sigh of relief, I realized she sounded normal. "Nothing too much. Working on making my dream of opening my school a reality."

"I can see. I called you on your cell phone and you didn't answer. Making this dream into a reality got you into a zone."

Erin said it better than I could. I had been in a zone when it came to my feelings and to Travis. Tonight was an extreme instance of being in that zone.

As I chuckled to lighten the conversation, I said, "Don't call when you see me on the Essence's Awards. This school is going to be one of a kind."

"It had better be. It got you temporarily in a space," said Erin with slight disgust in her vocals.

"Anyway," I said to brush the focus off me. "How are things with you and the mister?"

"All is well. I must say, he's been consistent. I know it's early in the game, but I'm happy with what it is now. I don't cramp his style and he's not all in my face. It's wonderful how well balanced it is at this time. Astonishingly, he hasn't pushed up on me to be intimate with him. We've had some toe-curling kisses and that's been enough. It feels lovely to be courted," said Erin.

I felt her ecstasy. "That's what I'm talking about. Ezekiel appears to be a rarity, Erin. I'm looking forward to visiting his spot Saturday. It's this weekend, right?" I asked.

"I'm going to confirm with him sometime tomorrow and I'll let you all know. I know ya'll will enjoy yourselves. I look forward to everyone finally meeting him," said Erin with a smile bursting through the phone.

Erin deserves the best. As a project manager with Georgia

Power, she has her career in perspective. She has been on some shaky grounds when it comes to relationships and love. Hell, who was I to talk? Look what I succumbed to tonight.

"Let me know. Maybe Michelle, Sonya, and I will ride and can get lost together."

"You're not going... Hold on," she demanded, as she clicked over to her other line. "Not to be rude but you know I gotta go," she said, with glee in her voice.

"Oh, it's like that now? You're going to kick me to the curb for some brotha?" I said jokingly.

"At the time being, yes ma'am." Erin and I chuckled some more. "I'll talk with you later."

It felt good to have normalcy back in my world for the moment. My actions had been too disgraceful to even repent. I knew I needed to get myself on track, but I didn't want to. I wanted to see where it would take me.

I'd lived a life as straight and narrow as a pushpin. To take pride in my character was what my grandmother instilled into me. She always said, "When you die, it's not going to matter what you got or where you went; it's going to matter on who you were."

Gran preached that to me and my brother all the time. I didn't want for nothing, when it came to material things. Gran didn't have a lot, but she would spoil me every now and then. I didn't expect anything from her, but her time and that was worth more to me than anything in the world.

When she died, my world came to a halt. I felt as though my insides were sucked up with a vacuum, making me ache. My emotions were a blanket of sadness and uncertainties: that suffocated me with one breath.

I cried for days. I moped for weeks before I was able to cry for joy. They were tears of joy, knowing that I was blessed to have had Gran in my life. No, I wasn't ready for her to go. I recognized I was selfish to have never imagined my life without her.

All that I did as a kid was mirrored to make her proud of me. I wanted to be able to give back everything she gave to me, and more.

I think of her all the time now and wonder if her proud, light brown eyes watch over me. I know the way I have been acting recently is something she wouldn't gloat about.

"Gran, I apologize for my actions lately. Yes, I know better than this," I said with disgrace in my eyes and tongue.

CHAPTER THIRTEEN

The summer had turned into a scorcher. Today's temperature was expected to hit ninety-eight degrees, per my favorite meteorologist, David Chandley. Being in the downtown area, it was going to feel worse because not much air whisks through the tall high-rise buildings.

It seemed as if the attitudes between Andrea and I had transposed between us. Andrea lifted herself and had become very active with the children. As for myself, I had become a tad bit lazy. Far from trifling because I still cared for the kids; however, the enthusiasm for being at work was agitated by my thoughts of Travis.

To get myself to a peace-filled state of mind, I walked over to pick up my favorite baby, Jordan. He lay in his crib, cooing to himself.

I sat with him in one of the rocking chairs that were arranged in a row. I could hear the noise around the large room, but as I began to stare into his eyes, my surroundings disappeared. I saw nothing but stillness in Jordan's eyes.

Sadness thumped my spirit. Was there doubt in myself, of achieving pure happiness? Overwhelmed, I exploded with anxiety to be all of what my heart desired Maré to be.

Jordan's face became blurred from my tear-filled eyes. To collect myself, I began to run my fingers through his hair, to get into his unsoiled spirit. As he smiled, so did I. All the corrupted feelings began to leak out slowly, like a flat tire.

"Ms. Maré, can I hold the baby?" asked a stringy haired toddler name Brittni, as she ran onto my foot.

"Oh, no, babies are very delicate and they aren't to be played with."

With her lips poked out and her left finger heading towards her nose, she asked, "Can I touch him?"

Brittni was the most persistent child there. All the kids ask a thousand and one questions, but not her. She'll wear you down. To prevent it from getting to that point, I wanted to see where she was trying to go.

"You have to be very, very gentle. Feel how I touched your arm and how gentle I am. That's how we touch babies." I could see excitement on her face.

Brittni cocked her head to the right as she caressed Jordan's left arm very slowly. All of her focus was on making sure she followed my directions.

"Ms. Maré, I did it and he smiled at me. That means he likes it?" she asked.

"Fantastic job at following directions. He really liked it. Now remember, you don't touch babies without an adult. Okay?" I instructed, with a demanding look and soft voice.

"Yes," as she skipped off to the play rug.

"Phew," I muttered to myself.

That could've been an all-day saga with her.

These kids take me out of that tunnel of negative thoughts. It's impossible to remain there with children camped all around.

I returned my attention to Jordan's eyes. "Thank you for helping me." As I talked he was cheesing at me. If he only knew how much he'd helped me, Jordan would probably charge me.

I looked up and there was his mother. This woman looked phenomenal, as she sashayed in my direction.

"How is my little man?" she asked, removing him from my arms. "How are you doing, Maré?

"I'm doing good, thanks. As always, Jordan was perfect," I said. I marveled at her Toni Braxton's 1992 haircut.

"Jordan will see you all first thing Monday morning. I have to be to work earlier than normal. I plan on picking him up earlier, so he doesn't have to be here any longer than usual," she said.

"We'll be here. You have a good weekend."

There she went. She had a Jones' New York flair about her style. With all she had going for herself, she was still down-to-earth. With Jordan's cheerful personality, I could tell his parents gave him much love.

I wondered if Travis's wife was like her, the "corporate America" sister who's very successful, yet who hasn't lost reality of whom and what she is. Black. As handsome as he is, there isn't a doubt in my mind his wife stands out, as well.

CHAPTER FOURTEEN

"You need to make a right at the next light, which should be North Decatur Road. The directions say you'll see it immediately on the right hand side," instructed Sonya.

We made it down to Erin's new man's café, to see what was going on. As Michelle drove and Sonya co-piloted, I enjoyed the ride in the backseat. Not too often do I have the opportunity to be chauffeured.

It was a beautiful night. The sky was pure dark blue and accented with sparkling stars. They lit up the sky as if they were fragments of diamonds. A light gust of warm summer wind made me feel spotless, inside and out. It's amazing how the night air can set the mood of an evening.

As usual, Michelle had her stereo blasting. Being in the back, it sounded like she had it turned up to extreme. Not to hear her mouth, I rolled with the flow.

"Wake up, Maré," yelled Sonya.

"What are you talking about? Can a sister just chill? Damn!" I said jokingly.

"Leave her alone, Sonya. I'm surprised she even made it out tonight," said Michelle. She glared at me in her review mirror.

"Whatever, nobody ain't thinking about ya'll." I closed the car door.

Downtown Decatur was packed. We'd never been down there together, just kicking it. I was looking forward to seeing what was going on.

"Whoa, Erin's man doesn't have it going on, does he?" asked Sonya.

To her surprise and ours, there was a line at his spot, Café Sacrifice.

"I'm glad Erin hooked us up," I said, as I stepped onto the curb.

Already Michelle was speaking to the man at the door. Erin placed our names on the list so we could walk right in. I guess we were VIP.

I could see the man looking at a piece of paper as Michelle

pointed to it. Just that quick, she motioned for us to come on. I could see the attitudes on some of the faces that were in the line. I probably would have had one, too, but not tonight.

"This is very nice," said Sonya as she looked around.

Erin's description didn't give the place any justice. Maybe it was the vibe we were getting by being there. Whatever it was, I know we all loved it.

"Let me call Erin's cell, to let her know we are here," said Michelle.

There I was in a black-owned establishment that spawned an air of sophistication. It was nice having a northern flair in the south. But as I absorbed more, it seemed like it had a taste of west cost, too.

Aztec colors set up the entire café. Straight ahead, like Erin said, was the bar. Each table was illuminated with a single chrome coil, dispensed from the ceiling and holding a light the size of a fist. White linen tablecloths were a beautiful touch of elegance.

I continued to mull over the style of this café as I noticed Erin, smiling and waving erratically.

"Hey, there's Erin over there," said Michelle, zipping up her purse.

We had VIP treatment for real. Ezekiel rolled out the red carpet for us. We sat in the best seats in the house. Each of us were impressed with the bottle of chilled wine awaiting our arrival.

"Erin, your man had already won me over with the cut in line treatment. But girl, it's on with this wine," said Sonya, with laughter in her words.

"Thanks, Sonya. Tonight is the hot night for him. He said he's been working hard to promote the café so he could grab the right clientele."

"I'm truly impressed with his décor. How did he get all of this set up?" I asked, as I continued to pan the room.

"I know. He did a fantastic job. He said he had a vision and this is the outcome. Let me go get him."

"I'm so happy for Erin. I hope this works out for her. Ezekiel has brought a much needed new flavor to the A-T-L. And has the capability to be successful," said Michelle.

"Most definitely. I know Adrian would love this place," added Sonya. She poured herself a glass of wine.

"How is . . .?" I was interrupted by Erin.

"Everyone, this is Ezekiel. Ezekiel, these are my girlfriends, Michelle, Sonya, and Maré. The sisters I talk about," stated Erin, as she smiled and held his lower back.

"Thanks for coming and checking the place out. Yeah, Erin talks about you guys all the time. It's nice putting a name with a face," he said, looking into Erin's eyes and grinning.

"We're happy to have been invited," proclaimed Michelle. "We're very impressed with everything."

"Yes! You have a winner here and I hope the best of luck for you. I'll make sure to pass the word around," praised Sonya, as she placed her purse on the back of her chair.

"Thank you so much for your compliments. They mean a lot to me."

I returned my attention to our conversation and away from the stage jazz band. "I'm glad to have a chance to officially meet you. We've heard a lot about you and your café. Like they were saying, it's very impressive."

"Erin said you all were very supportive. I can see why you're her friends," said Ezekiel, as he was tapped on his shoulder. "Enjoy yourselves. I have to attend to some things."

Ezekiel walked off quickly with one of his employees. I assumed so, being that the brother was wearing a crew shirt embroidered with Café Sacrifice on the back.

The time came when the attention was focused on the spoken word artists. Many of them were good, but some I didn't like.

Erin leaned into the center of the table and whispered, "This sister right here is good."

"Good evening, everybody. For those who don't know me, you can call me Sister Purpose. I got a poem for everyone tonight that I want you to feel:

Your House

Is there a chance that I can be your house?
I can see all the detailed thought that
Is placed there, no doubt.

Water my soul, so my spirituality can grow.
Prune my mind, to see its uniqueness.
Open the door to find a path that will allow me to
Walk beside you, may it be carpeted, vinyl or wooden.

Paint my mind of the images of your world –
Only those you wouldn't dare
Smear or blot on any other girl!

Replace those fixtures of my heart
With some the things you did from the very start.

Drown me with the overflow of creativity
To better represent your house to those
Who are there or somewhere near
Share the time to mow away any
Doubt or negativity

And fertilize me with culture growth
And security
The time put into this house, will not be
In vain
To become your house, to watch you enter
May it be sunshine or rain

Everyone applauded her skillful flow and use of imagery.

"Thank you, my people. Like I said, feel it and think about it. Peace," she said, exiting the stage. She tossed up her peace sign to the audience.

"She was nice. I liked that piece," Michelle said. "Erin when are you going to get up on that stage and recite some of that love jones poetry to your man?"

"How you know I haven't already?" asked Erin, as she blushed.

"Handle your business, Miss Thang," I said, as I cheered her on.

"Anyway! When are you two going to get up there?" asked Erin, eyeing both Sonya and myself.

"I would love to, but I don't have the nerve. Hell, Adrian hasn't even read half of my pieces," said Sonya looking to her left, as she pondered. "What about you, Maré?"

"That's not me. I like to write to release my thoughts. I can't imagine sharing my innermost thoughts to you all, let alone strangers."

"Okay, it's here whenever you're ready. I'm sure Ezekiel won't mind," stated Erin, before walking off.

This was another perfect night with the girls. As usual, we represented ourselves in the most stylish and mature manner. For black women, we enjoy . . .

"Maré, have you noticed the brother, three tables up and to the left? He has had his eye on you for a minute," insisted Michelle.

"Not really. I made eye contact with him once and thought nothing of him. If he likes what he sees, he can make his way over here," I said in a nonchalant tone.

I must say, the brother was attractive, but more is needed for me to go crazy these days. Sad to say, I didn't feel needy when it came to having a man in my life.

"Maré, don't act like you're not interested," Michelle said.

"Look at him, with his flawless smile, dark auburn tint, and his full round eyes," whispered Sonya, with a touch of lust.

"How is everyone doing this evening?" asked Ezekiel, returning to the table.

"Everything is great," I replied as I looked at his huge smile.

Ezekiel began waving his left arm. "Come on over."

Surprisingly, it was the black Adonis whom Sonya found attractive. He was in the flesh and not three tables away. From what I could see, nothing was different up close.

"My sisters, this is one of my homeboys from Virginia, Hollis," said Ezekiel, grabbing his friend's left shoulder roughly. "These are my girl's friends."

Hollis must have had some interest in me because he was very eccentric with his glance. He acknowledged all of us, but his eyes paused on me much longer than the others.

I found it appealing to my inner child, of needing and wanting that attention. I love flirting; it gives me an illusion of my attractiveness and allows me to play.

However, I wasn't quite sure what to do with him, if his interest was real. I knew that Travis already had all of me, even though he was unaware of it. The feelings I had inside could not be easily erased and replaced.

Michelle and Sonya stepped away to head to the bathroom, so they said. It was their plan to leave Hollis and I alone. I'm sure with high hopes, they expected something to come about between us.

He moved into the seat next to me. "How ironic is it that you know my friend Ezekiel? You caught my attention, when you entered through the door. I had no idea how I was going to approach you. My boy really hooked you guys up."

"I really don't know Ezekiel. He's dating my friend Erin, so we're here through her."

"Okay. Are you enjoying yourself so far? I must say this is a hot joint. I like the upscale flava."

So far, Hollis seemed pretty cool and someone who I would normally have interest in. He's attractive, like Sonya pointed out. As we continued to converse and played the questions game, a thought came to my mind and it had to be asked.

"Are you living in Atlanta or are you still in Virginia?" This question would clear things out, quickly.

Looking and speaking with this brother, I didn't have a reason for not pursuing the possibilities. To keep everyone off my back, I had to act like a desperate, single, black woman.

"As a matter of fact, I am sorta doing both. The company I work for in Virginia is in the process of relocating here and I'm working to get that completed. I'm here in Atlanta, unofficially," he said, as if he saved the day.

"Are you leaving family and friends behind? I'm sure you're going to miss them."

"I will, no doubt. But with this job market being as saturated as it is, I have to go where the money goes. My mom and dad are fine with it. You know family. Now they have somewhere new to visit."

As we laughed together, I could see Sonya and Michelle making their way back to the table. You would have thought they had fallen in, being that they were gone for what seemed like weeks.

Hollis began to return to his seat. "You are fine where you are," said Sonya. She winked like she was doing me a favor.

Apparently, Michelle ran into a guy she met some time ago. They had lost contact and they were catching up on old times. She went on about how this dude was the best and how happy she was that she bumped into him tonight.

The evening proceeded and everyone had a ball. I was so impressed with Ezekiel; I didn't have the time to be envious or jealous of Erin's relationship.

"I would like to call you sometime and take you out," Hollis professed.

That's not what I wanted to hear. I didn't want any more confusion in my world at the time. But living this double life was hell.

"That sounds cool," I said, trying my hardest to be genuine.

CHAPTER FIFTEEN

It was the break of dawn on the following day and I could see the smog clouds rising over the city of Atlanta. I guessed it was going to be a bad ozone day.

I woke up with Travis on my mind, wanting to know how his weekend was going. I cruised on highway I-285 and there was little traffic. That's about one thing that was constant—traffic.

My eyes popped out of my head as I cruised through the neighborhood. My memory must have been an Intel Pentium, to remember how to get back there. Travis's neighborhood looked quaint with the sunlight peeking over the horizon.

Every yard was meticulously mowed, not one weed to be seen. It was extraordinary to be in a community where every homeowner maintained their property. Just riding down the street gave me a home-felt feeling.

There it was—Travis's house, and it was manicured from yard to trees. The beautiful, plush green grass magnified the huge maple tree in the center of the front yard. The house stood out as well, as the tempered blue painted home was accented with burgundy storm shutters. The two-door garage accentuated the his-and-her image.

I drove past the house, trying not to bring attention to myself. I turned onto the same street as I had before. The entire subdivision looked like photos out of a *Better Homes and Garden* magazine. As I did a three-point turn, there was a slender, blond headed woman mowing her lawn. From what I could see, everything was intact in her yard.

Two houses away from Travis's, I decided to park over at Dunwoody High School, diagonally across from his house. I sat in the huge parking lot, not a soul in sight. It was me and a small school of birds chirping, as they played in the nearby trees.

As I stepped out of my car, I saw an old man with a white tank top and black shorts jogging along the front of the school. He appeared to be focused, with his mp3 player on his right arm.

I was not sure what I was looking to gain that morning. Did I really believe I would see Travis in the midst of his comfort zone, home?

I dropped my head and looked at my sneakers. "This is crazy."

The front door opened and my breath was taken away. It was her. His wife walked out the door.

My entire world came to a stand-still. I wondered what she looked like and if I would ever see this woman, the one who stole Travis's heart before me.

She walked down the red brick steps. She wore a silk blue robe and black bedroom slippers. I stood there gazing at this woman from across the street, through shrubbery. You'd think I was right next to her.

Her dark beige skin accentuated her petite physique. I could only imagine how elegant she would be in her best dress. Her short-cropped hair added a metropolitan touch. Just looking at her, I could tell she wasn't from Georgia.

She ran her hand through her hair as she leaned over to retrieve the newspaper. Turning to head back into the house, she glanced through her neighborhood.

"Damn!" I said in a low voice, as my heart raced with excitement and anxiety. "I can't even playa hate on her. She is beautiful and that's her get out of the bed, pillow face, and stink breath, look."

The world that Travis had was perfect. Perfect.

As I got into my car and drove off, I noticed a kid who looked to be about fifteen years old beginning to mow his lawn.

I made it back to the main streets. My cell phone rang. "Hello."

"What got you up and out before noon?" asked Erin.

There she was again with the damn questions. When will there be a time when no one cared about my location!

"Just out running errands." Aggravation was on my tongue as I replied.

"Erin, I really enjoyed myself last night. That café was out of control. I give Ezekiel many props on it. And you looked pretty happy, too."

"I know. He did a wonderful job and I pray that it continues to multiply. It seems as if you made a big impression on his boy Hollis. After you left he was asking about you. Wanting to know if you were single, about your personality, if you had any kids. It was like playing Trivial Pursuit."

I knew my response to her statement was going to be analyzed from A to Z. My intention was never to hurt anyone.

"For real? Who was he asking, you or your man Ezekiel?"

"Me, while Ezekiel and the crew cleaned up."

"What did you say?" I asked, not wanting to be in this conversation.

"You know—the standard. She's a really cool person. At this time she's single. I told him that you're an independent woman. That may scare most brothers, who aren't ready for you."

"Um . . . We'll see! He has my number and he knows what to do with it." Hoping he would thrown it away.

Erin continued to run her mouth about nothing. My cell phone beeped in with another call. I didn't feel like being on the phone with her, let alone talking with Hollis, so I ignored him.

I came to another realization that my feelings were deep for Travis. Most days on the highway, I'd hit at least seventy miles per hour. Today was an exception as I cruised. I wasn't in a rush, as a sixteen wheeler passed me.

Over and over, the image of Travis's wife spun through my head. What I did today was like a scene out of a movie. Every day I experienced new thoughts, ideas, and actions. I was alone in this world of pandemonium I had somehow fallen into.

No one knew the script or the dialogue, but the main characters were right there in my face.

CHAPTER SIXTEEN

"Yes, may I speak with Hollis?"

"Hey, thanks for callin' me back," he said, with cheer in his voice.

That's the single life. To have anticipation of someone feeling you, as much as you're feeling them. If that's the case, then you are overjoyed to chat with them on the phone.

Men anticipate, just as much as women do.

"You're welcome. I'm not a rude person," I said, as I giggled softly.

"I really enjoyed talking with you last night. After you left, I had to do a run-down on you. I drilled your friend Erin with a lot of questions."

"I guess her answers were to your liking. Is that how I made it to the phone call level?"

He hesitated to reply. He wasn't quite sure where I was coming from. "I wouldn't say that. I was curious and I wanted to talk about you."

"Hmm . . . Let me get my information from the man himself. I already know where you're from. How about the basics: children, age, career, single, and expectations."

That came out of nowhere. My technique in flirting wasn't usually so straightforward. I liked how it sounded. Hell, I sort of turned myself on.

"Okay, you got me. Um. I'm thirty-three years old. A single black man, that includes no wife or girlfriend. I don't have any children. I'm a consultant with a software firm. Finally, my expectation is getting to know you, Maré. How did I do?"

Hollis would've been a contender a month ago and could've been a champion. But now my world circled around Travis, whom I knew could be mine.

"Sounds pretty nice for the basics. I want to be real with you. I like to take things slow. Not feeling cornered to be something that it's not. I hope you can understand me?" I asked, questioning the clarity of my statement.

"I most definitely understand. I agree we're too old for that. I would like to take you out Tuesday evening."

"Uh-um, that's not a good time for me. How 'bout Wednesday?"

"I'm fine with that. I'll give you a call early in the week, to make some dinner arrangements," said Hollis, with strength projecting through the phone.

I sat there with the phone in my hand as I ended the call, questioning myself. I asked myself, why I would allow someone else into this triangle of mass confusion?

"Damn. I don't need Hollis stressing me." I dropped my face into the palms of my hands. I knew I could only provide conversation and a possible friendship.

I had yet to deal with the reality of Travis. Who's to say I would ever be his type of woman? He made it clear that he enjoys my conversation. And when I didn't show up at the bookstore for those two weeks, he noticed.

Was that really saying anything or was it wishful thinking on me?

If I ever felt alone, it was at that moment. I had no one to share my thoughts with. It was as if the entire world was looking in on me from the outside of a glass bottle. They couldn't touch me or feel me. I stood alone with determining my distorted behavior.

My doorbell rang. I saw it was Michelle as I opened the front door. "What's going on?" she asked.

She walked through the short foyer. I hate unannounced guests, and even more right now. God knew I wasn't in the mood for a visitor, let alone Michelle.

"Michelle, what brings you to my neighborhood? And no phone call?" I asked, walking to the sofa.

She looked around the living room. I had made many changes since her last invitation.

"I like this room! You got some skills in decorating. You put some things together that no one would ever think of."

I already knew that, but it was nice to have that confirmed by an independent party. Michelle will let you know her true feelings, nine out of ten times.

"Thanks. What brings you by?" I repeated, as my mood calmed.

"I was invited to a cookout and I wanted to know of you wanted to ride with me?"

"Not today. It's too hot and I've been up since, like six- something this morning," I whined, showing agony in my face.

"Why were you up so early? You and dude weren't knocking

boots?" she teased.

"Whatever. My body woke up and was ready to go. I think now it's hitting me and I'm coming down." I wanted her to leave.

"So tell me, what's up with—what's his name?"

"His name is Hollis. Nothing to scream about. We spoke a little a while ago and he seems pretty cool. We made plans to get together sometime this week."

"Umm… Gone then. Now everyone is all coupled up, but me," she said sadly.

"Anyway." I tried to dilute her thought with reality. "The only real couple is Sonya and her husband. I haven't even gone out with dude and Erin is still in the honeymoon stage with Ezekiel," I yawned.

For a brief moment I wanted to tell Michelle what I was going through. I could feel me inside of her at the precise moment she spoke of not being a couple. Somewhere inside of me, I felt she could relate to my agony, but I knew I couldn't trust anyone.

I wondered if there were other sisters out there who felt like Michelle and myself. How far would most women go to reach Mister Right? It's seen on the news and in movies everyday, where women stalk, kill, and harass. Was that me?

CHAPTER SEVENTEEN

I brought an extra set of clothes to work on Tuesday. I wanted Travis to see me in a sensual way. It's a known fact that men are visual beings, so I had to make him see me, too.

"Good night, Betty," I said, as I ran out of the room swiftly after work to grab my clothes.

There I was with my best gear on that has caught the eye of many men. I felt seductive in my curve-fitting, lavender Jones New York number. The polyester blend dress with the diagonal cut V-neck and the hem stopping above my knees flaunted my essential body parts.

I added a delicate scent to my neck and to the back of my knees to draw more attention to my presence.

It felt sort of weird being overdressed, but I knew I had to do more.

As I walked to my car, there was Eugene, the janitor, standing at the main exit, peering through the glass doors. He waved to make sure I knew that he saw me. Old men are just as bad as women, plain nosy.

****

Looking through the bookstore for Travis, I found excitement racing through my veins.

"Maré!"

I looked to see Travis waving me over to the espresso area.

Travis stood to pull my chair out. "You look fantastic. Is there a special occasion?"

I was lost for words. He ogled at me. What was I going to say about being dressed up? I didn't know what to say.

"Thank you," I replied, as I blushed. If I were white you would have seen the hives. "Today I had a conference with several parents. I like to look professional."

"Again, I want to say how beautiful you look."

I wasn't sure if he was being kind, but the lingering look in his eyes made it feel genuine. That topped it off, like candles on a birthday cake.

"Awe, thanks. How was your weekend?"

"Not too eventful. I spent time around the home and with the Mrs."

I had a visual of the Mrs. this time. Recalling her beauty reminded me that this tactic was worth it. Strangely, I wanted to know her name. Was her name as inviting as her appearance? I wondered.

"Nothing wrong with taking time for yourself. I don't think you ever really spoke about your wife. What's her name?"

"Kayla is her name. We've been married three years. How about you, married or in a relationship?"

There it was, the conversation I wanted to discuss on our initial meeting, but not including his wife. It was surprising to me how much I wanted to dig further.

Looking disheartened, I said, "Neither one. I'm a single woman in Atlanta. Quality men, like yourself, are hard to find."

"An educated and beautiful sister like you is rare. I don't know what's up with the black man today. If I myself was single, believe me, I'd be interested. There's too much game playing going on here; too much sexing and not enough dating." There was that fire in his eyes.

He blew me away. He found me mentally and physically attractive.

"Well, that's how it goes. I'm sure your wife was happy to leave the single life behind her. She got herself a diamond."

"Kayla is a wonderful wife. She gave up a lot for our relationship. First, moving here from D.C., then taking her career to another level. She's currently writing a screenplay for her alma mater in D.C. It was a struggle to get where we are now."

"That's impressive, a screenplay. Has she written anything else?"

"She did a lot of small stuff, nothing too major. This is her largest project."

We spoke candidly about his wife and it felt like we were becoming friends. Sporadically, my mind went south of the border. Could I kill someone? Could I kill his wife, Kayla?

Why would I kill her? I thought to myself. It was staring me right into my eyes. Travis. Did I truly want . . .

"Maré!" said Travis sturdily. "Looked like you were in another world. Are you okay?"

"Oh, I'm fine. Something just crossed my mind. I'm sorry for not paying attention. My wheels began to turn in my head. So, your wife spends most of her time alone at home? How does she like that?"

"At first she found it difficult. I thought she could work outside the home, too. But she wanted to be able to write at the drop of a hat. She connected with a few college alumnus from George Washington, so that helps out a lot."

"She really must be into her screenplay. I would think being amongst others would help her in writing. I'm assuming it's fiction. Is it?" I asked, as my eyebrows rose.

"I believe so. I try not to force my opinions on her, as long as her decisions aren't affecting me. Kayla does a great job of taking care of the house and me. But enough about me. Let's get back to the men out here who have not valued your strengths and beauty."

Travis knew how to warm my spirit, not only with his conversation, but also with his presence. No matter what I obtained tonight, it would never be enough for me. I would want more.

We spent another hour or so discussing relationships and dating. He continued to be stunned as to why I was single.

I hoped that he didn't get the idea that it was me, that I must have some sort of major issue that scared men off. I know what I think when I meet a man who appears to be marriage material and they are thirty or older. Believe me, my thoughts are either commitment issues, a player, gay, or selfish.

This was the first time I felt beautiful in Travis's eyes. The evening at the bookstore was my version of a night on the town, including theater at the Fox and dinner at Colby's Steakhouse.

A soft, gentle midnight breeze took my heart when Travis touched my hand as he laughed. Was I imagining a connection or was it reality?

CHAPTER EIGHTEEN

"To my listeners, I will be taking the cause of 'Be About It' to Chicago, with hopes in becoming syndicated. I'd like to thank each of you. We have proved that African-Americans do care about our communities, youth, advancement, and, overall, our well-being. Each of us are on this earth to serve a purpose. I hope we continue to open and fill these hearts with a purpose. In two weeks, myself and a few of my staff members will be on the move."

As the DJ cued in the mechanical applause, he said, "Travis, I must admit, my social awareness has been lifted with your existence on this show. Yo, people, this brother knows what he's talking about. Don't sit out there and do nothing, because the time is now. Good luck, man."

The station faded into a commercial.

It had come to the point where I didn't lie any more on Wednesdays; Betty and Jennifer didn't ask any questions.

The entire day, my mind was focused on Travis's statement on heading to Chicago in a few weeks.

My chin set in my right hand, "Hum . . . I wonder if he's taking the Mrs.," I said. I looked over the classroom in deep thought.

For the first time, the unconscious thought had surfaced to an actual consideration.

The thought of killing Travis's wife. I could do it and make it a perfect crime.

Looking out at the steaming black asphalt outside, I repeated, "I can do it. Study and research is all it takes."

"Ms. Maré, will you play Candy Land with me, pleasseee?" begged Staci.

With the epiphany blazing in my head, there was joy to play Candy Land.

Gazing down on the pigtailed little one, I smiled with the reply, "Staci, let's play."

We played the game for what seemed like hours. I won a few times and let her win the others.

After a full day of work, I returned home and waited for Hollis to pick me up.

With the great day I'd had so far, there wasn't a need for this date. Being a woman of my word, I decided to go.

"Hell! You look magnificent," said Hollis as I opened the door.

"Thank you. You're not looking too shabby yourself," I told him, making sure to keep all signals straight.

"This is a beautiful living room. Did you do this yourself?" he asked, with a look of amazement.

"I sure did."

"I'm impressed. I'm going to have to get you to do my spot." Hollis smirked as his eyes lingered on me.

"I'm not sure you can afford my prices," I said in a laughing tone.

He rolled out the red carpet to awe me on his first opportunity. We drove to one of the more dynamic restaurants in Atlanta, The Sundial, located at the top of the Westin on Peachtree Street.

I had only heard of it from others. What I could see so far was beautiful. The most amazing experience was the moving of the restaurant. As we sat there, we revolved at the pace of an elderly woman strolling across a street. I was able to get a beautiful view of the night's skyline from any angle.

It seemed as if I was on cloud nine; the wine added to the euphoric evening. I was being treated like I, as a woman, should. I felt beautiful, like the bomb, and I knew I was untouchable.

I knew I controlled the entire evening. For once I allowed myself to be that sister who many don't care for. You know, the one who walks with that air about her, the overly confident one, the one who wants everyone's envy. Yeah, that was me tonight.

Many would call her a bitch because they fear her strength, and at the same time, they admire it.

Hollis did a great job holding his ground when it came to the conversation. Then he got caught up in a lie.

"So you are relocating here with your company?"

He licked his full set of lips to get them moist. "Yeah, the company I work for is opening a store here."

"Hmm."

"What's up with the, Hmm?"

It was time to get into action and become that detective. If men only knew how much women love to mess up their game.

"Oh, nothing," I said, as I paused. "So what company is this?"

"It's a software store that's running strong in the northeast region called Software & Things. They decided to open a chain or two down south."

Brother told me he was a consultant with a software company. A retail chain and an actual company are not the same. *Hmm, let me bother him.*

"Okay. How does being a consultant fit into this department store flow?"

He appeared like he wasn't moved with the questioning of his stories. Then he started rubbing his chin. I remembered Dr. Phil saying that was a tell sign someone was lying.

"You know, the company decided to use my experience to assist in this move to Atlanta. I provide input on the stores here. I'll be managing this market. With hopes of doing well, I can branch into other states in the southeast."

Um . . . I'm not even mad at him because this is a black man, advancing. What angered me was his misrepresentation of his job. How can you go from a consultant to a retail manager? He obviously needed to boost up his male ego. Hollis is a pure M-E double S.

Already knowing that this was nothing major, I let it go. "Sounds like you are doing it. Handling your business. Let me put it like this: handlin' yo bizness."

We laughed, as if I was Chris Rock. Wine can make the driest comedian sound funny.

After a wonderful evening, Hollis drove me home. I invited him in, I don't know why. Let me be real—the drinking got my hormones racing. I knew I still had control tonight.

I fell into his trap: those full, soft, and shapely lips. I love to be kissed and knew that's what I wanted. For me, this was out of my character. What had been my character lately?

Hollis's large hands caressed my back. I could feel him squeezing me as I fell further into his kiss.

I moaned from the explosion of pleasure. "Travis."

Hollis paused and pushed me away.

Unknowing of what went wrong, I looked up to see Hollis. Infuriation was engraved on his face. At that moment I realized there weren't any substitutes to Travis.

CHAPTER NINETEEN

The alarmed blared like a trumpet in my ear. "It's time to get up already."

I rolled over, moaning like a three-year-old being awakened in the middle of the night. Heavy consumption of alcohol wasn't a good idea, and getting to bed late didn't help either.

"Maré, what are you going to do?" I asked myself.

I left a message on Betty's voicemail, letting her know that a sister wasn't making it in today. Then I rolled back over to continue where I left off.

Once I took a few more minutes of shut-eye, I gathered myself. Nothing was planned, other than recovering.

I was in a pair of cargo pants and T-shirt, driving up I-285. It was like a magnetic energy; it pulled me to go to Travis's neighborhood. I couldn't do anything but go.

Each time I drove through the neighborhood, I felt baffled. The maturity in the neighborhood was seen by the fullness of the trees.

Just as I turned onto Vermack Road, there was Kayla, pulling out of the driveway. I slowed to give her an opportunity to back out. I didn't want to bring attention to myself.

I pressed on the accelerator to pick up speed, and from the side road a car pulled out between us. Visible to the near-sighted were the words, "DeKalb County Police Department."

As we came to the traffic light, I sat there gazing through a police cruiser's cage into Kayla's black BMW. The police didn't trouble me. With the bright sun burning in my eyes, I reached for my shades.

The light turned green. She turned left and the police kept straight. I followed Kayla onto Mt. Vernon Road. Finally, I got the shades on my face. This was another scorching summer day.

"Phew, it's like Africa hot. I hope ol' girl isn't on the road too much longer," I muttered.

My distance remained visual as she began to grocery shop. I appreciated the needed AC. Being that not too many woman run in and out of grocery stores, I decided to pick up a few needed items.

I'm not an Bruno's shopper, but they had a few items on sale today. Picking through the grapes, I noticed the customers. Many appeared to be "well-to-do." They had to be, to afford these prices.

Bewildered, I was in the same checkout line as Kayla, separated by an elderly woman in a tattered straw hat.

"How you doing today?" asked the smiling cashier.

"I'm doing well. How about yourself?" Kayla asked, as she dug through her purse.

"Eh, it could be better, but it could be worse. You don't miss a beat on these weekly Thursday specials."

"Hey, I have to take care of business, and part of that is saving money." They both laughed.

Rudely, the old lady reached around me to grab one of the tabloids. No "excuse me" or "pardon me." If I was to come off with an attitude, I would be wrong. I feel young or old, use your manners.

Continuing to dig through her leather purse, Kayla said, "I can't believe I left my cards in my other wallet."

With annoyance on her face, she began to make out a check. I sat there, up close and personal, seeing this woman's face.

I could see all the particulars. What I had seen before was magnified. She was even more stunning. The personality she displayed seemed to be laid back. I couldn't see Travis with some stuck up woman. I was unable to see her penmanship, as she filled it out for forty-eight dollars and thirty cents with her left hand.

"See you next Thursday," shouted the big-nosed cashier.

Kayla pleasantly waved back as she pushed her shopping cart out the automatic doors.

The old lady was in the way. I didn't have time to waste with this. I'd better . . .

"I can take you ma'am over here," said a Hispanic guy on register four.

I quickly made it to his lane and urgently placed the few items I had grabbed on the counter.

My eyes roamed the parking lot to see if Kayla had already pulled off, leaving me behind. For the first time, I wasn't collected in my thoughts. I should have remembered where she parked and I wouldn't have had to strain.

This wasn't going to work if I was going to be slipping like this.

I became very miffed about failing to keep up with Kayla.

"Just stupid. I don't have breathing room for stupidity," I chastised myself, as I rolled the empty cart to the rack.

My eyes caught her walking from the adjacent cleaners. I couldn't tell if it was men's or women's clothing she was carrying. I knew I felt a sense of amazement, seeing her walking through the parking lot.

"Thank you, Lord."

How vain of me to thank Him, when the actions I was partaking in were unacceptable. Wrongfully so, there was a sense of joy in my soul, ready to continue in the hot pursuit.

Seemed as if it had gotten hotter and I wasn't going to have sweat rolling down my stomach. The air conditioning took a minute to kick in, like a wild donkey fighting its way out of a box.

I expected her to return home, being that she just bought groceries. But it seemed like she had her day planned. Who was I to organize her schedule?

I cruised over a speed bump and Kayla jumped out of her car. She walked into the post office.

She didn't take much time, as she exited with a handful of mail. Kayla sashayed back to her car with finesse.

I looked down at the gas gauge and I had about a quarter tank of gas left. With the air on, that was going to dissipate in no time. The hotter it was outside, the less cold air the AC pumped out.

I continued up Womack Road as Kayla turned onto her street, Vermack. I drove into the nearby high school's parking lot and pulled around to the front.

I caught the garage door slowly closing behind her.

"I'm following this woman like I know what I'm doing."

My face dropped into my hands and my fingertips racked down my face. I took in a deep breath through my nose; then blew it out my mouth. The air felt brisk to my fingers.

Peace was around me and I enjoyed the moment I allowed myself to catch. I knew this wasn't a time to relax or the time to slip up again. The time was for me to listen and learn. Every second, minute, and hour was becoming crucial.

I don't know what came over me. Maybe it was the realization of the act that I was about to perform.

"Snap! It's four already," I said, as I propped myself up in my seat.

"There's no way I can make it downtown now. Damn! How did I let this happen?"

A tad bit perturbed, I put the car into drive.

I could see the garage door opening and there was Kayla backing out.

"Hmm . . . where is the sister going now?"

CHAPTER TWENTY

I plopped on the sofa. "Man, following her was like work. I might as well had gone to work."

Like any other day, not a moment to exhale before someone was calling. I wasn't in the mood for a full-fledged conversation, I thought. *But let me answer the phone before someone starts crying about my inconsistencies.*

From the Caller ID I could see it was Sonya. "Hello."

"What's up? How was your date with dude?" she asked.

It was a great time for me, but who knows how Hollis felt after my blunder, I thought.

"It was pretty good. He tried to put his best moves out there. He took me to The Sundial and it was lovely."

There was a moment of silence, which seemed like minutes. "So are you digging him or not?" she questioned.

Sonya has a habit of wanting to get straight to the point. Then there are times she wants to marinate in the story.

"He's okay."

"Huh, what's wrong with him?" Sonya inquired.

"He has issues. Following the night we met him at the café, he said he was a software consultant. Sonya, I found out last night, he's in the retail business. He's supposed to be managing the software stores they are opening here."

"What? Why didn't he just come with the truth in the beginning?"

Crossing my legs as I lay back on the sofa, I told her, "I don't know, but I do know, that's a major sign. It begins with small contradictions; then comes the major ones down the road. I don't need to be wasting my time. You know?"

I had to give her something for not wanting to fool with Hollis.

"I understand exactly what you're saying. You don't have time to be dealing with a fake brother. Hell, be who you are. All these stupid games men play are just trifling."

Sonya wanted her girls to be in happy relationships like herself. She knew we were getting older and our biological clocks were tick-ing. I know she is thankful to be out of the single life.

"Well, at least I had a great dinner. The Sundial was marvelous. I suggest that you and Adrian eat there. It's very romantic, but pricey." I turned on the television. "If you speak with Michelle before I do, fill her in, so I don't have to."

"Okay, girl, I was calling to see how the date went last night. I'll holla at you later."

With the TV on mute I sat there in deep thought. This was the first time I was able to sit and think about the epiphany I had yesterday. Was I really going to go through with it?

At that moment there was breaking news.

I un-muted the television. "Suspect has been captured for the murder of the Hall County woman, which occurred six months ago," said the news anchor.

"With the evidence he left behind, he was bound to be captured," stated the police chief.

My eyes and ears were wide as the length of a sixteen wheeler. "That's what I'm talking about, the lack of smarts and know-how. He left behind fingerprints and they found hair samples at the scene. Crimes committed on a whim have a lot of mistakes made," I said to myself.

But I knew I had to do better than that. My life was on the line and so was the love of my life.

Every so often, the doubt of my capabilities penetrated inside my mind. I knew who it was. Gran was speaking to me. She was my angel, who kept me from harm.

I fell to the floor, to my knees. "Gran, I know what I'm about to do is wrong. You've seen me in some bad moments, but the worse has yet to come." A few tears began to roll down my face. "I need your armor of protection around me."

Only way I knew to get it done right was to watch some movies that contained murderous plots. Movies tell you, show you what, and how to do everything.

I remember when the movie *The Money Train* with Wesley Snipes and Woody Harrelson came out, there was a copycat from a scene. News reported that someone sprayed gasoline on a ticket booth operator in New York and torched them. I'd never thought I would be looking to movies to give me guidance for crime.

Not knowing what movies to really get and not wanting to ask anyone, I just poked around the suspense section of the video store.

Recalling that Michael Douglas was in a few murder-filled plot pictures and so was Richard Gere, I sought out their films.

I became bothered by how much time it took to locate some flicks.

"I can take the next person over here," said the kid with braces behind the video store counter.

I pulled out my membership card and cash as he scanned the movies.

"*A Perfect Murder* and *The Talented Mr. Ripley* are five-day rentals. And the other two are due back by twelve P.M. on Saturday," he said.

CHAPTER TWENTY-ONE

As expected, all eyes were on me the next morning when I went into work. I knew I just should've called in again. Whatever they dished, I had to be strong and take it.

Carrying her clipboard, Betty said, "We missed you yesterday. The kids asked about you. Are you feeling better?"

"Yeah, I'm doing better, thanks. Betty, again, I apologize for not making it in."

"It's okay. I don't think you hardly ever miss a day and for you to have called in, you must've felt pretty bad," she said with sincerity.

I felt my time that day was being wasted. I needed to be working on getting my plan together. So far, the two movies I watched last night, everyone scrutinized all elements before they committed their crime.

In *The Talented Mr. Ripley*, not only did he kill the guy, he took over his identity.

All that I do—must to be flawless.

"Do you have any plans this weekend?" asked Jennifer.

I felt like she was fishing for something. What exactly, I couldn't say. Normally, we speak cordially, with a hello or how are you doing, but that was it. On a few occasions we have enjoyed conversations about our alma mater.

There was a touch of intrigue in my expression and voice. "Nothing to scream about. Most importantly, getting some rest."

I distanced myself from the possible rat. I knew it was a harsh description, but rats are always on the move, looking and sniffing for something. So, to prevent any mixed gestures, I thought I'd steer clear of her.

Right now, no one could be trusted. I must question every person's intention.

I began to play with a few of the children at the jigsaw table. Like clockwork, I was lifted from my suspicions by playing with them.

A full day of work and I rushed home to continue my movie marathon.

"I'm too happy that it's Friday." I threw my purse on the sofa.

I checked my messages and astonishingly, Hollis called. I would've sworn that I was dismissed.

Motivated by the last movies, I made it back to Travis's neighborhood.

I drove in a heavy downpour of rain. When I returned to my favorite spot, I turned off the engine and the lights. My vision wasn't clear. It was blurred from the rain rolling down my windshield. The trees and houses had a wavy appearance, something like entering the *Twilight Zone.*

Again, I sat in the Dunwoody High School's parking lot, watching the house. There was a beam of light coming from the right upstairs window.

I leaned back for a minute and listened to the rain tapping on the car. The steady flow of drops sounded like tiny feet tap-dancing across the top of the car. I could imagine thousands of Savion Glovers.

As I listened closer, I found a steady beat that was aligned with the slowing beat of my heart. Then I brought myself to a focal point. I was beginning to enjoy being out there, watching.

At almost one-thirty in the morning, it was pitch black in the house. The only light on was the outside light at the brick steps. I looked closer at the house and noticed one of the garage doors wasn't shut all the way.

"I wonder if that's like that all the time?" I questioned, as I started the car. "If so, I can probably enter through there."

Drowsiness began to take over.

I made it to the four-way stop and turned, when out of nowhere I saw a pair of blue lights flickering in my rear and side-view mirrors.

The rain slacked off, as my grandmother used to say, as I pulled onto a side-road. I kept my hands at the twelve o'clock position on the steering wheel. I wasn't trying to initiate any more havoc than had I already.

The police officer motioned me to roll down my window. "Ma'am, how are you doing this morning?" he asked.

To be honest, I was very concerned.

"I'm doing fine."

"We received a call from a concerned neighbor of a suspicious car in the high school parking lot. They said it was there for a long time. Was there any particular reason you were there?"

Caught off-guard by the question, I found an answer. "I like it there. It's so peaceful. When I came across it, I just gravitated back to it, for meditating."

The officer looked stunned by my reply. "Let me see your driver's license and registration."

I took in many deep breaths as the officer performed his investigation.

"Ms. Alexander, you are pretty far from Decatur. I would suggest you find somewhere closer to you for your meditation," he said in an authoritative tone, as he returned my items.

CHAPTER TWENTY-TWO

I learned a lot last night from my brief encounter with the law. That was the last time I would be suspected for any wrongdoing. I sat in my big blue chair taking notes from each movie, pausing the videos and studying the characters on the thirty-two inch screen. Listening to every statement made.

"I have to make sure that I don't leave any fingerprints behind." I grabbed the back of my neck. It was pretty tight.

I'd become very parched, so I jumped up and headed to the kitchen for something to drink.

I was struck with a loud thought. *The gloves I saw at Sports Authority would be perfect. Yeah, those are the ones. The gripping and flexibility.*

I smiled as I poured a glass of water. I felt like I had come into my character. There I was in my kitchen, nodding my head from a reflection. Arrogance filtered through my veins. What was I, a character? It really didn't matter. I had to become whatever allowed me to get the job done.

"I can do this," I said with confidence.

I spent the entire day brainstorming and bouncing ideas off myself. It became fun and I was beginning to love the challenge.

Sunday morning, I found myself drowsy from the overpowering of my brain. Maybe I didn't want to follow through with my promise to Erin to attend church.

I didn't deserve to be there. My spirit was so stained from sin, I felt reluctant to even go today. But I knew Erin would question me if I didn't.

The beautiful cathedral gave a scent of purity. The stained glass window behind the pulpit was astoundingly designed. There was Jesus with his arms opened wide and the words, "Compassion, Pentecost, and Kingdom," shone brightly.

Ignorantly, I feared that my transgressions would be removed because I was now in the house of the Lord.

Making my way down the aisle, I saw Erin in the front half of the church. We always sit on the main level because the balcony gives us a detached feeling. But today I wouldn't mind being up there.

"Good morning, Maré," Erin greeted, as she gave me a hug.

Trying my best to shake myself, I asked, "What's going on?"

"We really haven't spoken since your hot date with Hollis, so how was it?"

I gave her the same run down I had given Sonya. I was apprehensive of Hollis telling Ezekiel what I had done that evening. And everyone knows how couples do, tell everything to each other.

The male gender is so controlled by their ego, dude probably wouldn't tell his friends that a sister called out someone else's name. It was something I prayed for.

Writing out her check for tithing, Erin said, "I'm going to ask Zek what's up with his corny friend."

"Girl, don't bother him with it. We're too old for this 'man in the middle' mess. You know? I don't want him to see me as some hard-up woman."

No one needs to know how hard-up I am, except me.

The Cathedral at Chapel Hill don't play when it comes to getting their praise on. The choir did a great rendition on Byron Cage's "The Presence of the Lord is Here." The vocals filled the atmosphere to where you couldn't help but feel the spirit.

"*. . . The presence of the Lord is here . . .*"

Erin was clapping like she felt it in her, and so were a whole lot of people in the congregation.

There was a time I'd be right there with her, but not today.

Before long, the Bishop had put the word on us for today's sermon.

Standing before his mixed church members, the white clergy adamantly said to us that we better listen up before we all perished unsaved.

The words he preached were real. Saying that each and every one of us has the same authority as Jesus. We have to believe and know that we are God's "son." When you know that God is your father, you don't have to ask, you have the power to receive what is rightfully yours.

I could hear "Amen" flying off the mahogany wooden frames.

In a baby blue hat, a church member ran up and down the aisle. She stepped so high her knees were visible to us, two aisles over. Her right arm swung haphazardly.

Nothing stopped the Bishop. He kept on sharing the word. Teaching us on getting to where many of us wanted to be. Completeness.

Erin nudged me when she agreed with each prevailing statement he made.

This was the first time I couldn't hear what he was saying. Had I allowed the devil inside me, to the point where he had taken over? But I was not really worried. Per the Bishop, God forgives us for all our sins.

"Girl, he was preaching today," said Erin, after the service.

Playing off her energy, I agreed, "You know how he does. He keeps it real."

Unlike myself. I was wearing a mask.

CHAPTER TWENTY-THREE

Time was winding down to the day when Travis would make his trip out of town. My plate was overflowing with tasks.

"I heard your show last week. And now you have the possibility to be syndicated? I know you're filled with joy."

This was the quietest day yet at the bookstore, so it seemed. I couldn't recall any other day since my attendance that had been as melancholy.

Maybe it was me. I would have to expect that all I'd been going through mentally, physically, and spiritually would affect my body. Had I become so disengaged to the world and overly focused with my dilemma?

Wearing a blue dress shirt with a white collar and a two-toned blue tie, Travis answered with joy, "I'm oblivious to my happiness."

"Whoa, not Travis, taken by surprise," I said with a smile.

Smiling back in response to my smart-alecky remark, he said, "Yes, I'm taken by surprise. I'm filled with so many dreams. To fulfill each dream, I sketch out a plan to bring them into a reality. Maré, I thought I'd accomplished my dream. To make it to an altitude of having my show heard outside of Atlanta is above a dream. It's a miracle."

Looking into Travis's eyes, I could feel the euphoria of his new opportunity. He appeared as if he was walking on air.

A sense of pride ran through my body. I caught myself before I allowed my eyes to water. I just wanted to hug him and not let go.

"Wow. I'm sure your wife is looking forward to the uplifting moment. Not to forget the shopping in Chicago."

"Kayla cheered, but she won't be on this trip. She seldom travels with me, when it concerns work," stated Travis.

"This is more than just work, this is a triumphant moment for you and our people. The media and radio have been trampled by negativity for too long. This growth opportunity means people are tired of being fed spoiled milk."

He had a look of gratitude as he scratched his head. "Thank you so much for the positive feedback. What you said means a lot to me."

My intentions weren't to stir up disorder in his marriage. That was far from my mind. I wanted to let Travis know how I felt about this monumental time in his life. If his wife treated it casually, then, so be it.

To know I was able to lift his spirits with my feelings and words thrilled me.

"You're welcome. Making sure you knew how I felt," I articulated. I boldly reached for his hand.

Butterflies ran through my body, as if hundreds were released from a jar and happy to be set free. They couldn't flutter their wings fast enough to escape.

Travis allowed my hand to remain there for a few seconds. To me it felt like forever.

"I appreciate it," he said with warmth in his eyes as he cupped my hand with his, then did a friendly shake to end the physical contact.

I needed to know more about his wife and her habits. To return to the neighborhood again would be hazardous.

"Kayla will probably enjoy her alone time. Men don't know, but women look forward to their men leaving," I said with a chuckle. "We don't have to worry about nobody but us."

"Hmm—she said that, but not as clearly and direct as you did."

"I'm telling you. She doesn't have to run errands or cook for you. You better listen to me. How long are you going to be gone?"

My head bobbed and right eyelid rose to my hairline.

"About three days," he said, laughing at me. "You're probably right. I'm sure she'll keep up with her aerobics classes. Kayla acts like she'll die if she misses her Friday evening writer's group."

I would've never imagined that I'd be able to digest a conversation about his wife. Like I said, I had to become whomever to get the job done.

Probing for information was no challenge. Men are easy targets when it comes to getting answers to questions. They are even easier when you're not sleeping with them. Travis wouldn't have a reason not to share in friendly conversation about the differences of the genders.

"It'll be her little sabbatical. A bottle of some quality Merlot, light some candles, and tune out the world in a nice, hot bubble bath."

Nodding in agreement, he replied, "That is so Kayla. That's even her preferred type of wine. She'll probably indulge in that on Friday night, after a full day, and getting home late, wine will top it off. What's that, a universal thing for women?"

"Pretty much. Some of the things women do are common." I laughed.

CHAPTER TWENTY-FOUR

I stepped out of the taxi in front of the school to get my car and my cell rang. Travis fixed his eyes on my purse.

Ignoring the ringing, I kept my eyes on him. "Thanks again for the ride. I should be just fine."

"Please be careful. Have a good evening," he said, appearing somewhat annoyed in his voice and eyes.

The taxi pulled off and I opened my purse to answer the call. I would've thought it would've ended by now. I guess cellular companies must have increased the ring time by a hundred.

"So you can't call a brother back," said the strong voice.

Not even focused, I replied, "Huh?"

"Damn, it's like that? I must've really been nothing but an 'in the meantime'."

Catching his voice, I was shocked to even hear from Hollis again. I felt he had served his purpose for me that evening. Me calling out Travis's name put a period to even a possible friendship.

"What was it for me to say that wasn't said that night? It was a very awkward situation. I thought you had dismissed me after that."

He was taken by my straight-forwardness and obviously didn't know what to say, being that there was a break in the conversation.

"I'm not going to lie, it did piss me off. I had decided to scratch you off my list, but something about you, I really liked. Maré, I wanted to get to know you. Who is this guy? Is he your man that you're not telling me about?"

There are times when men can be just like women when it comes to dating. Hollis not seeing the signs, that I had some possible issues, frustrated me. Him thinking that he had an opening to be my man was where I didn't want him to be.

As I merged onto the busy highway, I told him, "I'd rather not discuss that. Like I said in the beginning, I'm a single woman. There's nothing more to say about it."

Insanity must've taken over. I had an available man, so it seemed, who wanted to know me. And here I was, scheming and plotting to kill someone's wife for his love. The heartbreaking part about it being that he may not love me in return.

"I can understand that and I will not press you. My boy Zek asked about the date. I didn't know what to say because everything was cool."

"What an idiot! You see me with my blinker on and you still won't let me over," I snapped, with full aggression in my voice.

I still didn't know what to say. It has never been my character to shoot a brother down when I'm not interested. Like everybody, I just don't answer or return calls. This was different because Hollis and I had a tie between us: Erin and Ezekiel.

"I've heard about the road rage down here. Don't hurt nobody," said Hollis, to lighten the mood.

"Making sure nobody hurts me. You'll see it for yourself. Right now, you are still in the 'I'm trying to get there and find it' stage."

We laughed and chatted a little longer. Nothing more said about what would be between us. I think we both felt obligated to keep the lines of communication open, for the sake of our friends.

Making it to my exit, my thoughts returned to where my heart was. Travis.

With the days going by quickly, I knew I needed to get myself in check; and to do that I needed to know if that garage door was always open.

I knew it was unwise for me to return to that neighborhood, but I felt it would be safe. It would be a drive-by, literally. This time no parking or peeping.

I made it back onto I-285, with about thirty-five minutes to get to my destination.

The beautiful night was clear of clouds. I had the air conditioning surging to cut through the hot, humid evening. The car struggled a little to get into gear, but it wasn't unbearable enough to be without the air.

The long day was beginning to take a toll on me. My right leg began to pulsate with a slight cramp. With one hand on the wheel, I bent over to rub it. That really didn't help physically, but mentally it did.

I prayed aloud, "Oh, God, let me just ride past here and be okay." I prepared myself with bottomless breaths.

There I was, cruising by with hopes to go unnoticed by the soul who did on the last occasion.

I made it to the front of Travis's house. There were a few boys dribbling and tossing a basketball.

I cut my eyes to the left to satisfy my inquiring mind about the garage door. Swiftly, I located the teenage boys heading towards the school.

I drove out as smoothly and easily as I came in.

"My ride won't be used when I come back. I can't afford for someone to finger my ride as the car they saw on that night. No, it's not going to work like that."

With another trip back to my side of town, a million thoughts ran through my head. Many possibilities and not a lot of time.

"How much time do I have left?" I asked myself, making it back onto I-285.

CHAPTER TWENTY-FIVE

"Ms. Maré, I need to go potty," begged the snag-a-tooth little boy named Brett.

Eight fifty-two read the big-faced wall clock. I shifted my attention back to the snag a tooth kid because of the tugging on my shirt.

Time was running and it wasn't good for me. To leave the classroom consecutively would draw attention. I've drawn enough of that.

I grabbed the back of Brett's head as I directed him towards the door. "Let's head to the bathroom. Let's put some pep in your step."

Shoving him down the hall, he began to trip over his footing. I wasn't really concerned as to his well-being, other than him using the bathroom; I wanted to get it taken care of.

Brett could've bathed and brushed his teeth for the time it took him to potty.

"Ms. Mare, why are we walking fast?" asked the puzzled-faced kid.

These darn kids today are so perceptive, and to make matters worse, they call you on everything they notice.

"Just want to get back to the classroom," I replied with a smile, as I stroked his head.

"Oh."

Brett darted through the door as I opened it. Back to the playing blocks.

This time the big-faced wall clock read eight fifty-eight as I grabbed for my purse. As I began to walk out the door, I looked back to see Betty staring at me with uncertainty in her eyes.

I tuned into the show, like a fiend, and Travis had already begun his show.

"I would like to challenge everyone to write down at least five things that concern you, as an individual. It can be teen pregnancy, homelessness, illiteracy, education, or whatever. Out of those, pick the one thing you vow to work on for change. We have too many able bodies, sitting around complaining and not doing anything. We are all leaders."

The ideas and methods he uses are simple to every man or woman. I've yet to disagree with any statement he has made.

"Who are you waiting for to fix your community problems? Someone who doesn't live there? Get your act together, then look for reinforcement. Remember, I'll be in Chicago next week to bring our show into syndication. Your help is needed. Please visit our website at www.beaboutit.2ya.com to share your thoughts and ideas. We all know strength comes in numbers. I believe one is better than zero."

My soul was ignited once again by this man of strength. As he continued, I felt different on this day, as if my space was being invaded. Not sure what it could've been, I dismissed my crazy thinking.

I leaned over to pick up my bag; there in my peripheral vision I saw the bathroom door partly open and a pair of tan Easy Spirits. Startled by the interruption, I jolted my body back up.

"Betty!"

"I'm very concerned about you, Maré, to a point that it can't be overlooked. Follow me to my office," she ordered, as she held the door for me.

I couldn't be mad; I had been out of my character. At this juncture, my craziness had already been determined.

As we walked in silence through the corridor, I could hear the squeaking of Betty's orthopedic shoes echoing with each step. I only had a few more steps to get a story together. A believable one, that is.

A ray of sunshine lit up the small corner office space. She kept her desk crowded with papers and folders. Cramped into the office along with her desk was a yellow plastic chair. I sat in it.

"Maré, the behavior you have been displaying lately won't be tolerated any longer. You know my feelings when it comes to work ethics. But you also know how understanding I am. This is your time to clear the table," Betty commanded as she twisted a pen.

Taken by the situation, my voice weakened. "I apologize for my behavior and I know it hasn't been up to par. Betty, I enjoy working with you and the children. It hurts that my credibility is dwindling."

"You're disrupting the class each Wednesday morning with your abrupt dismissals. Maré, you are constantly lying about why you're leaving the classroom. Then I find you in the bathroom this morning," scorned Betty.

We both sat there with our heads held low, as if we were fearful to look into the others' eyes. I know I was.

"Betty, I apologize. That was never my intention to be disruptive."

"What is it that you want? Do you need something from me? I'm telling you, this is your last warning," she said without sympathy, but with soft eyes.

"I understand your position. Time to get myself back in check is all I need. Betty, I promise you, I will be back on the horse, riding like a pro. And it won't take long. You know I love my job," I professed, as I wrung my hands together.

She smiled as if she had nothing but love for me. And with her smile, I was able to breathe a bit more naturally.

"Don't let me down. This is your first and last warning, Maré. Don't take my kindness as a sign that I won't take the next step, if this activity continues."

After I returned to the classroom, I stared outside to the busy life. I knew it was going to be okay. There wasn't going to be a need for collectiveness.

Like Travis always says, "Don't complain about it. Be about it."

CHAPTER TWENTY-SIX

"Yes, I would like to know the cost for a two-day car rental?" I asked.

"Ma'am the price depends on your usage. Are you planning on driving locally or long distance?" inquired the gargled voice.

"It would be local."

It felt weird coming straight home on a Thursday afternoon. I would've rather been with Travis, but taking caring of business would insure my desire of seeing him every day.

Throughout the entire day, I could tell Betty was happy to see me back to my "normal" self. She smiled with pride and winked several times. The excessive attention got on my nerves somewhat, but I didn't allow it to put me on the edge. There were more important things to take care of.

Clearing his throat, he said, "We have a special right now where you can rent a car for only nine dollars and ninety-nine cents a day. This covers forty-five miles a day. Now, any overage will cost you an additional dollar and sixty cents per mile."

"Okay, that sounds pretty good. How can I hold it? I would pick it up Wednesday evening."

"We can reserve it in your name or you can go ahead to confirm the reservation with a major credit card. You must be at least twenty-five years of age," said the gargled voice.

I paused for a moment—I really didn't want my name on nothing, let alone using a credit card. Doing any of that, I would be setting myself up for failure.

"Um . . . I don't have a major credit card," I said in a flustered tone.

Again he tried to clear his voice, "I'm sorry. You must have a major credit card."

Frustration overcame me faster then the batting of an eye. Ignorantly, I had allowed the fictitious plots of the movies to take over; I had not thought for myself.

"Thank you," I said. I ended the call.

Furiously, I began to find all of the major car rentals in the Atlanta phone book. I turned page after page and called number after number.

I sat with the cordless phone in my hand, as *'major credit card is needed'* ricocheted in my brain from every rental agent I spoke with.

"Damn it! This wasn't part of the plan. This wasn't supposed to be this difficult. Stupid movies! What made me think it was that easy." I became livid.

I stood and walked to the sliding glass door. The sun had begun to set and I could see fireflies light up one by one in the brush of trees off the deck. It is so funny how you have to catch them at the right time and now was the right time for me. The beauty of these bugs amazes me every time I see them.

My frustration began to dissipate, which allowed me to brainstorm. I knew it was important to stay focused. For the first time, reality struck. This was going be a true challenge.

I headed back to the phonebook knowing I was on mission that must be completed. With more of an expectation in mind, I continued to call. In this city, too many people have bad or no credit and there had to be someone who has tapped into that market.

On my last leg, I said once again, "I want to rent a car for two days. Before you go into the cost, do you require a major credit card?"

After calling over thirty locations, I had to cut to the point.

A woman replied, "No, ma'am, it's not a 'must,' but we would prefer you to use one. To rent a vehicle without a major credit card you must give us a deposit of $250.00, plus the rental cost. Once you've returned the vehicle, you'll get your deposit back."

I closed my eyes and quickly reopened them as by head fell backwards onto the sofa cushion. I was ecstatic that my persistence paid off; however, there was no time to reflect on it.

"How much are your rental fees? This will be for local use."

Typing on her keyboard, she quoted, "It will be fifteen dollars and ninety-nine cents per day, which includes thirty-five miles a day. If you go over the miles, it's going to cost you a dollar and ninety-five cents per mile. We also have accident insurance for an additional thirty dollars per day. We strongly suggest to all of our customers to get the insurance. It covers you for loss, theft, and accidents."

No and bad credit people have it rough. With my good credit, I could have gotten a better deal. But I had to remember it was about getting the job done.

Letting out a sigh, I said, "That's fine. No, I don't need the insurance."

I provided the requested information. My name was still needed, which I was leery of giving. I told her to give me the economy size car. It didn't matter.

"Ma'am, your total due at the time of pickup on next Wednesday evening will be two-hundred and eighty-four dollars and twenty-two cents. Your return time is forty-eight hours from your pick up time. We'd like to thank you for choosing Mega Car Rentals for your rental needs."

Who would have thought this would take the entire afternoon? Not me. A sense of relief blanketed my body from head to toe, as I sat in pure silence. It felt as if I had just run the hundred-yard dash four times back to back.

This was the beginning. I had much more to complete and time was clicking.

"What's next on the agenda?" I whispered to myself. "What's next?"

CHAPTER TWENTY-SEVEN

"If you're looking to get to the top end of the perimeter, then I-85 North isn't it," said the traffic reporter. "Two lanes have been shut down due to a tanker spill. Alternate routes around this area . . ."

I turned off the radio because there wasn't a need to follow the other routes. Sometimes I forget why I love Atlanta so much, with the traffic mayhem.

"It's Friday, I'm stuck on Peachtree Road. I'm nowhere close to getting home," I complained, rubbing my forehead.

Like clockwork, whenever I'm in unbearable traffic, one of my girls calls. I'm not sure if it's always a good thing.

"What's up?" asked Erin.

"Girl, this damn traffic. I don't know why I didn't take MARTA today," pouting through the cell.

"Where are you now? If you aren't too far up Peachtree, maybe we can meet up for some drinks."

Erin seemed unlike herself. A true friend can tell when something isn't right. I would like to think that I was her true friend, being that the tone she used sounded lifeless, but she tried to put something to it.

I felt it would be better not to say anything right then. I'd wait until we met up.

"Might as well. I'm not going anywhere, no time soon. Where are we trying to go?" I asked, turning on my right blinker.

"The Shark Bar is pretty close. You think you can maneuver that?" Erin asked with laughter.

"Oh, you got jokes. I can maneuver that and that free drink you owe me. Thank you very much."

I could tell she had something on her mind, so I made a point to get there.

The Fox Theater was at the next light and I needed to turn around. Traffic became uncontrollable and straining; too many cars and not enough space.

"Honk—Honk." I heard as I jumped in front of a Dodge truck.

Either you take it or sleep on it. That's the mentality that I'd inherited since I moved here. People in this city aren't friendly when it comes to blinkers.

The side roads were congested, but not as much as Peachtree. My head began to throb and I was in need of a drink after that twenty-minute saga.

"What took you so long?" laughed Erin.

"You'd better shut it up, Ms. Straight Shot," I said in a sarcastic tone, putting my keys into my purse.

Erin wasn't far from here or my job. With the restraints on my schedule, we never had the opportunity to eat lunch together. Her hours are so crazy she spends a lot of time working.

"How many?" asked the frail host.

Looking back at me, "Just two," requested Erin. "Should we do the bar or get a table?"

"Let's get a table so I can grab a bite, too." I peered at the dining area.

The thin waiter sluggishly showed us to our seats.

The Shark Bar is a hot spot. The layout of the joint is quaint, nothing too lavish about it. It has some character. You can see it as soon as you come through the door, with the bar immediately on the right. Later tonight it would be packed.

On the opposite side is the dining area. The lighting is soft, but with loud music. That's the one thing I don't like about this place.

Tilting my head to the left, I asked, "What's going on Erin? I can see it your eyes."

Taken by my direct approach, she stuttered, "I-I-I don't know. I may be taking this out of context."

Ezekiel was written all over this. Women don't have many problems until they have themselves a man. Not to generalize it to all women. Let's say my women friends.

"What's going on?" I asked again, impatiently.

"Maré, I think Ezekiel is seeing someone else."

"Huh? What makes you think that?" I concentrated on removing the dumbfounded look from my face.

"Tell me if I'm taking things to an extreme. I told you how I liked his consistency and the respect of each other's space. We still haven't had sex. Okay! We have spent many nights together, may it be my place or his. For the past couple weeks, he hasn't stayed over and he hasn't invited me over."

"Well, Erin, have you asked him about this, to why the change?"

"I have, not wanting to sound like a nag. All he has to say is that he has been tired from the café. Saying that it has gotten busy lately," she said with a look of uncertainty.

I truly didn't know what to say. I wasn't in the mood to deal with Erin and her insecurities. She has allowed them to break up many good relationships. Right now wasn't a good time for me, being that I didn't have any patience for the drama.

"That could be it. The night we were there it was packed and people were waiting to get in. I'm sure it's somewhat wearing on him," with assurance in my voice.

The waiter finally made it back to us with the standard water. In the midst of our conversation, he dashed off.

"Maré, I can accept that. So I offered to come down to help him out, where I could. He almost bit my head off when he yelled NO!"

The frail waiter squatted at the table as he took our orders. It seemed as if his mind was frail, too. We had to repeat the order at least four times. I wasn't sure if he even got it right.

I hated seeing Erin like that. It amazes me how another being can control the light switch of joy within another. For about a month, she was elated with this man. I didn't want to bring up that he hadn't committed himself to her.

"To be honest with you Erin, the only thing you can do is take care of yourself. The best way to do that is to let him know how you feel. Now, if he isn't receptive of your feelings, that's a different story. Let him know and the ball will be in his court."

I could tell that wasn't good enough for her, but I was proud of myself. That was good advice.

"Your food will be out momentarily," said the waiter.

"Where are the bathrooms?" I asked.

I made my way towards the bar area and could see that it had become exceedingly invaded already.

Turning left at a wooden column, I noticed a gentleman who looked like Travis from the back. Disregarding him, I continued on my journey.

"Excuse me, are you in line?" I asked a voluptuous sister.

She barely acknowledged me, but she nodded. You would've thought that the halter-top she was wearing belonged to her daughter.

Making my way back to the table from the bathroom, I glanced back to the bar and my eyes had not deceived me. To my amazement, there was Travis sitting at the bar drinking and laughing with some guys.

My instinct was to walk over to make my presence known to him.

"Can I afford to have Erin see me and him together?" I murmured to myself.

I was seeing the lion in his natural habitat and it was a beautiful picture. I couldn't distinctively hear his laugh, yet with his huge smile and the head toss, I could tell it was hardy.

The exuberance he displayed was a Memorex moment. Travis's character was as distinctive as the Seven Wonders of the World: self-defining; unique; everlasting; one of its kind . . .

I continued to walk with my eyes on him.

"Excuse you. You are in my way. Are you going to the bar or what?" asked the same tight-fitting halter top woman, with attitude.

CHAPTER TWENTY-EIGHT

My attention was absent from Erin's dilemma as I rejoined her at our table. The minute image I could grasp on Travis, my eyes were on it.

It was hard work getting Erin to perk up and to have a positive attitude on her situation. She seemed a bit peeved at my distraction.

"Maré, your attention has seemed divided for the last hour or so," she said. Her face creased like a child's not being heard.

"Uh. . . I don't know why you think that. Maybe I'm a little tired. I apologize." I made another quick glance towards Travis.

As her eyes followed mine, she continued, "Is there a brother you want to holla at, at the bar? Don't let me hold you up."

"What are you talking—?"

Placing the ticket on the edge of the table, "Is there anything else I can get for you ladies tonight?" asked the waiter.

"No, we're fine." I looked at Erin. "Thank you."

Exhaustion rushed through my body as we made our way out the front door; there was a faint call of my name. I knew the tone and I knew I couldn't expose my two worlds to one another. Determined, I didn't flinch to Travis's shout.

Tonight was meant to be more productive and not eventful. It dawned on me how unplanned occurrences can either be a positive or a negative.

Atlanta is a large city and every so often I run into an acquaintance, but who would've thought I would have seen Travis? *Could I have been in his circle before and never crossed his path?* I thought.

With the night turning to morning, I knew I had to work on my plan. I popped in a movie, which was on its fourth time being played.

My eyes bulged widely when I loudly spoke my mind, "I'm overdue on these two movies!"

I jumped up to see the rental days on the movie covers. With all that life had put on my table, I had forgotten to look at what I already had.

"Shoot, I'm going to be four days late on these damn things.

How did I let that pass me by?" I griped, as I stomped back to the sofa.

Not too happy with my forgetfulness, I continued with *A Perfect Murder*. My pad and pencil were in my bag across the room.

There wasn't enough strength in me to hold up my heavy eyelids. I knew once I laid on the sofa and set the lighting to a dim glow, it would be all over. My eyes fainted closed.

Startled by the ringing telephone, my eyes popped open. I could barely see from the brightness of the television.

"Hello," I said with agitation.

"What's up? You can't call anymore?" asked Sonya.

I was still a bit groggy from the brief intermission of sleep and the last thing I needed was mess. Thinking over Sonya's question, I guessed it had been a week or two since we had last spoken.

It appeared as if my days and nights were folding into one and I was unable to differentiate one from another. I would've returned those movies if I knew Monday from Thursday.

"What are you talking about?"

She seemed put off by my tone. She slashed back, "I haven't heard from you in over a week."

Listening to her attitude, I felt as if she took my lack of communication personally. You would've thought it had been months.

"Sonya, we spoke the other week," I said, as I yawned.

"You really haven't spoken to Michelle and barely Erin," she stated.

Why did it matter who I spoke with, on what day, and at what time? It bothered me that they felt the need to talk about me behind my back.

I quickly became annoyed by the grade school conversation. "Sonya, I just came from the Shark Bar with Erin. She called me and wanted to do drinks. I'm not sure what all the hoopla is about. If I can call you, then you can call me. I'm tired as hell."

Sonya didn't have much to say. Women have that need for attention from all, may it be a lover or a friend. I think she felt left out of my world.

"I was seeing what was up. Everyone was concerned."

"Well, say that, rather than coming at me like I had done something wrong. If you want to talk, then just call," as the agitation rung in my voice.

The phone filled with pure silence and for a brief moment I allowed my eyes to close. The day had been tiring and I should've just let the phone ring.

"You're right."

We were two friends on the phone at a loss for words. All this came from miscommunication and insecurities. What a day for the insecure friends.

Confusion set in my head after I hung up with Sonya. I wasn't sure what the expectations were of my friends. Each and every one were at different levels in my life.

Erin knows me better than all, yet she still doesn't know me. Michelle knows me less then all of them, but she can be a joy to hang out with. And Sonya, whom I have much in common with, hasn't experienced me at a time of struggle.

When I've had times of struggle and those around me had insight to it, there was an opened window to me. Not many of those windows have been opened and Erin has been through a few with me.

A second wind hit me, so I decided to grab my pad and pencil.

CHAPTER TWENTY-NINE

Not much time and a lot left to do. There I was at the traffic light on a beautiful Saturday morning; a small school of birds lined themselves on the power line. One of the birds lagged behind as he tried to find his place.

There were a few white smidges in the sky, but purity dominated the view. I felt life in the air as I returned the videos.

I rolled down the window. "Let me take care of everything today," I planned aloud.

My "to-do" list seemed long and somewhat complicated, being that I wanted to keep my trail clean. I decided to make my purchases throughout the metro area. My first destination was Sports Authority.

"Welcome to The Sports Authority," greeted the red-headed guy.

I nodded and smiled as I walked past him. "Dude must really love his job. He was as chipper as the first time I came through," I noted to myself.

This time I was a paying customer and knew exactly what I wanted. I searched through the football gloves. I had to locate the ones from before, with the grip and flexibility.

Mumbling to myself, "Which ones were they? They had to be youth size."

"Is there anything I can help you with?" asked a smiling female sales associate.

Stunned by the interruption, "Ah, no. I'm fine, thank you."

It seemed as if I was there forever looking for those damn gloves. I became frustrated, an emotion that, made a regular appearance in my life. I stopped in the middle of the aisle and took a deep breath.

"Relax and do the damn thang!" I continued to look.

Sorting through the gloves, my eyes latched onto the ones I wanted. Anyone passing by would have thought I had won the lottery, as I did a little jig.

As I exited the aisle, my attention was more open and I focused on a cage of basketballs. I placed the gloves on the floor and grabbed a ball. Looking around at the pretty much empty store, I began to dribble. I shot a few hoops into the display goal.

"Hello, did you find everything okay?" asked the steel-mouthed cashier as I place my items on the conveyor belt.

"Thanks. Yeah—no problem."

"Your total comes out to thirty-seven dollars and forty-five cents," she cited. She placed the basketball last into the bag.

Making sure not to leave a name behind, I handed her two twenty-dollar bills.

I skipped out the door and was headed to my next destination. Slowly driving over a speed bump, I saw Sonya and Adrian pulling into a parking spot. Not sure where they had come from, I floored the car.

"Whoa, I wonder if they saw me. Last thing I need are questions."

I made it to TJ-Maxx off Pleasant Hill Road. Still somewhat early in the morning, the traffic wasn't overbearing.

I headed straight to the boys' department in need of a disguise, something that would throw off anyone's perception.

I wasn't sure what to wear. I saw a cool navy blue Polo baseball cap. Searching through each rack of the boy's clothing, I decided to get a pair of basketball shorts.

Looking at the sizes, I mulled to myself, "I gotta get them big and with a draw-string. This will work, with the silver and black."

Continuing to search through the clothing, I found a hooded shirt. It somewhat coordinated with the shorts and I liked the price.

I put the two items up against one another. I thought it was a good combination and it gave off the scent of a teenager. I nodded my head in agreement with my thoughts.

I had become a bit drained from all the driving. The feeling wasn't there for the travel to Marietta. Cobb Parkway had become busy, which was no surprise, being that people don't stay inside around here.

With the sun beaming through the windshield and fatigue creeping up on me, I pulled into the nearest strip mall. There was a Payless. I thought, *I could buy some sneakers there.*

I hadn't been in a Payless Shoe Store in over a decade. I strolled through the boys' shoe section. Today must've been my day. They had a sale going on; almost all of the sneakers were on clearance.

There wasn't a particular style I cared to have, or color. I wanted something that fit my disguise. Out of nowhere, a thought came to my mind to get the shoes a size and a half bigger.

I made my way back to I-285 and I was ready to put my head in the parallel position. To keep myself pumped up, I decided to play my favorite song. If there was a song that fit my life right now, I would say, 'Bottle & Cans' by Angie Stone. Now I don't know if I agreed with all of it, but I felt it.

I bobbed my head to the beat and the air conditioning kicked out as much cool air as it could. I got into a zone and wasn't aware as I sang along.

> "... I'd rather be pickin' up bottles and cans (if you can't be my man)
> I'd rather be homeless in the streets with no food to eat
> I'd rather be facing twenty to life (if I can't be your wife)
> Now I know that it seems like I'm crazy for you
> That's what love can do ..."

My mind took over and began to swirl with thoughts. Was I ready to accept for Travis all that Angie sang about? Was I prepared to except the worst? Was Travis worth it?

"Why am I tripping like this? This is just a song," I said.

I'm not sure if I reassured myself. However, I knew that it was a "go" and nothing could bring doubt inside of me. What I felt for this man was real.

Driving at the speed of eighty, I looked over at my passenger seat to look at my shopping bags.

CHAPTER THIRTY

Slept like a bear last night. I did a Michelle number; I turned off the ringers on my phones. I felt invigorated, something I hadn't felt for some time.

Just as I turned the ringer on, the phone rang. I looked at the Caller ID to see Erin's number. I knew she was calling about church. I wasn't up to it. I wanted to be lazy and lounge around the house.

I decided not to answer to prevent me from hearing her pleading or me lying. There it was on its sixth ring, which seemed like sixty.

Tossing my pillow onto the sofa, I saw my bags on the floor. I decided to try on the gear to see what I looked like.

I tossed off my old, raggedy green nightshirt and put on the hooded T-shirt; then I put on the shorts.

I began to feel myself intertwining into my deviant character. It was like how Clark Kent felt when he displayed his chest with the large letter "S". I knew there was another me, but with my outfit on, my mission was becoming more real.

I felt divided inside, something I had to hide. Too many days and nights I had cried, but soon Travis would be all mine.

Amazement about my capabilities and what I'd come up with so far moved me.

"Yeah, you got this. Handle yourself and it will be all right," I said, reaffirming myself. I began to remove the shorts.

I had not yet decided on how I was going to kill Kayla. It was important to keep it quiet and with little to no struggle. Shooting her wasn't even an option.

I pondered in pure silence continuously, even replaying the movies in my mind, from *Murder by Numbers* to *Unfaithful*.

Each movie had a different plot when it came to committing crimes. Only one was in the heat of passion and the others were calculated. I knew I couldn't become too confident of myself, just enough to do it.

"How should it be done?" I asked myself. "Should it be an attempted burglary or rape?"

I knew those weren't doable. To burglarize the home, I would have to take items from it and I wasn't going to add more to my plate. All I needed was to have stolen evidence in my possession. And to rape her, that would be barbaric.

"I can make it look like a suicide. Yeah, that is it." I smiled to the idea. "I'll look up info on how most people commit suicide."

I jumped to my feet to turn on my computer. I couldn't imagine life without the internet. All of the information I would ever need, right at my fingertips.

Logging onto the internet, I typed in my search criteria: "How to commit suicide."

The search located over two hundred-thousand related websites. *If it's not here, then it's nowhere to be found,* I thought.

The first link contained an article about an Italian man who tried to hijack a plane headed to Paris. I continued to search further.

For a brief moment, I thought I clicked onto a possible informative site, but it turned out to be the site of a rock group with the name Commit Suicide.

The more irrelevant links I opened, the more annoyed I became. Who would've thought I would find so many links for suicide prevention and religious scriptures?

To this point, the easiest task had been picking out my disguise. I selected link after link and it appeared the majority were on how to prevent it. A lot of sites saw this subject as a joke.

I came across *The Practical Guide to Committing Suicide.* My eyes were tired and the long guide made them even more so.

The site shocked me. I never expected to see excerpts of people sharing how they tried to commit suicide. Many tried slitting their wrists, which they failed. Who would've thought there was a correct way to slit your wrists?

I was overwhelmed by all the information. I think those who had attempted or contemplated suicide were on the site giving suggestions saddened me.

Indecisiveness was my feeling on the method.

"Would it be feasible to kill her with carbon monoxide?" I said aloud. "That won't work. I have to knock her out first."

Jamming a pencil up her nose sounded ridiculous. Where did they get these ideas?

Slowly, I leaned back in my chair as my eyes remained on the monitor. There it was: valuable information. It read that mixing bleach and ammonia was toxic, moreso if inhaled as a concentrated gas.

It was a beginning to my crime. I figured that I could use a high dosage of the combination to put her out for the count.

A smile swept across my face, as if to say, "Again I'm victorious." I knew this was going to take place, without a doubt.

CHAPTER THIRTY-ONE

"What got you so happy today?" asked Eugene as he swept the hall.

"Life in itself. Just life," I replied as I smiled.

I wasn't conscious of my mood and that it was visible to anyone. It may have been that the joy I felt was so thick it couldn't be sliced away. Today had gone fantastically and it could only get better.

"You got yourself a boyfriend?"

He has a tendency to probe on matters I find personal. He reminds me of an old woman sitting on a porch in a rocking chair and watching the running of the neighborhood. I bet Eugene could tell me stories about the on-goings around here.

"Like I said, it's just life," with a little flair in my voice.

He stepped closer to me. "I's wondering. I saw you some weeks ago, running out of here all dolled up. I been round long enough to know when a woman got herself a man."

He tried to steal my joy, but that wasn't going to happen. With the reek of liquor as usual, it concerned me that the smell may attach itself onto me.

I began to walk away, telling him, "You have a good one. Stay out of trouble."

He looked at me with the eye of a cobra, as if he was raring to attack me. Sometimes he liked to insinuate situations and he was good when it came to the white teachers. They fed into his "old man with wisdom" antics.

I felt nothing but pure excitement as I waited for Travis. It had been a week and I knew he was probably eager to get to Chicago.

Before I left work, I tried to glamour myself up by putting my hair back in tack with my brown hair clip. I sprayed a little Mango Mandarin body splash on my neck; I walked through a mist I spread in the air. Wanted to catch his attention, but not overdo it.

I could barely hear my surroundings when I got to my destination; the store was amazingly loud today. I took notice on the table tent that there was a book signing this evening. Everyone was piled up to see this author who had written a series of war novels.

Through the full store, I saw Travis making choreographic steps through the crowd. I could feel my smile clear out the entire room. I hoped my basic outfit was okay. When it comes to children, it's not a realistic expectation to come to work jazzed up and leave jazzed up. It's not feasible. I did my best with my hip-hugging jeans and my form-fitting cropped baby blue shirt. I wanted my breasts to catch his attention tonight.

"Hey stranger," he said with a smile.

"How are you doing? Are you ready for the big day?"

"As ready as I'll ever be. I've done all my research and created my personal proposal as to why we should become syndicated in Chicago. I can only do my best and put the rest into God's hands."

He sat there with a blaze in each eye and I don't think anyone could remove them.

He seemed a bit put off by the noise. "What's going on in here today? They must be having a book signing tonight." He scoped out the store. The center of his forehead looked like the veins in a leaf.

As I pointed, I said, "Yeah, there's a book signing."

"I don't like to be swarmed with people and disturbed at a book-store. I came here for a nice hushed atmosphere. Would you like walk over to the CNN Center and find a quiet place in there to talk?"

Inconspicuously, I took in two deep breaths. I had to do what-ever it took not to burst out with joy.

"Sounds cool with me. It looks like this won't be over no time soon," I said with calmness in my voice and ecstasy in my soul.

I walked down International Boulevard with my man, Travis. For the first time, I truly measured the height of this man. Being that I was five feet, five inches, it appeared as if he was like a skyscraper. Yet, he was distinctive with his presence and he glided with each step.

"It was madness in there tonight. I feel people should be more considerate for those who are there to read or whatever. Not focus-ing on self. I forget, we live in a self-absorbed society," said Travis, as he held the door for me.

We located a quaint little deli shop that could barely seat eight people. It was large enough and quiet, for Travis and me.

"Can I get you something?" asked Travis. He reached for a menu. "Might as well eat while we are here."

The last thing on my mind was food. Tonight it was him and me alone, away from our standard meeting place. I got the chance to spend time with him before his trip tomorrow.

"I think I'll get a little something." My leg brushed against his, as I crossed mine.

Reading over the menu, I imagined that his appetite was monstrous, but healthy. Behind me I could hear the passers-by in the atrium; it was minimal compared to the bookstore.

This was the first time we were in each other's presence and there was silence. He decided on his meal and I just melted inside.

Placing his attention on me, he asked, "What is going on with blacks in the media?"

"What do you mean exactly?" Without doubt, I knew he was going to enlighten me. I placed my menu to the side.

"It seems like we are being portrayed in the most negative light the majority of the time. Let me give you an example. We as African-Americans have a cable network whose claim to fame was to cater to us. Now, BET has struggled a great deal and it had some flaws back in its start-up days. It became better with some great shows in the *mid-nineties*. Looking at it now, it's worse today then when it first came on. There is nothing of substance on that network," he proclaimed.

"Travis, time has changed, and no one has taken the lead with our generation to bring some form of a revolution. Farrakhan, he started the Atonement Day, back in what, 1995? That lasted for about two years. BET is reflecting what many have allowed to be the forefront of their lives: materialism."

Briefly, disturbed by the pot-bellied server, we placed our orders. I could tell Travis had a lot on his mind that he wanted to get out. I wondered if his wife allowed him to bounce off issues of the many topics we have engaged in. Or was she not fully engaging in the conversation? He seemed so hungry to talk.

Acknowledging the man, I read my order, "I would like the Caesar salad. Can you please add some extra dressing?"

"Sure, that's not a problem. How about a drink?" asked the man, as he notated on his pad.

"I'll have a medium Coke. Thank you," as I gestured to Travis at my completion.

Anxious to return to the conversation, Travis gave his order, "Yeah, let me get a grilled chicken sub, with light mayo, no onions or salt. Make that with wheat bread and a medium Coke."

The man quickly turned back to us and asked, "Does anyone want chips?"

We both shook our heads with no interest.

Travis continued, "Let me get back to you. I know you know,

and I hope everyone else knows, time has changed. Are we allowing all the hard work put in before us to go down the drain? It was only about fifty years ago when blacks were made to take demeaning roles in the media. The only parts given to us were butlers, valets, or maids, any part that made us look ignorant." His tone deepened.

I could see he was hurt by the turn of events of our people. At that moment, I saw more of his lion traits than ever before. His eyes softened, just a tad, from a deep question inside of "why"?

During our action-packed dialogue, the server placed our orders in front of us.

Sipping from my straw, I engaged his topic. "If you ask people, they will tell you, we have made it. We have it all in control. We've become content with what we have. We're our worst enemy because we expect less of ourselves, as individuals and as a people."

"Maré, we have to open our eyes to how the media is a propaganda against ourselves. Out of all the networks, to find an uplifting non-fiction story is like finding a contact lens in the sand. There isn't any balance on this plane. None whatsoever!" Travis debated. He took another bite of his sandwich.

Right then and there, when our conversation came to a halt, I felt like we bonded emotionally with what he just said.

CHAPTER THIRTY-TWO

My cell rang as I entered my dollar bill into the MARTA token machine. Knowing that my time was strained, I couldn't afford to get caught up in girl talk. I peeped at the LCD to see that it was Michelle, whom I hadn't spoken with for a minute.

"I'll have to call her back," I told myself. I reached for my change and tokens.

I made my way into the sub station to find the route to take to pick up the rental car. By now, I would think I'd be savvy when it comes to taking the train, but I just use it to get to work.

My destination took me up to the Chamblee Station and all I had to do was get on the northeast line. MARTA makes its map easy as hell. They have two colors, orange and blue, and only four options, north, south, east, and west. Just have to know where you're going.

Slightly tired, I made my way onto the train. It amazes me each time I ride the train how it gives me an illusion of living in a large metro city, like New York or D.C. I love looking out the window and seeing the city as I move.

There I was, peering at a railroad car as I heard, "Lindbergh Center."

That was the next stop. I could tell who was getting off by those shuffling to get themselves prepared. It can be quite easy to stare at people. I want to know sometimes what is going on in their worlds.

I relaxed as the people exited and entered the train.

"Dude, I'm telling you, she's cheating on me," said a grunge-looking teen on his cell. "Come on Dale, why would you think I could make something up like this?"

He was a character. I thought, *How does a parent allow their child to leave the house looking like that? With his hair spiked in purple and orange; his fingernails painted black and gray; and his clothing three sizes too big, the boy reflected death.*

Picking in his nose, he spoke loudly, "Dude, I hear what you're saying. There're only so many times I can show up at a party and she's up in another guy's face. You remember that party that Stanley threw? We walked in and some dude is grabbing all on her ass, and what is she doing? Laughing."

I, as well as everyone else around, could hear the anger in his voice. He was in his own little world. The grunge kid said what he felt and maybe because he was hurt by this girl.

I returned to the scenery as I propped up my right leg on the metal ledge running along the footboards. It was beautiful to see the Georgia Tech skyline in the day. When we traveled through the tunnels, that was when I felt like I was in a major metropolis city. There's enough graffiti to be seen on the passing walls.

"Dale, you're not making any sense to me. Why is it that you are taking up for her? Dude, I have to talk to you later because right now I'm becoming pissed with you, too! I got other things to do. Give me time to think about all this. I'll call you later," he instructed with fluster in his tone, as he ended the call. He slid backwards to allow his head to press onto the window.

I could tell he was drained from whatever he was going through. Why should he be? He was a teenager and he was already experiencing the difficulties of relationships. God knew I wanted to say something, but it wasn't my place.

We made several more stops before the conductor announced, "Chamblee."

This was the second to the last stop on this line and everyone piled off. Along with everyone, I made my way to the main street, New Peachtree Road.

The rental place was a few blocks up the street and I was ready for my hike. The sun tearing down on me, I became perturbed.

"Man, it's hot out here. Can I get a breeze or something," I bellyached. I stopped at a light.

I waited for the pedestrian sign to flash for me to walk. I noticed how busy everyone looked as they sped by in their cars. The world stops for no one. I continued and I could see the car rental marquee about two blocks away.

From the heat, I had began to perspire on my stomach and under my breasts. I knew I was almost there as I took my right hand to remove some of the sweat.

"Yes! AC," I cheered in a soft voice as I entered Mega Car Rentals.

"Hello, is there something I can help you with?" asked the full-nosed and small-eyed lady behind the counter.

"Yes, I'm here to pick up my car rental," I replied. I began to dig for my driver's license.

"Okay, may I have your name please?"

I was annoyed with having to use my real name, but I told her, "Maré Alexander."

The full-nosed and small-eyed lady typed away at her keyboard. My eyes roamed the small space and found a water cooler. I was past parched as I gulped down four small cups of water—if they were four ounces.

"Ms. Alexander," she called.

I swiftly turned and made my way back to the counter. I held out my hand to give her identification. "Here is my—" I said.

"Ma'am I don't see a reservation in the system for you." She looked up to discern my possible reaction. "I continued to search to see what we had available at this time and it appears our stock is already spoken for."

I closed my eyes and took a deep breath to maintain my composure. "I called here last week, last Thursday, to reserve a vehicle. The young lady informed me that the amount would be two-hundred and eighty-four dollars and twenty-two cents, being that I wasn't using a credit card."

Time was of the essence. I wasn't moved by the incompetence. I knew I wasn't leaving without my rental.

"Oh! You're renting through the cash deposit plan? Let me look in our files. I apologize. We have that information located in our file cabinet," she clarified, as if I was reassured.

Not finding her cute or reassuring, I gave her a look like she was going to get a beat down, no matter what. I watched as she scuffled through the files. I propped my head up with my arm on the counter.

"Here it is. I'm so sorry for this inconvenience. I would like to give you half off on your second day of rental. That would make your new total two hundred and seventy-three dollars and twenty-three cents. And you already know, you will receive your deposit with the return of the car." She smiled with pride.

I gave her a smirk as if to say it was never any fear that I was leaving without a ride. "That sounds fine with me. I would like a receipt with that information."

She typed up the information and I reviewed it like Michael Jordan would his Nike contract. All looked fine and she pointed me to my rental. There it was, a gray Dodge Neon with two doors. Could the car be any uglier?

CHAPTER THIRTY-THREE

The air conditioning was on full blast as I made my way home. It was true what Gran always used to say, "The heat will take away your energy." At that point, I was ready for a night of deep sleep.

"Now how do I want to do this? My car is at the train station," I said, as I was getting closer to home.

I drove around the Indian Creek MARTA parking lot to find my car. There was an ugly Neon, just like the one I was driving, pulling out of the parking spot next to me. I took the space and stepped out.

I looked around the rental to make sure everything was intact. I walked over to my car and started it up. I stretched my neck up towards the rearview mirror, to see if I was looking like I felt. My eyes were red as an apple. I relaxed my neck and put the car into reverse.

"I gotta get home and take care of everything else. Make sure I get everything organized. After that, I gotta get some sleep," I said aloud. "Damn, should I call Michelle back tonight?"

I entered the house and the sofa was calling my name. I knew I couldn't stop for one second because I would be down for the count. I dropped my purse at the entrance in the foyer.

"Let me get my toxic mix together," I verbally planned, as I walked towards the pantry. Everything I needed was sitting on the floor.

I grabbed the facemask package to put one over my mouth and nose. I didn't want to experience the fumes. I grabbed the bleach and ammonia and placed them onto the kitchen counter, next to the sink.

Slowly, I poured the bleach into an old 409 bottle. I began to perspire, bringing to my attention that the air conditioner wasn't on. I walked to the living room to turn it on. As expected, the system kicked on immediately, with the thermometer reading eighty degrees.

I put my attention back onto pouring the bleach into the bottle. "They didn't say how much would be needed. I'll just do half and half," conversing with myself.

My body temperature began to cool. I think having that facemask on made me hotter than normal. I clutched the ammonia steadily as I began to mix it with the bleach. I could hear a slight sizzling noise. My eyes widened with amazement.

I put my clothes into my backpack. I went over each item to make sure I didn't forget one thing.

"Okay, I got the shorts, shoes, shirt, gloves, facemask, baseball cap, and the mix I'll leave out for now. Is that everything?" I asked myself. I looked around the bedroom. "Rag—a rag for the stuff."

Darting off to go downstairs, my left ribcage made contact with the corner of my metal sleigh bed. "Ugh-um-Ugh. Damn-damn-damn!"

I made it to the pantry and I was still crooked over with pain. To make matters worse, what I thought I needed wasn't even there. *Making* my way back upstairs, I thought on what I could use. It wasn't a major element; I needed a rag or cloth to put the mixture on.

I placed the bag and basketball at the bottom of the stairs. I sat to finally take a breather. Yet I knew the night was still young and I had to keep my trail clean, so I'd better call Michelle back.

"What's going on Ms. Williams?" I asked.

"The question is, what's been going on with you? We haven't spoken in a while. What have you been up to?"

Not quite sure what she knew, I wanted to make sure I covered myself and not be too evasive.

"Nothing too much. Had some drinks with, um, Erin last Friday, down at the Shark Bar. Other than that, nothing to scream about," I said, as I laughed. Wasn't prepared to go into the Sonya conversation and who knows, she may have been aware of it.

"Same here. Did you ever hear from Hollis again?"

Not sure where she was going with this question, I answered her honestly. "Yeah, the other week. I told him how I felt and that I had no problem being his friend. That's all I could see with him."

"Sonya told me what he did. I was shocked to hear that. I don't understand it. You sure you can't get past that? He may have been, you know, nervous, Maré."

I felt as if she was being too intrusive and that she may have had a motive. I really wasn't feeling the twenty-one questions game tonight. Why did I feel the need to answer her questions about my decision?

"Michelle, I really don't want to go into that right now. I made my decision and feel that's that. It would be nice to get some support, rather than feedback. If you're interested in him, I'll give you his number," I said in a facetious voice.

I could sense the tension I just created beginning to brew inside

Michelle. For me to snap on her like I did wasn't my character and she was not prepared for this side of Maré.

"Hold up, I must've missed something," said Michelle with attitude. "Where is all this flip lip coming from? I don't know and don't care at this point. You better check yourself because I'm not trying to curse you out right now. So whatever you got going on, I'm going to let you go, so you can resolve it."

Damn, I wasn't trying to start up a fight with her. I just got tired of her questions and they seemed more interfering then usual. There I was, angered at myself and happy with what I told her.

"It's not even like that Michelle. I'm tired and there are times I need my girls to be behind me one hundred percent without trying to fix it. You are pissed at me and whatever I say, you're not trying to hear."

"I'm going to let you go. Heard you and I'll holla at you later," she said unexpectedly, still with anger in her tone.

From the drain-filled day and the stress-filled conversation, I felt my emotions beginning to run over. Before I knew it, I began to cry. There I was, sitting on the sofa feeling alone. My world was filled with so much and yet it was empty. I had been so focused on getting everything in order that there wasn't any time to be with me.

Alone with myself, I sat filled with distress. I felt lost. "Gran, I feel so empty inside right now. Why Gran—Why? Can anyone ever love me as you did? I need the attention, understanding, passion and love that you had trademarked in each hug and kiss."

CHAPTER THIRTY-FOUR

Awakened by the bugle horn-sounding alarm, I opened my eyes and reached over to shut it off. There I lay on my back in the bed, in complete darkness with the day in my mind. I knew I needed guidance and protection.

I stared up toward the ceiling as I prayed, "Oh, Dear Heavenly Father, I know you already know my plans for this day. I'm somewhat ashamed of asking for your protection throughout the day. Please guide me in the right direction. Today's prayer is different than the days before. God, you know why. Help me."

I took in a deep breath as I allowed my eyes to close. Humiliation ran through my body from asking the Lord to be with me in my time of sin. How could I have asked that when one of the Ten Commandments is ". . . thou shalt not kill . . ." But I knew I needed protection.

I made my way to the MARTA station. I drove until I located the rental car; two huge SUV trucks sandwiched it in. I found a parking space two rows over.

My mind was preoccupied with what I knew was about to take place tonight. I didn't think this would bother me. Could it have been the turn of events on last evening? But now I needed a place that would take all my troubles away. I headed to work.

When I entered the classroom, Patrick bomb-rushed me with open arms. "Ms. Maré, look at what I made."

The blond-headed toddler grabbed my hand and I went along with him. The moment was like entering a different world and lately I had taken it for granted.

"Let me see what you have here." I placed my purse on the table and took a seat. "Wow! Patrick, you drew this all by yourself? Look at all the pretty colors—green, blue, and yellow."

With a smile that tied behind his head, he said in a cheerful voice, "Yes. And I picked the colors, too."

"You did a great job. I'm proud of you," I praised, as I rubbed his back. "Let me put my purse away, okay? You continue with your masterpiece."

I love it when I feel needed and wanted. These children make me feel as valuable as their favorite toy. Then there are times they will switch up on me and that's when I return to reality.

I found myself swallowed up by the joy of the children today, as if I hadn't a care in the world. I felt serene within myself. The room made my life seem imperishable.

"Maré, I want to thank you for putting me on the right track this summer," said Andrea with humility. "Monday is my last day and I hope we can do lunch."

There I was, cramped into one of the kiddy chairs while I reorganized the painting utensils. I looked up, "That sounds fine with me. I'll let Betty know and maybe she can give us some lead way on time," I said, as pride rushed through my heart.

The day was flowing ever so heavenly. Had God answered my prayers, or was Gran trying to say something to me? All I knew was, I wanted my days to continue like this.

I felt no confusion in my body or heart. Life appeared simplistic and real. As the children napped, I began to write out my thoughts onto a piece of green construction paper.

All I Want Is To Be Me
To be me is all I want
The freedom to air without care
The ability to talk without wondering who is there
All I want is to express my ways of happiness
Without bringing any confusion or madness.
To have a deep sense of peace within me
All I want is to be me

It seemed as if I lost a portion of myself when I became knotted with the affections for Travis. But I knew once all was completed, I could return to that part of me.

I made it through a beautiful day, which was nothing but a positive sign to me. As I walked onto Luckie Street, the smoldering heat hit me like a bee sting. The vapors and smog hung low in my face. It had to be one of those bad air quality days. The lingering cigarette smoke blown into my face by a blue-suited yuppie sure didn't help matters.

There it was, a constant reminder. I can always be found by my cell phone.

"Hello," I said, walking with the crowd of pedestrians.

"Hey. What are doing this evening? If you're not busy maybe we can do dinner or something."

Erin was in need of some of my time and tonight wasn't it. I very seldom denied her the support that she needed. However, she knows I'm not a weekday girl. That's not me, but I would open my home to her for some conversation.

"Oh. What's going on? How are you doing?" I asked.

I could hear her speaking to someone, "I really don't know, Maré. I really don't know. I'm trying to keep a grip on what I have now and still have room for more. It seems like life is smothering me. Some of it includes Ezekiel. Hold on, my manager is calling."

A thought ran in my mind and made it to my lips, "I hope I haven't gone over my minutes."

I held there on the line as I bobbed my head to the classic jazz hold music. I knew I was going to have to tell her no. The needless lying was getting to me, when it came to Erin. She may never know. I will. What can I say to . . .?

"Maré! Forget about it. I'm so sick and tired of this job," she said with distress.

"What's going on?" I asked, with pure delight in my mind.

"My manager got me working on this stupid project with him. You would think he would know how to create and develop all the documents he needs for the weekly margin contribution meeting. Anyhow, he feels some of the data on the reports needs to be re-worked. Which means my butt is here tonight." Frustration filled her voice.

"Don't let them get to you. You know you are good at what you do. Take everything they give, for your own benefit," I said in a consoling tone, as I stood a few feet from Peachtree Center.

"I know. Let me go, but I'll talk to you later." Erin sighed heavily through each word.

Right then and there I turned off my cell to alleviate any more distractions. I had to be alone for the remainder of this day. I couldn't even allow myself to reflect on the mood of Erin because I knew she was taking it to an extreme.

CHAPTER THIRTY-FIVE

My pulsating showerhead helped remove some of the knots on my back; the water's warm touch relaxed me. I didn't allow one inch of my skin to go un-caressed. Sometimes I think it would be nice to do the white-girl thing and allow my entire head to be submerged by the water and not have to do anything with my hair. That thought only lasted for a millisecond.

I prepared myself for the evening. Preparing my hair was very important because I must appear to be a boy. I folded my hair upward and put on a skullcap.

Then I tossed an extra set of clothes into another bag and a few extra items that had come to mind on the train ride home.

In the full-length mirror, I marveled at myself in astonishment. I wanted to get a visual from every possible angle. I posed and turned; front to back and left to right. I even stepped back to practice the masculine walk. I knew once I left the house, Maré was no more. The character of the night had arrived.

The humid night was beautiful, as the half-moon rested low in the sky. I cruised to the music of the world. As I turned onto Flat Shoals Parkway, there were the flashing lights of a fire truck. I pulled to the right as it sped by.

I became a bit warm, so I rolled down my window. I reached behind to roll down the back one, too. The cap on my head, I'm sure, was the culprit of my rising temperature.

It seemed as though nothing fazed me. Everyone on the highway was driving like they were in the Indy-500 and I was someone's grandma stuck in the middle.

"This is where I'm no longer Maré. Let me grab everything and head to the car," I said, to reaffirm myself as I entered the MARTA parking lot.

I decided to park several rows over from the rental. The car was where I had left it. I threw my bags into it and cranked it up. My heart almost jumped out my chest when the radio came blasting through the manufactured sound system. The last thing I wanted to hear was some R. Kelly. Catching myself, I turned off the radio to continue to drive in silence.

Traffic was jammed at the Ashford-Dunwoody exit. Taking notice of the clock, I couldn't understand what could be going on at eight o'clock. I finally made it onto the main street; I could see all the traffic turning into the Crown Plaza-Ravina.

"That's where the gala is," I said, accelerating with the traffic.

It had been a week or so since I'd been in Travis's neighborhood. Tonight wasn't about sight-seeing or just peeping. This was about taking care of business.

Driving down the road I had come to know, I noticed that it had been newly paved. It was so fresh that the centerline wasn't complete. It was enough to divide the street. I felt as if I had been missing out on life in just the short time I hadn't visited.

I slowly drove past the house and everything appeared exactly as I remembered. The outside light lit up the red brick steps of the house.

At the next major road, about two blocks away off Mt. Vernon, was a church, where I decided to park in a dark portion of the parking lot.

My eyes peered upward towards the cross on the temple of the Catholic church. I could only imagine how enormous it was; maybe the outside appearance was reflective. I lacked fear and was unable to acknowledge my presence. My emotions weren't in existence. I might as well have been a computer, filled with information and nothing more.

I unzipped the book bag to make sure I had everything. I didn't want to bring attention to myself, so with each item, I ran my fingers over it and looked intently in the dark. There was everything I felt I needed, from my gloves to my toxic mix.

I took a deep breath and recited one of Travis's quotes, "Lead, Follow or Get out the way."

With the basketball in my right hand, I opened the door and stepped out.

It was a surprise to see how busy the street was. The cars zoomed up and down Mt. Vernon. Is there a place in Atlanta where everyone sleeps?

My eyes zoomed southward to patrol my clothes, to make sure I was intact. I threw on my baseball cap to conceal my face. No one could make me out as a female, let alone as Maré.

Crossing over the busy street, I dribbled the basketball. My technique wasn't at the varsity level, but it was nothing to sleep on, either. With each bounce, the sound echoed in the air. It sounded like a cadence.

It felt invigorating to be outside my world. I was in this neighborhood disguised as a teenage boy and no one knew what was about to take place. The street was lit up from the lights inside each home.

Tossing the ball back and forth in my hands, I could hear the crying of a baby. I would've thought it was being killed by how loud the cries were.

Crossing over the street opposite Travis's house, I checked on the time. It was about twenty minutes before nine. I knew time was growing near. I made it to the high school's basketball court.

I placed my bag on the ground and began to shoot some hoops. I started out at half court; then my adrenaline began to increase with each lay-up shot. Before I knew it, it was going on nine o'clock and I had extended play to full court.

Gathering my bag and myself, I began to walk towards my destination. I wanted to go unnoticed from that moment on. I held the basketball under my left arm, looking to see what was going on in the neighborhood as I made it closer to the street.

I darted across the street and I faded into the night's dark and shrubbery on the edge of Travis's yard. I quickly made my way to the garage door that was left ajar. I dropped to the ground, forced the basketball through, and began to inch my way into the space.

My body made it, up to the point where the book bag met with the door. I slid back out and removed the bag from my shoulders. Once I did that, I made it inside easily.

I was inside of Travis's garage and there was his truck. From what I could see, it was well maintained. They kept all of their equipment organized.

I could hear the squeaking of a car's breaks.

"Okay, Phase Two complete. She should be here soon," I whispered.

To shield myself, I hid underneath his truck. In the hot night and the stuffy space, I began feeling halfhearted about this night. Thoughts ran through my mind about what I was doing. I was somewhat amazed at what I had already done.

Stuck under a truck and breathing heavily wasn't my field of dreams. Was doubt running across my mind or was it fear?

CHAPTER THIRTY-SIX

I knew I had to use my down time because it was valuable. I laid on my stomach and my elbows, pressing heavily into the cement; I contrived a way into my bag.

Wanting to be prepared, I secured the facemask around my neck and allowed it to rest on my forehead. Placing the gloves on each hand topped off the gear and I was ready physically.

Even though I was emotionless, somewhere in my head I was thinking of turning back. Not sure what it was, but I knew I couldn't.

Using my book bag as a pillow, I rested my head. Before I could get comfortable, there was a glare of light seeping through the cracks of the garage doors. I could hear her pulling up and the garage door lifting. The lights from her BMW brought clarity into the dark space.

"I don't know about the changes when it comes to the plot, but I know this play is finally flowing for me," said Kayla. "With Travis gone, I'll be able to work on it a bit more intensively."

I could hear her voice bouncing in the garage. There wasn't any pleasure in listening to her phone conversation, let alone speaking of Travis.

"Yeah, I'll be here a couple days while he's out of town. I'm happy," she said, laughing aloud. "Let me get off this phone, so I can grab these bags."

It was time to put my plan to work and to execute it perfectly. I didn't have time for doubt or mistakes.

I listened as she grabbed the grocery bags from the car. I timed it, to allow myself one last breath, prayer, and thought.

With caution, I began to roll from under Travis's truck. I doused the rag with the ammonia and bleach mix. Walking towards the door to the house, I could see that it was cracked, making my entrance effortless.

Making my way into the door, I began to anticipate the job. I was wondering, *Could it go through without a snag?* Placing each step with prudence, I knew I wasn't turning back.

I stood in the sunroom, which connected the garage and

kitchen, watching her put away her day's shopping. It wasn't much; it must've been extras.

The kitchen was beautiful from what I could see. My eyes remained on Kayla. She was wearing a hazel linen outfit. She had kicked off her mocha Kenneth Cole shoes at the entrance.

Before another moment passed, I jumped into action. Her back was to me. I wrapped her arms with my left arm; it tangled her up. Before Kayla knew it, my right hand followed with the rag drenched with toxic fumes over her mouth and nose.

All the strength I could muster was ample to hold off her struggling. Each time she jerked her head to get away from the fumes, I pressed the cloth harder into her face. She moaned and attempted to scream.

What seemed like an eternity was about a minute and a half. Kayla's body began to lose its vigorous intellect to fight. Her head fell forward and her body slumped in my arms. It took more strength to hold her lifeless body.

I placed her onto the kitchen's hardwood floors. I stood there staring at her, wondering if she was truly dead. To make sure, I poured more ammonia and bleach onto the cloth and put it to her face. I sat there, at the top of her head, holding it.

"Damn—my hat fell off and I didn't even notice," I mumbled through my heavy breathing. I reached for it near her left calf.

I thought that she was out and it was a victorious night. My body was as lifeless as Kayla's.

There I stood, in his home. I could've only imagined what the inside looked like from the outside, but now I was there.

"This is too beautiful," I said, awed. I began to walk around.

The black appliances and the wood countertops coordinated well with the breakfast bar's black Corian surface. My mouth was wide open as I toured the house. The dining room's exceptional style was unquestionable. It was painted in a dusty eggplant color. The table's wooden cream color brought light to the room; the place sets coordinated perfectly with the walls.

"I bet the bedroom is remarkable." I walked up the stairs. "This is going to be me, very soon."

My eyes popped opened from the shear loveliness of the master bedroom. It was outrageous in size. The sitting area, which surrounded a fireplace, was breathtaking. The unmade bed couldn't take anything away from the room.

I knew I had to leave and that the tour was over. Making my way back downstairs, I heard the phone ring. There was Kayla on the floor and she faintly moved her head.

"What? I didn't see what I thought?" I asked myself in a whisper.

I remained composed. It was time to take it to another level. Without a moment to spare and thoughts running in my mind, I began to drag her into the family room. Again the phone rang with a tone of persistence. I knew it was important to finish.

Placing Kayla in an Indian style position in front of a green leather chair, I was in motion. I walked back to the kitchen and grabbed a knife.

I stood in front of this beautiful woman and for a brief moment I felt sympathy for what I had done. I was wondering if I should walk away. She never saw me.

CHAPTER THIRTY-SEVEN

The night was nothing but an out-of-body experience as I jumped into the Dodge Neon. The realization of my actions wasn't present. I became disconnected and I wasn't sure when I would return.

Turning the ignition, the car stereo began to blast again. I pulled out onto Vermack Road and crossed over Mt. Vernon Road. Driving down the street, I didn't acknowledge Travis's house.

"Michael Jackson is the man. I don't know what Whitney is talking about. Shoot! Bobby Brown isn't the King of Pop," I rambled. ". . . rock with you . . ." I harmonized along with the radio.

I continued to move to the groove of Michael's old jam. While sitting at the traffic light, my senses began to return. I'm not sure if it was the beat of the music or if it was just time.

"My God, what have I done?" I asked myself, as I sat in shock.

The world around me was no longer visible, until the driver behind me laid on their horn. The light had turned green. I became crippled by the events that occurred in that house. I was a runaway slave as I drove full-speed ahead.

Again, I hadn't an ounce of logic in my actions as I drove onto I-85 South. Was I wanting to get out of town? Where was I running to? My heart began pulsating as I drove, with my hands at the three and nine o'clock positions on the steering wheel.

I was truly nowhere near my home and wasn't sure where I was going. I decided to exit at Tara Boulevard. I had literally driven from one end of the city to the other, and most days I wouldn't drive forty miles in Atlanta without complaining.

My mind had surely taken over and I followed what it thought was rational. I pulled into the first gas station off the exit and drove back into the darkest vicinity of the parking lot.

I recognized that fear had crippled me. My eyes filled up like a monsoon and my nose ran like the Chattanooga River, constantly. I became angered for allowing myself to be scared. I punched the center of the steering wheel with precision; left-right and left-left.

"Why am I scared? Why am I feeling this way?" I posed to myself, as I ran the back of my right forearm against my nose. "Why did I have to take it further, as if the chemicals weren't enough?"

I sat there staring at the hands that were purely violent and, through the tears, I was able to make out a spot of blood on a portion of the gloves. Becoming hysterical, I started to disrobe in a frenzy.

Not allowing myself to calm down, it took three times as long to remove the clothing. I struggled getting the shirt over my head as I tugged roughly to get my left arm free. I yanked so hard my hand came flying out and hit the horn.

My attention was caught as I looked to see if anyone had noticed me for the first time. There were a few Latino men walking away from their van towards the building's entrance. It was a noisy strip and maybe no one took notice.

I cleaned my face, but tears continued to trickle down. I pulled out a pair of shears from my book bag and began cutting everything I wore. It was possible blood could be on any portion of the clothing.

"I have to get rid of this stuff. I don't want anything coming back to me," I sniffled. I continued to cut the sole of the sneaker erratically.

Looking at the pieces in the passenger seat, I knew what I had to do. Adjacent to the car was a large dumpster. I grabbed some of the cut up fragments and opened the door. As far I could see, no one was paying any attention to me. I tossed the items quickly and returned to the car.

The night was late and I needed to get rid of the rest, so I started the car. I was startled from the blasting radio, so I reached over and turned it off.

Making my way back north, I knew it was going to be a quiet ride home. Still filled with emotional turmoil, I hoped to get home by twelve. I then noticed the signs reading I-75 North. I had driven further than what I had perceived.

Driving along the highway, I decided to exit at Morrow Road to toss the remainder of the clothes. I spotted a dark strip plaza and drove to the back to locate its dumpsters.

I tossed the pieces and jumped back into the car. I picked up speed as I returned to the front of the stores. Out of nowhere, there was a police cruiser, sitting in the parking lot.

"Where did he come from? Damn! Okay, just remain calm and all will be fine." I drove over the speed bump, not sure if I should drive across the lot illegally or follow the law. There weren't any other cars insight. It was just Five–0 and me.

"I don't need a reason for him to look at me. Do this right."

The hectic evening was taking a toll over me. My body felt weak and my soul felt weary. All I could do was cry softly as I drove up I-20. The lights were bright and once again I felt alone. In a city as large as Atlanta, no one was near. The interstate was empty.

"What was I thinking? I gotta go to the train station to pick up my car. I'm ready for this night to end," I said drowsily.

I pulled into the lot, and there was MARTA police doing their rounds. He crossed over into the next lot and I pulled into the first available parking space.

I did a plain-view check of the car to make sure that nothing was left. There were a few clothing pieces that I grabbed and tossed into the book bag.

"Where is the basketball?" I asked myself. "Don't tell me!"

Too tired to become any more frazzled for the evening, I got out of the car and made it to my own. It was the first time that night I started a car without my ears being blasted out with music.

The concern of the left basketball began to weigh on my mind and I was disappointed.

"How did I allow this to happen?" I continued to question myself.

Was it in my best interests to return and get it? I knew I couldn't afford to revisit the scene of my crime. It would be pure stupidity. But what made that thought any more ridiculous than me leaving the ball behind?

CHAPTER THIRTY-EIGHT

My eyelids felt like cement blocks the next day; they had a mind of their own, and I agreed with them. I knew the day was going to be trying, but I had to keep myself on task.

"Ms. Maré, why are you sleepy?" asked a brunette toddler, staring at me.

"I didn't sleep well, Troy, that's all." I allowed my head to fall into the palm of my hands.

He crouched lower to look through my hands. It was like a game of peek-a-boo. There he peered at me with his innocent smile. His deep green eyes pierced into me with genuineness.

He made his way through my crossed arms and closed legs and gave me a hug. It was as if he knew what I needed. The hug spoke to me, saying that everything would be okay. My right cheek softly fell onto his silky dark hair.

Troy's embrace ignited me with a spurt of energy, but not enough to erase the previous turbulent evening. I knew life could be worse and I had to make the best of this Friday.

"Maré, the director and I decided to allow you to leave early today. You have your lesson plans to prepare for the beginning of school next Wednesday," said Betty.

In light of all I'd been going through, I had forgotten about school and my new incoming students.

"Thanks, Betty, I can use the time to do just that. Prepare," I said with a smidgen of forgetfulness in my eyes.

It shouldn't be much work to do. Like most teachers, I'll retrieve my plans from last school year.

On the train ride home, my mind became deluded with thoughts of going home and getting face down under the covers. It felt great to be riding and being able to rest.

Whenever I became immobile, my mind replayed the night at Travis's over and over; I tried to replace those thoughts.

From the battle of my thoughts, the wrong and the right, I fell into a light sleep. I seldom allowed myself to appear vulnerable in public places; that instance was an exception.

The squealing of the train brakes awakened me. Lifting my head from the window, I rubbed my right eye to clear my vision. Looking at the signage, I saw mine was the next stop.

I hadn't realized how drained I was until I walked to the parking lot. Walking around, I wasn't seeing what I came for: the rental car. Concern ripped through my mind.

"Damn! Where is the car? Oh, God, please let me find this car." I prayed, as my mind began to wake up.

I walked briskly through the lot and stopped from weariness. The sun attached itself to my left cheek. The fusion of the high temperature and the sleep depravation had me feeling as if I was losing my mind.

"I know the car wasn't towed. Please don't let that be." I turned in a circle. "Aw, man, why am I trippin'? I'm in the wrong freaking lot."

A few beads of sweat populated on my forehead as I walked to the other lot. I was too occupied in locating the car to wipe them away. I knew I was ready to get out of my jeans and cotton, half-sleeve, V-neck shirt.

It was right where I left it. A huge sigh of relief rushed through my chest cavity while I made my way to the car. I opened the door and my eyes did a sweep of the vehicle to make sure all was intact.

I turned the ignition and the radio came on at full blast. I reached to turn it off, but I detected the beat of the song. Moving my head to the intro, there were the lyrics,

"Everything is everything . . ."

"Oh, snap, that's Lauryn Hill. That's what I'm talking about." I turned on the AC and threw the car into reverse.

The music magnified me in some way. Out of any artist, when it comes to R&B or hip-hop, Lauryn has my respect. No one can touch her skills. With the air on full blast and the music blaring in my ears, I caught a second wind.

Traffic began to slow down as I made my way around I-285. The traffic inched along and I continuously tried to peer through the congestion to see what was going on up ahead.

My eyes dropped to notice the fuel gauge. With the trip around Atlanta last night, I only had a third of a tank left. With the halt of traffic and the air conditioning on, I was hoping I had enough to make it to the car rental place.

To use my time wisely, I decided to call Erin. "What's going on?"

"Hey, what have you been up to? I called you last night."

"Nothing too much, just checking on how you're doing. Have

you worked things out with Ezekiel?"

"I'm going to work on myself. You know what I've been through in the past, with Darren cheating on me and Marcus who constantly lied every chance to he got. I'm not going to allow the past to mess up what I have right now. It's a good thing," she said.

It was good to hear that Erin recognized her insecurities. They came from men who didn't value her strength and her character. She wanted this to last between her and Ezekiel.

"So you never mentioned anything else to him about his change?" I probed for more details.

"Nope. I thought about what you said. Then I had a night of reflection on me. Why is it that he has to be doing something wrong? You know? Filling my mind with negative thinking. He said he has been tired, then so be it," she said so profoundly.

"Wow! Sounds like you're handling things and it sounds like a winner to me. Dr. Phil says we have to look at ourselves first. It's going be okay," as I smiled with pride in my voice.

Knowing Erin, doubt may find its way back into her mind, but right now I knew she had recognized it and was working on it. I prayed that Zek treated her like the queen she is. She wanted to be married and was tired of the endless relationships.

"I can't promise that I won't question his actions again, but for now, it's going to be about me." She laughed. "So what were you into, Missy, yesterday evening?"

She couldn't leave well enough alone. Traffic still at the pace of an infant's crawl, I didn't want to lie to her.

"Girl, I had a long and tiresome day, so I must've been out." Hoping to curb her appetite on me.

"Where are you now? It's kind of late for you to be doing lunch."

"Oh, I'm off until school starts next week. So don't hate," I said teasingly.

"Anyway. Believe me, I'm not hating on you. What you got planned for the weekend?" asked Erin.

First thing that came to mind was sleep, sleep, and more sleep. I really wasn't trying to be out in the streets.

"Nothing too much, probably relax and prepare for my classes. Why?"

"I think Michelle and Sonya are trying to go out tonight or Saturday."

"Tonight is most definitely out the picture, for me." I got a view of what obstructed traffic. In the far right lane were two mangled cars. I couldn't decipher the make or model. I could clearly see the black car was damaged beyond recognition, like a soda can I would have crushed with my foot, back in the day.

"Maré, are you still there?" yelled Erin.

"Yeah, I'm looking at this accident that had traffic backed up. It's amazing to see the damage. I hope no one died," I said in a solemn tone.

"You be careful out there. There isn't a day that goes by without an accident—not a day. Let me go. I'll let you know what comes up this weekend."

Looking ahead, the highway was pretty much clear. Every vehicle sped off when they made it past the accident scene, as if they could make up for the twenty-minute traffic delay.

The car began to jump into gear to meet the vacant highway when my head jerked forward. It was a surprise that I didn't need at that moment.

CHAPTER THIRTY-NINE

Astounded by what I felt and what I thought occurred, anger started bubbling inside my veins. My eyes made it the review mirror to see a white woman throw her hands onto her steering wheel.

"What the hell!" I said in an irate tone, as I exited the car.

Walking to the rear of the Neon, I could see the damage of the other car, as images ran in my head as to what my car could look like.

"I'm so sorry. I apologize for my incompetence. This is so wild, I couldn't tell you how this occurred. The damage is solely on my vehicle!" rambled the overly tanned, tall woman.

Inspecting the dents and scratches, I replied, "I just spent about a half an hour in this traffic, due to a horrible accident. It's too damn hot to be out here waiting for the police to make their way out here or even finish that one up back there. You have inconvenienced me."

My patience was very high. Maybe I was happy that the rental car wasn't damaged. At the speed of a foot moving to avoid a falling knife, my mind registered the impossibility of me filing a police report.

"Again, I apologize. I have my . . . "

Tension railroaded itself inside me. "No, I don't have time! I can't afford to be dealing with the police and waiting. It really looks like your problem and not mine. My question is, how do you suggest we solve this in a timely fashion?"

My expectation was for her to ride off and deal with it herself. The damage didn't leave her with an un-drivable car. The busted headlight and bent fender on her new model Camry was minimal damage.

Astonished by my tone, she suggested, "I think we should file a report. My insurance company won't take care of my damages without one."

"You must didn't understand or hear what I just said. Let me put it like this. Being that you hit me from the back, you are at fault. As a matter of fact, I think my neck and back are becoming stiff," as the tension revealed itself in my voice.

There we stood in the second left lane. Passersby looked on to see Part Two of the traffic holdup on their journey. Even a few honked their horns. That's how it is in Atlanta, a lot of insensitive souls. Sad thing about it, I could relate to them.

"I never got your name," she said.

"Does it really matter? I never asked for yours."

Hesitant to by reaction, she said, "I'm not trying to be a headache, but I would like to handle this appropriately. I can see that this was my fault and time is being wasted here. I think I can handle this on my own."

Within the revelation during our conversation, my heart began to race to a preset beat of a metronome. Entering the car, I could feel my pulse in my neck. I looked into the review mirror to observe the tanned woman beginning to slowly pull away.

"Where is that cop going?" I asked myself.

There in the left emergency lane the cruiser proceeded with his lights flashing. Did the lady call 911 without my knowing? This was not a good sign, not at all. I slightly let up off the accelerator as the police continued in my direction. Before I knew it, he was three car lengths ahead me.

"Whoa! I could've sworn that was my ass," I said with relief.

I continued to Chamblee to return the rental car. Peachtree Industrial was a smooth exit off the highway. At the traffic light, I decided to search the car to make sure nothing incriminating was left.

All looked well except the fuel gauge. I pulled into the BP gas station, across from Lowe's. I didn't mind filling the car up, with the reasonable gas prices. I've seen prices as high as a dollar sixty-nine; so one forty-two was a blessing.

Inserting my debit card, I noticed the sign that read 'Use Debit/ Credit Cards Inside' taped on the pump's base.

"I can't stand it when they do that. It defeats the purpose of using the debit card," I said in aggravated manner to myself.

I walked toward the cashier to pay at the same time as another patron.

"Go right ahead," said the dusty looking old man.

Excepting his offer, I nodded. "Thank you."

The gas station attendant processed my card while the old man and I stood in silence. I grabbed my receipt and exited the store.

Returning the rental car ended my chronicles when it came to the killing of Travis's wife. I knew he would be returning sometime soon. Exhausted from the mission, there weren't any immediate feelings about his return; however, I was looking forward to seeing him.

I loathed the train ride back to Decatur. It seemed like the last twelve-plus hours had been trips up, down, around, and through Atlanta. Right now, I had seen enough of it.

"Oh, my God, I thought I'd never make it home," I said with exhaustion as I dropped my purse in the foyer.

I closed the door and headed straight towards the sofa. My early time off allowed me to get home to see Oprah shaking her guests' hands as the credits rolled. As I lay on the sofa, my body began to melt into the cushions, as I faded into restful sleep.

"We have breaking news!" said Monica Kaufman, anchorwoman, for Channel 2 Action News.

My eyes slightly peeled opened to see what the news reporter was speaking about.

A sense of importance was readable in her eyes. "There has been a dead body discovered in Dunwoody, on Vermack Road. We will keep you posted as we gather further information."

The television was barely visible through my eyelashes, but my ears were as alert as a deer's.

"What!" My eyes sprung open. "I wonder if it's Travis's wife's body she was talking about. It has to be!"

The time to relax was no longer available because of my racing thoughts. Sitting on the sofa I began to wonder if it was Kayla and how she was discovered? I hadn't really thought of the affect it would have on me, once she was discovered.

"Maybe Travis is home now," I said, with speculation in my mind. "I hope his trip was a success."

I became more inquisitive to who, what, when, why, and how of this reported dead body. The concern of me being fingered wasn't an issue. I was more captivated on how the story would be reported and the speculations.

With sleep last on my mind, I walked to the kitchen for a glass of kiwi-flavored water. For the first time in quite some time I was anxious for something or someone other than Travis.

The once lazy eyelids were vibrant and well percolated. I sat on the sofa horizontally with my back resting against the right armrest. I allowed the cool water to quench my thirst and activate my taste buds, as I took moderate sips from the white plastic cup.

"How long is it going to take before they come up with the full story?"

CHAPTER FORTY

As I waited patiently, my energy level began to drop. The news was going into its second half-hour of stories. Who knew I would be allured by the depiction of my work?

The news made its way back to the top story of the hour. Monica Kaufman restated her previous facts on the discovered body in Dunwoody as she handed the story over to the reporter on the scene.

The camera panned out to give a glimpse of the neighborhood and house; as it widened out from its close shot of the reporter, I knew where it was.

"I'm Jovita Moore, reporting to you from what appears to be a gruesome and saddening death that took place at this home," she reported, as she brought attention to it with her extended left arm, pointing in its direction. "It has been reported that this appears to be a possible suicide; however, investigators will wait until they have completed an autopsy to confirm."

A shot of chills ran though my pores as I paid attention to every word and every motion. The police and reporters were trampling the stupendous house. I could sense the disturbance that the house felt from the intrusion.

"I'm standing here with Detective Sabrina Crews. Detective Crews, what can you share with us about this death?" asked Jovita.

The detective stared straight into the camera lens as if she could see her listening audience. From the full camera shot, I noted she was a full-sized African-American with spotless skin. Being in a male-dominated profession, Detective Crews presented her femininity with her flipped hair accented with strawberry highlights.

Her lips were smeared with a splash of lipstick. Her light beige pantsuit completed her assemble.

"Currently, this appears to be a suicide. We're going to proceed in our investigation. There's a lot more to look into," she said in a monotone.

Jovita nodded. "Were there any other signs that this could be anything else?"

"Like I stated, we will continue our investigation to make sure all points are covered. Right now, we have just started and the initial crime scene says a suicide."

"Can you tell us who discovered the body?" probed Jovita. She returned the microphone back into Detective Crews's face.

"It's been reported that the body was discovered by her husband when he arrived home from a business trip," she answered, with a grim look on her face.

The camera once again panned out to capture the mayhem at fifty fifty-four Vermack Road. From what I could see, it was the most commotion I had ever seen in the neighborhood.

"I wonder if Travis is in the house," I asked myself as my eyes searched the screen for his face. "This is wild."

The news continued to cover stories in the metro Atlanta area and through out Georgia. I sat there staring into the idiot box wondering what was going on at the house. I hoped that I was able to keep everything untraceable to me.

Running my right index across my full lips, I closed my eyes and leaned back into the large chair. A day when I thought I would be allowed to relax was no longer a part of the agenda.

Slowly opening my eyes, I pondered verbally, "There's too much traffic on the roads right now."

Grabbing the remote control, I strolled through the other local news channels with hopes of seeing more. I hit almost every channel until I stopped and saw the house. Just as I thought, this was going to be covered by every news network.

With squinted eyes and wind-blown hair, a male news correspondent said, "We have a neighbor and friend of the victim. Is there anything you can say to shed light on this misfortune?"

The name Susan O' Conner flashed on the screen. I could see the grief in her eyes and heard it in her voice. She stood next to the reporter in her yellow tank top and full gray hair without a bit of concern about her appearance.

There was a light whimper in her voice. "Excuse me, I'm still in shock. Kayla and I just spoke Tuesday. She was looking forward to going home next week to visit her family."

"Were there any signs of problems that you can now look back on?" he asked.

Susan was working hard to maintain her composure. She cleared her throat on several occasions and wiped a tear from her eye.

She shook her head in disagreement to his question. "This was a great couple that had a great relationship. Her husband wanted her to take her trip because he didn't want her to be home alone."

With a lethargic look, he said, "Thank you. I'm Kevin Rowson, reporting live in Dunwoody for 11Alive News.

The network had mechanical difficulties as it delayed leaving the shot. I sat there watching him standing there in a suit and tie with the 11Alive symbol on his microphone, in the midst of the heat; behind was nothing but movement.

"Travis is home and I want to see him," I said with desire.

My feelings had resurrected themselves into full flame like a smoldering fire in the California wilderness. They lifted themselves even stronger than before. Could it be because I knew that the only obstacle was no more?

Yes, I was tired, hungry, and didn't desire to see the streets of Atlanta anytime soon. My craving to see Travis magnetized me to react. I felt impatient to see him on our regular meeting days. Like the first day I met him and like today, I needed to be replenished.

CHAPTER FORTY-ONE

Propelled by my soul, body, and spirit, I found myself driving on I-285. I knew that this wasn't a smart thing to do, but I wanted to do a drive-by. Who knows, once I got there, everything could have died down, with the news and police.

I had spent the last forty-eight hours in transport from one destination to another and I'd hated much of it. I knew I had to get the job done, and sacrifice was the only way to do it. Travis had spoken about that on a few occasions. Not many are willing to sacrifice to get what they want.

"Gran, I feel your presence with me. I thank you for keeping me safe last night. I know you're not happy with me," I said shamefully. "I've been what a woman should be and the men I've come in contact with haven't appreciated it. Then I realize, they weren't of my caliber, so how could they? This man is rare; please let this work out for me!"

I didn't know what was occurring, all I knew was that my grandmother's spirit was visible in the car. It began to scare me because I recognized how disappointed she was with me. My spirit felt unbalanced and heavy. It was as if my soul and spirit were separating like a Zip-Lock bag.

Petrified for the first time, I yelled, "What, Gran? What! You knew what I was planning, why now? Why do you want to become angry?"

It felt like the whole world was moving around me in slow motion, and the harder I pressed the gas pedal the slower I moved. I couldn't understand what was going on.

My cell phone rang once and stopped. Not thinking about it, a minute later, it did it again. Within a five-minute period the cell repeated itself. Each time I looked at the display there wasn't a telephone number visible.

Tears began to build up in my dark brown irises. "What are you wanting from me?"

What seemed like an hour was only fifteen minutes. I allowed myself to settle down. I had to hear what Gran was saying to me. The fear was making her voice incomprehensible to me.

Continuing to Travis, I began taking in deep breaths. I took in as much air as I could through my nose and held it. I could feel the tension through my shoulder blades. Rolling my head clockwise, I took another deep breath and my neck popped.

My grandmother's spirit was still with me, but not as wrathful. Memorial Drive exit was approaching as I allowed myself to hear her speak. Still unable to clearly understand, I exited the highway.

I pulled into the first gas station I came to and parked as far away from the patrons as possible.

"Okay, I'm going to sit still and listen. Let me hear you," I requested, as I closed my eyes.

The busy street that it is, I worked hard to block out the noise. To find the spiritual zone, I controlled my breathing by setting the pace. The rhythm smoothly made its way into my psyche.

"Beep—Beep."

I didn't allow it to disturb me. I was open and was hearing what was being said to me. The images I perceived were clear as a movie cinema screen. All that Gran showed and told me I understood.

Opening my eyes, I placed my hands on the steering wheel in silence. I knew what I needed to do and I started up the car. I backed out of the parking spot and headed back onto the highway.

"I have to remember, when I ask Gran for protection, to listen for her cues," I said aloud, as I cruised.

Driving in dead silence and in disbelief that my grandmother had spoken to me, I made it to the exit. I pulled up and stepped out of the car, still not sure what had taken place. All I knew was that I was back where I belonged. Home.

Peace of mind was what I struggled to find, and I found it with a bottle of wine. Music swayed in the air of the living room and it moved in a slow, walking pace. It felt as if I had found my freedom as I sipped from the thin-brimmed wine glass.

A gentle wind cut through the screened sliding glass doors. What brought me to this moment of serenity was unimportant; I wanted to absorb it all.

My big toe danced to the jazz melodies and slowly my torso followed close behind. I felt the ferments of the wine. I'm sure my tired body provided a lending hand. All I knew it was Friday and that my Travis was back home.

"Oooh—ooh—oooooh," I hummed to the music.

The ambiance was set on high and I knew I was going to fall into a deep sleep right in my chair. To prevent having to move, I sat the wine in its chilling bucket and the CD changer was set up with continuous music. I thought of everything.

"Damn! Who is that?" The secret night was disturbed. "Hello!"

I felt perturbed that I hadn't turned the ringer off on the phone. With certainty I came across in a tone, not welcoming.

"Dang! Are you busy?" said Michelle in an off manner.

"Nah, what's going on?"

She and I hadn't spoken since our slight misunderstanding, but I had known she would get over it sooner or later. As long as no one disrespects Michelle, she is cool with you. She doesn't know how to react when someone goes against her strong thoughts at times.

"I'm not sure if you spoke with Erin today, but, um, we had thought about going out tonight. So are you interested?"

"Oh yeah, I spoke with Erin earlier today. She was telling me about it. She wasn't sure if it was tonight or tomorrow. I was telling her I was going to get my rest on."

"Aw, come on, Maré! We haven't been out in a minute. You know we need to hit the scene to meet some men," in a pleading voice.

I knew my instincts were telling me to stay put, but my body screamed the need of male attention. And I was off until Wednesday.

CHAPTER FORTY-TWO

"Aren't you glad you made it out tonight, Ms. *Home Alone?*" asked Michelle.

She was right; I felt good about being among the living. God knew, it was what I needed. I thought about the last few weeks and my living as if I was a CIA agent on an undercover mission. I wasn't allowed any human contact, only of those who were a part of my "operation."

"Yes, Michelle, you were right," I said, with a smile on my face.

The club was filled to capacity, as to be expected at Club Nocturnal. It had become the "elegant" club of the ATL, and everyone who is anyone comes through, so they say. I had yet to see a celeb in here, but I did like the layout.

The neon glow of white lights really set off each bar, catching everyone's eye, even the non-drinkers. The split-level sitting area near each dance floor, complete with black leather sofas, added an upscale touch to the texture of the lightly dimmed, intimate areas.

As a lover of music, I couldn't help but notice the large floor-model speakers throughout the club on my first visit. It took me for a loop on a separate occasion when they threw club dancers on the speakers; they weren't needed.

We congregated in the sitting lounge of the club which was filled with an abundance of leather sectionals. I must say, this was an asset that couldn't be overlooked. My interest wasn't to be sitting too much longer; I wanted to hit one of the three dance floors.

"Hey, did you see the news today?" inquired Sonya. "There was this sister who committed suicide up in Dunwoody. Looking at the neighborhood and the house, I don't think she killed herself."

Jumping in quickly, "Yeah, I saw that. I think they're looking at the husband," added Michelle.

All my vital organs shut down as I sat and listened to the debate of Kayla's death, the death I caused. My eyes remained still as a statue and as focused as a hawk on its prey. An inkling of thought was nowhere to be found.

Sipping from her Alizé, "Maré, have you seen it?" asked Erin.

"Maré!" Sonya said sternly.

I knew in a flash of light I had to gather my poise and wits to cross over this bridge that stretched over dangerous waters.

"What?" I answered, as if they had lost their minds.

"Are you with us or what?" questioned Michelle as she placed her drink onto the quaint end table.

"I heard you, and I haven't heard about that story. W-w-why are you in my face like that?" I directed to Michelle.

Before I knew it, I had again crossed some invisible line when it came to Michelle and her ego. It wasn't intentional; however, she was too close to me. The yelling from them, the clubbers, and the loud music, were major annoyances.

With attitude written in her eyes, Michelle said, "You're really killing me with your smart-ass remarks lately. Is there a problem you got with me? It seems like every time, it's directed towards me!"

I was confronted with words of war and the last thing I wanted to do was hash them out at a club. Michelle will allow a few instances to slide, and this wasn't one of them. Sometimes, she can take things a tad bit personal.

My eyes skipped through the club and back to Michelle. "Why is it that whatever I say that doesn't coincide with your thoughts or how I should respond to you has to be taken in an offensive manner?" I asked her in a passive tone.

Sonya and Erin looked and wanted to know what was taking place. They sat there quietly sipping on their drinks, Erin with her Alizé and Sonya with her apple martini. Maybe it was something they both wanted to address with Michelle, and I was the voice of the people.

"No, it's not even like that and you know it. You come off like I invaded your space or something. Like when I was asking about your boy, Hollis. Damn, you'd think I was prying into something personal. If you don't want me to show interest or concern, then that's fine with me."

"Come on now, Michelle, it's not that serious. See it like this, if Sonya said the same thing, you would've shrugged it off and probably added a joke. Me! That's an entirely different story. Why can't I get smart with you and not be seen as a smart-ass?"

There were conversations taking place everywhere but with us. Michelle grabbed her drink and leaned back on the sectional. I was mad that I was the killer of the evening, but I knew it would blow over soon.

Looking at me with acceptance in her eyes, Michelle said,

"You're right. I need to work on not flipping on you like I do. You've evolved a lot, compared to back in the day. You're more flip at the lip, and, you know, Sonya and Erin have always been like that."

It took a lot for her to remove the binoculars and see the entire picture up close. I felt that the offset of our brief argument was right on time to move off the topic of the death of Kayla.

"Anyway, back to the conversation, before you messed up the flow," joked Sonya. "Recently, there has been an increasing number of deaths this summer. I'm not sure what's going on with the black community, but it's getting crazy."

Showing attentiveness, I said, "I agree. Like that day there were two stand-offs. There was one in Cobb County and the other in DeKalb. The police squad killed the brother in DeKalb. It's getting crazy and I bet it's the economy," I said.

"I didn't come to the club to discuss issues tonight. I'm here to dance and have a few drinks. I suggest we get up and head to the dance floor." Erin rose to her feet with her drink in her right hand.

I concurred with her because I had become bored and disinterested in the conversation. Without a doubt, this wasn't the place to discuss the death of Kayla.

I stood and a statement that Michelle made whisked through my head, of the police suspecting Travis.

"What's on your mind that has your face all squashed up?" questioned Erin.

I gave her a smile, and said, "Nothing—nothing."

The dance floor was packed, as usual. We didn't mind, as long as the DJ was playing the right music. The beats flowed and the songs connected like a carefully crocheted sweater.

I found myself enjoying the music and dancing with a short, butterball body type brother. As I threw my hands in the air, sang to the words of the song, my eyes became interlocked with Erin's.

With the live atmosphere and the overflowing dance floor, somehow she made me feel as if she was questioning me. I didn't break from my joyful composure and neither did Erin. It was felt in her glance, as if she was saying, "I know something is going on with you."

CHAPTER FORTY-THREE

A ray of sunshine pointed into my right eye through the natural woodgrain Venetian blinds in my bedroom. I felt like I had been dragged through a valley and every portion of my body touched each hill.

Feeling the throbbing of my muscles in each leg, I redirected myself from the fetal position into the spread eagle. I didn't want anything touching my body, other than the bed.

Unaware of the time, I rolled my head to the left and glanced at the clock. Just below eye-level on the glass-topped nightstand, the clock read two minutes after eleven.

"I need to get up," I groaned. "I can't stay in bed like this."

Neither a muscle nor an eye moved as I fell back into a deep sleep.

It was the first day I was able to rest and there wasn't one place I needed to be. My body sensed the calmness of the day ahead of itself. I'm sure it questioned why I went out last night when it was exhausted.

Soaring into an upright pose awhile later, I mumbled, "I gotta get out of this bed!"

I've always made myself get out of bed. If I was going to be lazy, at least it would be on the sofa. That's one thing my father hadn't tolerated, bed lounging.

Feeling the pulsating of my tensed muscles, I slowly tiptoed down the stairs with my pillow at hand.

"This doesn't make any sense, all this pain." I made it to the last step.

Saturday is a day I look forward to. As usual, it's all about chilling and me. Today wasn't going to be any different than the others, just that I was in agony.

Lying on the sofa and surfing through the television was sheer delight. I made it down in time to see one of my favorite cartoons, *Static Shock*. Every time I turn around, the WB network has changed its time slot. I'm not sure if it's because it's a black cartoon.

"Eleven-thirty two," I read from the VCR time.

I was engulfed in the episode as Static, the superhero, took on

The Meta-Breed, the foes on the show. When I first came across the cartoon, it impressed me to see a black teenaged super-hero. I have been tied to it ever since.

With all the cartoon stations on cable, I haven't found the need to watch them, as long as I have *Static Shock* and *Filmore* on Saturday mornings.

Curiosity struck me once it hit twelve o'clock, which led me to turn to channel three. One of my favorite news reporters, Diedra Dukes with Channel 2 Action News, was anchoring the noon news. She was covering the tribute to the late Mayor Maynard Jackson and the controversy on renaming Hartsfield Airport after him, as his legacy.

She continued with information on possible traffic gridlock due to events promoted by the 100 Black Men of Atlanta, in recognition of Maynard Jackson, the first black major of this city.

Many activities were in the making for the weekend, including a parade and the Tennessee State versus Florida A&M football game.

Still drowsy from the lack of rest, I began to yawn so hard that tears surfaced into my eyes. Using my red nightshirt, I wiped each eye, but the more I wiped, the more I yawned.

My eyes began to droop, but Diedra propped them up when she covered the story of Travis's wife's death. She recapped the facts that were provided on yesterday, so it seemed, until the tail-end when she added, "The police are investigating other possibilities of the death."

The news was filled with deaths, murders, and suspects being discovered, which I was a part of, unlike times before. I stared at the screen as they displayed a male with a buzz cut being transported for molesting and impregnating his thirteen-year-old cousin.

With the brief coverage on the story, I began to feel anxious about becoming Travis's new woman and living in his beautiful home. A smile crossed my face and disappeared like free beer at a football game.

"I wonder what other possibilities they could be looking into?" I questioned.

As I placed myself in an upright position on the sofa, my brain cells began bouncing out of control, as if they were two-year-olds on a sugar high. I went over everything I could that would make the police believe it wasn't what it appeared to be: a suicide.

Throwing my hands over my face, I bellowed, "Damn, it's the basketball! They found it and they know someone was there other than her."

My heart began pumping at the speed of a Dodge Viper doing one hundred and twenty miles per hour. It felt like it was about to kick itself out of my chest and there was nothing I could do about it.

No longer feeling rested or lazy, I jumped up, wondering if they were on to me. After looking at the news, I knew I was going to be next on the Most Wanted list.

"Calm down—I have to calm down. It's probably just police procedure to investigate everything, and that Detective said that on yesterday, anyway," I said aloud.

I knew I had to maintain my peace of mind and not nut-up on speculative information. We all know the news makes up stuff to make it read and sound fantastic. There isn't any evidence that actually points to me. The basketball may be overlooked.

Feeling a slight bump on my forehead, I continued, "I can't afford to be going through these ups and downs. I've done it. I have to face what I've done. But I got to have faith that everything will be all right."

With all the conversions that had taken place in the past few days, I most definitely needed some Travis in my life and body. Wasn't quite sure how much more of the emotional turmoil I could take without my angel somewhere nearby.

CHAPTER FORTY-FOUR

"What did you do yesterday?" I asked Erin.

"Probably the same thing you did, slept. Ezekiel came by later that evening and joined in on the sleeping," she replied.

We were in church; I knew this was right where I needed to be. With all the sinning and wicked things I'd done, I needed spiritual cleansing.

With a smile on my face, I asked, "Oh! So you and your man are back on track?"

"Yeah, it seems like that. Like I said the other day, I'm working on me. I forgot to tell you that he has been more open and back to his consistency." Erin nodded.

"What do you mean, more open?"

"You know, he has been sharing himself with me and it has helped me understand him more. He was telling me how his parents were and still are very critical of him and his brother. Everything he does has to be just right, to prevent the negativity of the folks." Erin placed her program in the pew.

"Wow! So he must feel pressured to achieve all the time. That isn't fun. Where are his parents and brother?"

"His parents are back in Virginia and his brother lives Texas. He and his brother left Virginia once they were able to do so. Now I'm able to understand why he was unable to accept me wanting to help him out. He is self-sufficient," she said with empathy in her voice, shrugging.

It felt weird sitting there with Erin because I wasn't sure what she really thought of me. Too many times she has given me an uncertain or questionable look; those occasions made me feel uncomfortable.

We got together as if there wasn't a question on her mind, and as if I wasn't fearful of her discovering my secret.

Allowing myself to be lifted by the words today, I was determined to concentrate on every declaration that Pastor Donald Earl released. The Bishop's nephew became a regular in the pulpit on Sundays.

Erin and I enjoyed the minutes of worshipping. The church became quiet as the Pastor made it to the pulpit. We were all ready for the week's assignment.

Placing his bible on the podium, he said, "Quit playing with dead stuff."

Knowing D.E., what many called him for short, he was about to educate us today. He stood in front of a congregation of over a thousand or more, with his gray suit and blue tie. The young, sandy-blond, crew cut, muscular built minister knew how to feed his sheep.

"God cannot use us in our destiny until we get rid of some dead stuff. I'm talking about addictions, past relationships, bad decisions. Ya'll feel me?" he asked. He took strides to the left side of the pulpit.

Erin tapped me and mouthed a few words that I couldn't make out or I wasn't trying to. I was there to hear the Lord and receive my confirmation that Travis was all mine. Like many other churchgoers, I came to be selfish.

"Do what God tells us to do when he tells us to do it. I think some of you all missed that. Let me repeat it. Do what God tells us to do when he tells us to do it," preached D.E.

The heads in front of us nodded in agreement with the Pastor. I agreed with him, too; however, I never know when it's the Lord or me. I know we as Christians can get into our own way.

The sermon stirred up facts and truths that I needed to hear. I wanted to speak the word of reversal into my life and into what I thought was dead.

Wiping his forehead with a white handkerchief, he shouted, "Let God separate those who won't support our destiny. Yoke ourselves with people who make our 'baby' jump."

Unbeknownst to me, a smiled painted itself onto my face. I felt that Travis was yoked to me. He has the capability to support my goals and desires to help me reach my destiny.

Erin leaned over to whisper, "You're smiling. D.E. must've spoke the truth to you."

"Anyway!" as the smile dissipated.

D.E. came to church to work, and he didn't take all morning to do it. He closed up his sermon and told us that there was a reversal coming into someone's life today.

I looked up into the rafters of the cathedral, seeking the reversal in my life. I was determined to let the death of Kayla go. I was going to accept that Travis was equally yoked with me.

CHAPTER FORTY-FIVE

"This is my last day to complete my first month's worth of lesson plans. I know my boss will be asking for them when I get into work tomorrow," I griped in a low voice.

Sitting at the bookstore table awaiting Travis's arrival, I continued to touch up my lesson plans. I wouldn't have an excuse for the lesson plans not being completed, being that Betty and my boss *allotted* me extra time. I must say, it really did pay off working the summer.

The bookstore became busy with a lot of customers; however, they would leave as quickly as they came. Maybe with summer coming to a close, people were returning to their regular schedules, where they rushed to do everything, rather than slowing down and breathing.

I looked at my silver wristwatch. "It's fourteen minutes to seven. Hmm . . . I wonder where Travis could be?"

Time continued, and I continued to wait for him to walk up to me with a huge greeting. I knew he was back home from Chicago and it was time for him to get back on track.

I located a clean piece of paper and allowed my thoughts to flow into poetry.

I Hunger

I hunger for your presence
Every second and every minute
No matter how much I get, I'm not finished
I hunger to have it all replenished

I hunger to hear your voice
To have it in my ear is my first choice
It's as distinguished as Rolls Royce

I hunger to have your arms around me
It gives me a deep feeling of safety

The bonding of our bodies & our breaths
A true symbol – to show we care

I hunger for our joyful conversations
They range from topics of furniture
To what happens in this nation

> *I hunger for all the simple things*
> *And major things that were mentioned*
> *Yet I do hunger for a sweet kiss.*

Reading through my thoughts and my feelings, a tear released itself. I felt alone. Quickly, I removed it from my lower eyelash. I gathered my books and other belongings.

As the time rolled around to eight-thirty, I decided to make my way home. I had to become mentally prepared for my new school year. I wrapped up my last task as my heart became flooded with emotions for Travis.

Walking in the night breeze-filled air, I could smell rain approaching. At the corner of International Boulevard and Marietta Street, I came to a complete stop and allowed the illuminated CNN logo about twenty stories up hypnotize me.

Taking in a deep breath, I forgot how bad the air quality was in the downtown area. The dark blue sky, the light whisk of air, and the electrifying night had taken me to a place of reminiscing.

There had been many evenings Travis and I embarked on this exact spot; we laughed and talked. Those times were sweet and full of memories.

"What you doing out here this time of night?" he asked.

I turned to see who was questioning my whereabouts. "Huh?"

You'd think he was FBI, from the way he snuck up on me in the night.

"Last time I checked, I was a grown woman, Eugene!"

"I was just asking, being that you been off for some days now. When do you return?" he asked with one eye squinted smaller than the other. "I think I seen you down here befo'. It was some Tuesday evening, just like this, with a fella. Was he your boyfriend?"

"Tomorrow. I need to go."

The beautiful night breeze was tainted even more with his smell of liquor. I think I was caught in the up-wind. There wasn't a need to acknowledge Eugene's remark because he was trying to agitate me.

He tipped his navy blue baseball cap. "I see you in the morning, rise and shine," he said with a smirk.

I began to walk off as I waved off Eugene's instigative comments. However, he had me somewhat rattled.

The unnerved feeling I got from Eugene was still present as I sat in my car. It was a rarity to get a good park in downtown Atlanta for free on the street and I couldn't even enjoy the moment.

Noticing a car waiting to take my spot, my mind continued to race with the "how did he" and "what ifs." I never know if what Eugene says is real or make believe. There have been rumors at work that he's not mentally stable, being that he was a Vietnam veteran.

"I got to get home and get some sleep." I turned the ignition. I checked my mirrors; there was a car waiting, but this was a totally different one. I could only imagine how many others had waited and drove off.

As I pulled out, I began to speculate if what Eugene said could've been true. If he did see Travis and me together, how much did he see and how much did he know?

CHAPTER FORTY-SIX

On the drive home, I felt pure hunger and thirst for Travis; maybe because there was an expectation for his presence today that wasn't fulfilled.

"How much longer can I go without hearing or seeing him?" I pondered, questioning my endurance.

It was uncommon for me to travel without music, but this was a night I wanted to think and feel. I wasn't sure what would occur and I welcomed what came.

"What am I going to do?" with urgency in my voice.

The more I thought, the more I wanted to get to Travis in some shape or form. It had been a week today since I last spoke with or saw him. The longest I had gone without seeing him was about a week or two, and that was by choice.

Waldrop is a very dark, curvy road, and the closer I got to home, the more I felt split between needing Travis's attention and wanting his company.

"I need to feel him tonight." I closed and locked the front door.

I dropped all my belongings at my feet and made my way to the phone books located in the coat closet. The huge volumes made it difficult to snatch from the top shelf, unless I wanted to injure myself.

The first book was the A-L Yellow Pages and the second book was the M-Z white pages.

"Come on now!" I said in an annoyed tone, as I reached again.

Holding the thick, five-pound book in both hands, I had struck oil. Stepping over the others I'd tossed to the floor, I made it to the edge of the sofa and took a seat next to it.

My thumb fanned through the pages of the book's B section and quickly made it back to the A's.

Licking my left index finger, I repeated, "Atkins–Atkins. Askew–Atkinson, I need to go back. Atkins!"

I hadn't thought of how many Atkins's there were in the Atlanta area, and now I knew. My eyes scrolled through the fine font looking for Travis's name.

"Travis and Kimberly. Is that it?" My eyes paced the page. "Kayla, let me see if it's under her name," I said, looking without luck.

I kicked my left leg from under my bottom and stretched it out as my head fell onto the sofa's arm. I felt like a loser with no hope to regain ground.

When I thought I was done, I jumped to my feet to make it to my computer. I recalled all the different search engines on the internet where I could locate people.

I felt hope towards locating his phone number and I just wanted to hear his voice in my ear. I had so dearly missed his conversation, his laugh, and his cordial touch.

So many Atkins's; I decided to do a search, and as expected, over a million were located. Not knowing which one was going to be a success, I clicked on the first link.

The website was clear and simple enough; it differentiated the available searches. With the three options, I clicked on 'find a person' and entered his last name, first name, city, and state.

I was still on dial-up, so it took a few seconds to populate, to no avail. It was unable to locate an exact match. The site broke the data into three sections, T. Atkins in Atlanta, T. Atkins in GA, and Travis Atkins in U.S.

I immediately clicked on the latter of the three, to see if my Travis was among the ten located in the U.S. Not one of the individuals were in Georgia, so I went through the remaining two sections.

Continuing through my searching, my eyes connected to the time on the computer monitor. It read fourteen minutes after ten o'clock. It had been my anticipation to be in bed by now.

Frustration was making its way up the hill and marching towards the peak. I could feel my neck muscles tighten. Somehow, I pushed that to the side and continued my chase.

I took my left hand to rub my neck. "This is it. I need to go to bed."

I thought to myself, *Of course it isn't going to be there, either.* With a need in my soul and determination in my mind, I felt the need to *pursue* further. There I sat on Anywho.com typing in Travis's name, closing my eyes to beg the Lord to help me.

Who knew if it was divine intervention or pure luck, because there was the information I was wanting. Right there, the fourth Travis Atkins was my Travis Atkins and at that very moment, I was feeling a bit looser.

I quickly disconnected my internet connection and felt overjoyed for not giving up. A smile embarked itself across my face and on my heart.

"Okay, I'm just going to call to hear his voice." I picked up the cordless phone.

Like a sixteen-year-old, I sat in front of my computer working up my nerve to dial the number. I was feeling excited, and that's something I hadn't felt in over a week.

I hyped myself up, "Let's do this!" I pressed the talk key.

I followed it by a star sixty-seven, to block my number in case he had Caller ID. There was a pause as I glanced at the number on the monitor. The feelings I was having were so interlocked, I couldn't understand them all individually.

Again, to take care of my short-term need, I began to dial the number. There was complete silence in the house as I waited for the phone to complete its first ring. It rang again as the time made it to eleven-ten.

"Hello," the dazed voice said after the third ring.

The sound of his inflection was nourishment. I couldn't put the phone down.

With annoyance dominating his tone, "Hello! Is anyone there?"

I wanted to divulge my identity and my feelings for him, but I sat there frozen as he hung up the phone. Not quite sure what was taking place, I redialed his number. I needed more.

Immediately he answered, "Hello! It's late in the evening, so whomever this is, please take this game somewhere else."

A tear made its way to the groove of my nostril while I held the phone to my chest. I wanted more than ever to hold him in my arms, and needed him against my skin.

CHAPTER FORTY-SEVEN

Wednesday morning arrived, and I hadn't gotten enough sleep to prepare myself for a full house of third graders, but I felt that it would be an easy day. With the changes this year, I inherited a teacher's aide for half of each day.

"Good morning, Ms. Alexander!"

"Good morning, Justin. Are we ready for school today?" I asked.

"Yes ma'am." He smiled and ran into the classroom.

I was back to where I could maintain my sense of balance that no one could take away from me. The love I received from students was therapy.

This school year, I decided to have a focal point on positivism, where we would be aware of what we said and how we said it. I placed a quote on the door of the classroom, "Words can make or break you," to allow students, even the parents and myself, to see each morning.

Nothing too major was slated for the first day other than allowing each kid to stand and share their summer adventures.

My new aide, April, mannerism's were lethargic as she made her way into the classroom. It was my first meeting with her; we had spoken Monday morning over the phone. The conversation had been to the point. I shared my goals as a teacher and educator.

"It's great to finally meet you," she greeted, flashing her full set of teeth.

"Yes it is."

It was my first time having someone in the classroom with me, and I knew it was going to start off uncomfortable for me. I needed to come to grips with it to prevent any negative reflection in my attitude.

"Maré, I haven't received a copy of your lesson plans, so what do you have scheduled?" she asked as she dropped her dingy brown tote bag on the corner of the desk.

I shifted through a bright yellow folder. "I apologize. Here's what I have planned for the first three months. It was a full summer working with the preschoolers."

"I bet you're tired. Okay, so today the kids will be sharing stories about their summer vacations?" April asked, adjusting the black headband in her red, thick, curly hair.

The morning began with introductions of April and myself; the kids did the same. I had seen many of the smiling faces in the corridor: running, playing, laughing, or talking. I wanted a great group of students that I could teach and who were ready to learn.

Without a skip in the beat, we rolled into hearing the student's stories. Of course, many of the kids were shy and timid, but as we began to have fun, they lightened up.

Vaguely reading her nametag, I asked Renee to share her story. She stood proudly, filled with a zealous personality, in her checkered blue and white shirt that coordinated with her navy capris.

"My father sent me and my brother to Orlando to visit my grandparents because he and my mom needed a break from us. Before he left, we went to Walt Disney World." She smiled and took her seat.

"What is your brother's name?" I asked as I noticed the wall clock.

"His name is Anthony and he's ten years old."

April filled into the question segment, "What did you see at Disney World?"

Renee gave a look as if we were getting too personal; however, she stood. I could tell she liked the attention and she knew how to play it.

I patted April on her shoulder and whispered, "I need to run to my car. I'll be right back."

With my keys in my left hand, I hustled in my pumps as they clapped in the empty hallway. Who would've thought that the teacher's aide would be a payoff for me? My strides became longer and faster; it seemed like I was in a tunnel as my steps echoed.

Exiting the school building, I began to make it across the black asphalt parking lot. Looking up, it appeared as if someone had brush-stroked the clouds into the sky.

The most remarkable image was the small rainbow in one of the clouds, adding an artistic touch. It must've been one of those crystal clouds that the weatherman mentioned last night on the news.

As I opened the car door, the heat fell out the car and I knew it wasn't a day to be sweating. First day of school, I had on beige slacks with a short-sleeve, button-down, turquoise shirt, and there wasn't a desire to funk it up.

I tuned the radio into 93.9 FM at eight minutes past nine o'clock. My attention was continued on the beautiful sky as the commercial ran on.

"For those who have tuned in with us this morning, our commentary will not be new, it'll be a replay of a previous show. We can never hear too much of a positive message from Travis," said the DJ. He segued into the rebroadcast of Travis's show.

I sat there in dismay, not knowing what was taking place with Travis and why he wasn't serving up his weekly meal of positive and thought-provoking discussion to us—hell, to me.

Taking the key from the ignition, I was unsure how much more I could tolerate not having Travis in my life. I needed normalcy from him, something we had before he left for his Chicago trip. Everything was at a loss. I was beginning to feel the same.

What I once reviewed as art in the sky looked liked garbage as my spirits dropped to a low. So often I allowed one thing to affect my entire mood, and the sad thing about it, I was aware of it.

"It's good to see you this morning," Eugene said as he held the door.

The last thing I needed was some meddling old man in my face smelling like a distilled brewery of cheap alcohol. No matter where I go in the building, somehow he finds me on my worst days.

"Hey, Eugene, thanks."

"What got your face all squashed up?"

"Nothing—nothing." I attempted to walk on.

"What was you doing out there? You got class to attend to?" talking to my back.

It was time, and had been a long time coming. The man never knew when to shut up and quit while he was ahead. He loved to egg everyone on at school, like punks. Everyone took it and then complained about it.

"Eugene, you're getting on my last nerve. If you know so damn much, then take note that I'm not in the mood for your Barnaby Jones questions. You don't know me and I don't want you all in my personal business. Okay? Can you understand that?" with force in my tone.

Stepping backwards, "You know what? I knew something was wrong with you. You all out in that car when you got class and now you want to get angry with me. I tell you now, young lady, I will continue to keep my eye on you. I done seen too much," with hesitation in his stance and a voice of authority.

"Whatever. You're just an old man who has nothing better to do other than being nosy and exaggerate stories! Who can believe what you say? They're not sure if it's you or the liquor talking." I fanned my hand at him as I turned away.

I could tell I hurt his feelings with my last remarks, but it was the truth. However, I knew it shouldn't have been said. His shame was as visible as the missing stripes of a faded Sergeant's uniform from the U.S. Marines Corps.

No matter how crazy I thought Eugene could be, I knew somewhere inside there was an inch of sanity. He was already nosy and I didn't need his extra effort. Who knew what he'd seen already?

CHAPTER FORTY-EIGHT

"What time will you be home?" asked Sonya.

"I'm not going straight home. What's up?" expressing interest, as I left work.

This was one of the times I couldn't tell what was going on with Sonya. What it could be was disturbing me, and I shouldn't have answered the cell phone.

"Um, I just wanted to see how things were going. Making sure you didn't let Michelle get to you Friday night."

"It was nothing, as always. Hey, I'm over it and I let it go last Friday." I stepped off the curb.

"Wanted to make sure. I don't want my girls fighting. I spoke with Michelle and she understood what you said that night at the club. Plus, she met some brother that night and he has been trying to holla," said Sonya.

That would be all I needed, for Michelle to get her love life on track, along with my other friends, which would leave me solo. I began to hope that Travis would be at the bookstore today.

"That's nothing new. I hope he can keep her interest and respect. You know how she does when it comes to men."

Pausing for a moment, as if to think, Sonya said, "You're so right. At least she can start on a relationship. We need to get you hooked up. You would think one of our men would have a single friend or two to hook you up with."

I could feel the fast pace of everyone around me, and I guess I blended in, stepping to get to the bookstore. That was where my attention had been all day. Sonya's call was an interruption.

"Anyway! Sonya, don't worry about it—," The cell flew from my right hand.

I cringed as the phone toppled to the ground. In a millisecond, fury slapped me as I looked to see what individual had run over me in broad daylight.

"Excuse me," said the dreadlocked man in a nonchalant voice.

I could only image what the phone would look like as I took four steps to pick it up. There was a huge gash on the side of it. Many scrapes from the slip-and-slide ride it took.

My eyes were filled with fire glancing at the Rasta wannabe as I could hear Sonya, screaming my name. I had forgotten about her being on the line.

"Sonya, I'm fine. I have to holla at you later," I told her, keeping my eyes on the prize.

"What's going on?" she asked with an uneasy tone.

"Girl, this dude just ran into me and jacked up my cell. I'll holla at you later."

The anger had settled itself in my throat and wouldn't be budged. I didn't want a scratch and dent phone; I wanted some form of compensation from the rude boy.

"What's wrong with you? The sun is brighter than a two hundred watt bulb and you still ran into me. Look at my phone, I don't want this," I said, closing in on his personal space.

"Yo, I'm sorry my sister. It wasn't intentional and we know accidents happen. I apologized, what more you want me to do?" he said with hesitation.

In the middle of the sidewalk, people continued to pass us by. Standing there bickering with Dreadlock, I inhaled enough exhaust fumes from MARTA buses and cars to fill a football stadium.

"What I want you to do? The question is, what do you want to do, since you caused the damage!"

I recognized that Rasta hadn't raised his voice one time and lacked any visible emotions.

"Sister, my eyesight is pretty much gone. I can see shapes and everything is a blur. What I want to do is get my eyesight back. It doesn't help being in denial every day. My denial has caused you damage," said the man.

I felt like an idiot, ranting and raving over a stupid cell phone, when a man couldn't see. My compassion made itself available as I dropped my head in shame. He couldn't have been more than thirty-eight years old, to look at the man.

Like everyone around me, I had conformed to material things, and I knew then and there I was on empty.

I waited to see Travis's smiling face and to breathe in his air. My thoughts continued to go over the incident on the street as I thought about what got me to this impassionate place. I knew it could be solved. Travis had more pieces to the puzzle than I'd realized.

I waited impatiently for him in our spot at the bookstore. An hour and a half past, still no Travis.

****

The night was motionless. The quarter moon sat low in the sky, and I sat in my driveway crying. I knew the beginning of my period aided my emotional roller coaster, but I also knew it was because I needed this man.

Not once had I thought again about Kayla. Why would I, when she was no longer an obstacle to Travis?

"I'm hurting so much right now," I cried, sniffling through my tears. "I yearn for you so much that it makes me sick. Where are you? What am I going to do? Don't you know I need you more than ever before?"

I was at odds with my emotions and my needs as I made it into the house. I stood in the foyer feeling as if I had been dismantled, and the only way to assemble me would be with a rare wrench.

The days became harder and longer to deal with the more I sought Travis's love. I knew I would get some form of his presence today. I wanted to feel his voice vibrate throughout my body.

I grabbed the sticky note containing Travis's number. I entered star sixty-seven, to block my number. The phone pressed against my face like a newborn baby. I could hear it begin to ring.

After the second ring, I heard, "Your call has been properly delivered, but the party you are trying to reach is not accepting calls from callers that do not allow delivery of their telephone number . . ."

I sat at my kitchen nook with a speck of light from the living room peeping through as I stared out the window, with the phone still to my ear. There was only dead air. What I knew to be a guaranteed filler, was no more.

The silence was disrupted by a call waiting beep. Not caring who was on the other line, I slung the phone towards the refrigerator. My kitchen was smaller than most master bathrooms.

It lay shattered on the floor, and I was losing my mind. I knew I wanted to be with this man and he needed to know.

I stumbled over to my purse as I headed to the living room to grab my keys on the curio trunk. I made it out to the car, tears surging and everything distorted, emotionally and visually.

It was a miracle that I made it to the neighborhood gas station. My eyes were overflowing as I dug through the glove compartment. Rummaging in the mess, my hand felt a tissue. I wiped my eyes and cleaned my nose. The high volume of customers at the Quik Trip made me hesitate.

I exited the car and made it to the payphone.

"All I need is to hear your voice," I said, as the coin raddled down the slot.

CHAPTER FORTY-NINE

Friday morning, I was awakened by the high-pitched alarm clock, an act that didn't take much effort due to the sleepless night. I hadn't been in any condition to drive last night, or in the right frame of mind.

I lay in the pitch black room filled with hope and optimism for the day coming forth. Deep within, I was trying to build buoyancy for Travis and me. Slithering its way through my pores, like a tick, was doubt.

"Oh, Heavenly Father, I come to you this morning for strength, wisdom, knowledge, understanding, and courage. Guide me through this day and provide me with all my needs. Lord, I ask that you forgive me for my sins. Please, God! Please allow everything to work out for Travis and me. In Jesus' name, Amen," I begged at five-thirty in the morning.

The train ride provided me time to think with a clear mind. It was too early to be filled with emotion. My dilemmas were compounding and no one could deal with what I was going through but me.

"I told him to go on," said a man in a thunderous voice.

Just looking at him, I would assume his life was worse than mine. He sat across the aisle from his partner, laughing and talking. I was having a pity party and there was this brother who had a few front teeth missing, twisted nappy hair sticking from under his raggedy baseball cap, and a leg brace.

Why would I think he had it worse than me? Like many Americans, I determined his joy of life by his physical appearance rather than what was inside. Who was to say he didn't have the very thing I wanted: love.

My mind wandered as my eyes bounced through the train. *Does everyone have love?* Somewhere, I thought, *I lost sight of my true values and me. Am I nothing but rhetoric? Was I wearing a mask? Who knows—I sure don't.* I never wanted to conform to the materialism of society, and somehow I think I was slipping into the abyss. I thought to myself, *How real am I?*

Looking out the window, I asked myself, "What is my purpose?"

Life had a greater destiny for me than what I could see or even imagine; however, my patience had began to run low when I met Travis. I took my destiny into my own hands and right now my world was standing on a tightrope. At that moment, I couldn't afford a misstep.

Everyone trampled off the train, except the missing tooth man and his friend. They continued their conversation and chuckled, seemingly without a care in the world.

I could see the cars speeding through downtown and impatient people on the sidewalk. It was time to become real within and committed to making a change, no matter what. I needed to have a purpose in life.

Diagonally, two attractive MARTA officers entered my peripheral vision. They continued in my direction as one pointed at me. From ten yards away, I could see the serious manner upon their faces.

If guilt had a name, it would be Maré. I became petrified as their pace towards me quickened.

"Hey! Stop—Stop!" shouted the stockier officer.

Both officers began to run and my mouth dropped in apprehension. What did they find to connect me? In the immediate time, I was attacked by my vivid imagination.

The two officers got closer, but they passed me. I turned to see what happened and there were other officers near the turnstile strong-arming a male to the ground. I could still hear the beating of my heart and nothing could bring it to a place of calm.

No matter how much I tried to convenience myself that I could handle whatever came my way, I knew deep inside I would lose every piece of mental stability I had if I was found out.

Once I made it to work, I was greeted. "How are you doing this morning?" asked April. "Your spirits seem a little low."

Having someone in my space was the reason I didn't desire a teacher's aide. Now she wanted to be a counselor and solve my problems. Each word, feeling, and emotion was carefully watched, and I had to have a believable response. When it was just the children and me, we'd smile and hug.

"The day has been fine. I'm not sure if it's lack of sleep or if I'm catching something. I'm glad it's Friday though," I replied, making eye contact.

Honesty hadn't been available to me for some time. I knew that my mind was on what took place at the MARTA station. My ability to lie at the length of a red ant has allowed me to do so quite often.

With the time winding down, I was prepared to get home and relax. Unlike last week, I wasn't going to allow anything or anyone to disturb my weekend.

Leaning over my shoulder, April said, "Maré, if you like, I can watch the students if you want to leave now. There's only an hour and a half left in the day, and they're all working on their descriptive stories."

Noticing the compassion in her gesture, I felt like I should take off and get home to collect my thoughts, get myself on the right track.

"April, are you sure that you'll be okay? You don't know how much I appreciate it," I said, as my eyebrows rose to my hairline. "Your late half-day schedule has it purpose."

Shushing in a humbling manner, "It's fine with me. There's only an hour or so to go and everything will be just fine."

I gathered my things to make it home, with hopes of beating some of the Friday afternoon traffic. Before leaving, I said my good-byes to the class and directed them to show April the same level of respect as they did me.

So far, my kids had been very mild-mannered and attentive; they were a different breed of beings this year.

The train ride seemed quicker than usual. I was ready to get home and vegetate my weekend away.

My car was compressed with heat, so I rolled down the two front windows in the MARTA parking lot. As I stretched my left arm behind me to roll down the window, my cell phone rang. I reached into my purse to notice that it was Hollis. It was a surprise!

"Hello." I wondered what was going on.

"What's been going on? I haven't heard from you. I've been thinking about you, so I decided to call," he said, in a mellow drone voice.

I was hesitant to see where he was coming from. I hadn't expected to hear from him and his voice sounded inviting to me.

"Nothing too much. How are you doing?" I asked, making my way out of the parking lot.

"I'm doing good. You've been on my mind and I wanted to talk with you. Has anything exciting been happening?" asked Hollis.

Surprisingly, he put a smile on my face. "Thanks for thinking about a sister. I've been pretty much working and relaxing. As a matter of fact, that's where I'm heading now—home, to relax."

He and I both laughed as if we hadn't missed a beat or weeks since our last conversation and the awkward moment. The male attention was on time.

"I feel you. I'm about to head up out of here in another hour. So, are you still seeing that brother?" he inquired.

"What brother are you talking about? I know you're not bringing up the embarrassing moment!"

"No, I'm not bringing that up, I'm wanting to know about the man in your life," he said, with a more definite voice.

Again, I went over the same information with Hollis that he already knew. To be honest with myself, I stayed on the phone with him because his voice was a snack. It was nowhere near Travis's and the conversation didn't even receive a score of two from the Russian judge, but it was beneficial.

"Why are we going through this again? Hollis, I've had a long week and I'm not up to this today." My voice had a speck of whining.

"I apologize, sweetheart. My intention wasn't to cause you drama. I was calling because I wanted to take you out, if not tonight, maybe tomorrow," he confided.

The person nowhere on my mind was Hollis, and at the state I was in, missing Travis, I didn't need to be in his presence, free food or not. I recalled how his lips set me off. Me desiring Travis even more would only be hazardous.

"Thanks. This isn't a good time for me, right now," I told him.

"Maré, you're making it hard for a brotha. But that's okay, because I know what I like. Nothing comes easy." Hollis ended the call.

As I made it to my driveway, Hollis helped me decide that I needed to get myself a plan together. I could no longer wait for Travis to magically appear to me, like he did before.

I wanted to hear Travis say that he thought of me, and I knew I could get it done.

CHAPTER FIFTY

After the derailment of my emotions and expectations, my concocted sabbatical allowed new life to enter my world. The clarity I attained was like crystal: valuable.

Every phone I owned was turned off. I placed messages on my voicemails that I was okay and I hoped everyone could respect my privacy. There was a need for the disclaimer; I would've had the GBI, FBI, DeKalb Police, and any others that my friends would've called knocking at my door.

My body rested and so did my mind. Then I focused on what was needed to get to my desired level with Travis. I knew failure wasn't an option. I knew he was meant for me.

I reset the mood from last week, with the music and wine; allowed my body and soul to be free and become one again.

By Monday, I felt rejuvenated throughout the day and it was visible to all in my presence.

"For a Monday, your spirits are high," observed April.

"Today was a good day. Again, thank you for Friday. I was able to get some needed rest over the weekend," with gratitude in my voice. "It was about me, me, and then me." I laughed.

School ended, and as I made my way out of my classroom, there was Principal Quincy Graham coming up the empty hall. As always, Mr. Graham made sure he dressed for success.

I said, "Good afternoon, Mr. Graham," as we reached each other.

"Hello. Maré, do you a few moments?" he asked in his white dress shirt and yellow tie.

Never had a visit from him, other than my initial start date here. He had stopped by with a cordial hello, but never at the end of the day.

"Ah, sure." My lungs felt like they were covered with syrup.

We took a few steps back to my classroom. We stood just inside the doorway and I tried my best to keep a clear face; I didn't want to show any fear.

"Maré, since you've been here, you have excelled with your students and have also been a model teacher. I'm sure you were unaware of the policy on this matter. It was brought to my attention you left early on Friday." He spoke melodically.

"Yes, I did. I wasn't feeling well at all, and April, my teacher's aide, offered to remain with the students for the remaining hour." I noticed his posture hadn't adjusted.

I was unsure what was going on, or about to go on, and how he found out, but it wasn't a game. I felt uneasiness present in the room and I wanted it to go away. Questions began to run in my head.

"It's against our school policy to leave a class unattended without appropriate supervision, and teacher's aides aren't appropriate. I'm aware that this is your first time working with one and I understand. I'd like for you to stop by in the morning to sign off on your understanding of this rule." He dropped his hands to place them into this pockets.

"I'm sorry. I hope I didn't get April into any trouble. She was trying to be helpful." I eyed him.

I wanted to know how this could have gotten to him and why?

"Everything is fine." He patted me on my right shoulder.

To me, it was odd that Mr. Graham knew about my one-hour early disappearance. To fathom that April would burn me like this began to piss me off. I inquired about her status with hopes he could shed some light.

I wasn't going to let this hold me down, so I mentally returned to my weekend sabbatical to find the center of my soul. I had more important things to focus on, like my mission to check on Travis. Time had been wasted fooling with Mr. Graham, when I had somewhere to be.

****

"Thank you," I said to the short gentleman who held the glass door.

I made my way through the door, where a security guard behind an enormous desk greeted me. He stood and I would've thought I was at a club, being that he had the look of a bouncer.

"Good afternoon. Do you have an appointment?" he asked in a Barry White tone.

"No I don't."

"Are you here to see someone?"

"Yes, I'm here to see Travis Atkins," I announced, placing my forearm on the desk's countertop.

"What's your name?"

"It's Maré Alexander. Hum, just say Maré. Never mind— Maré Alexander," speaking rapidly.

The officer directed me to the sitting area as he dialed up Travis to let him know he had a guest. Even with his deep, strong voice, I couldn't make out what was being said through the side conversation taking place near me.

Two white women in the waiting area were very loud and not aware of it. Their voices ricocheted in the lobby, up to the two-story ceiling. This was my first time inside the *Atlanta Journal-Constitution*, or the *AJC* as it's called.

The black leather chair gripped my bottom like a good sock to a heel, and my eyes just marveled at my surroundings. I have never worked in a corporate setting and could only imagine what it was like. The only insights I got were from my friends.

The front glass walls allowed me sit still as the world outside continued. I would've thought I lived somewhere in New York City, how everything captivated me.

I believe that my awe was more from nerves and uncertainty about my going to Travis's job.

The security officer motioned to me and said, "Ma'am, Mr. Atkins is on his way down."

CHAPTER FIFTY-ONE

I heard the elevator indicators going off constantly, and each time I looked, someone else made their way through the lobby. The traffic seemed to pick up, with more people roaming in the atrium.

Right outside the building, a police car sat with its blue lights flashing. Two men were standing at the rear of the squad car. To get a better view, I twisted my torso, which made it more relaxing.

"Maré," sang the voice.

A quiver exploded through my body from the voice, the same sensation heroin addicts receive with each fix. Just the deliverance of my name from his diaphragm was filling.

Untwisting my body, I saw him standing over me, tall and full-framed. His skin was beautiful, his attire, his hair were all still the same, but I could see something missing in his eyes.

Again he sang my name, "Maré, what are you doing here? I was taken by surprise when security told me that you were here." He took a seat in the adjacent leather chair.

"I apologize for coming unannounced," I said with an awkward smile. "But I was concerned about you and wanted to know if all was okay. I hadn't seen you at the bookstore for some weeks now. The last opportunity I had to listen, your commentary was in re-broadcast mode." My tone softened and became filled with gentle-ness.

"Thank you so much. You could never know how much that means to me," said Travis, his head dropping an inch or two. "It's hard to say what has been going on in my world and this isn't the time or place."

I saw something noticeably different, as if his soul was absent from his body. What I saw I didn't expect. I wanted to revitalize Travis to another level and I knew I could. I could bring the flame to an inferno, into his eyes; replicate the hunt of a hungry lion into his spirit.

"I understand! I wanted to see if you were okay and let you know I was concerned. Even though we only spoke at the bookstore, I felt a connection with you. If there's anything you need, feel free to call on me. I hope all works out with you." I reached out to touch his left knee.

"If it was that easy. I thought of you and wanted to let you know that I've made it into syndication for Chicago. That's slated to roll out next quarter," he shared, as a small smile flashed on his face.

There it was, the statement I wanted to hear; that he thought about me—Maré. I knew all I had gone through wasn't futile. He told me that I had a place in his life because he thought about me, especially when he was victorious.

"Fantastic! I knew you were going to do it. Without a doubt! I don't want to hold you up."

"Oh no! Don't worry about that. You were a pleasant surprise and sometimes the spirit needs those." He nodded. "I'm trying to get back into the swing of things, and I don't think the bookstore will make its way back into my regimen."

A brick found itself inside my stomach and my heart was underneath it. There was pressure building up to close the deal, you know, to make my "friendship" boundless. The bookstore had become our place to meet and evolve into one another.

"I'm sad to hear that, being that I enjoyed our conversations and you kept me motivated. Hmm, I'm not sure what a sister's gonna do without the special attention."

With all the motion and voices in the lobby, he still knew how to make the surroundings disappear. His eyes were on me and so were his ears.

"We'll stay in contact. As a matter of fact, I'd like to take you out for dinner, to thank you for this kind gesture. You didn't have to stop by here. People get lost in selfish living. I love to see selfless acts," lectured Travis.

I hesitated to play the "no thank you," and then he says, "I insist" game. "Aw, thank you. You know you don't have to."

"I know that and you know that, so how about tomorrow?"

"Th–that sounds fine with me," I stuttered.

As always, Travis walked me to the door, and this time he hailed down a taxi for me. I couldn't believe that we had exchanged cell numbers and I was about to go an official date with my man.

CHAPTER FIFTY-TWO

I floated on cloud nine to the tenth power. What took place was indescribable. No words, not one word, could I use. I didn't dare to look back, for fear that I was in a dream and if I looked back he wouldn't be there and I'd wake up.

The joy I felt radiated like rays of the sun. It couldn't be dodged unless you went into a building, but anyone within twenty feet felt it.

As expected, my cell rang. I hadn't returned any of the messages left from the weekend. Time for the crew to check in. I'm not sure if any of them would know how to function without me in their lives.

"What's up?" I said in a cheerful tone.

"No, the question is, what is up with you? You the one who cut all communication this weekend. What's up with that?" asked Sonya.

"Just needed some solitude and I had to get it by any means necessary."

"Solitude! Solitude from what?" she said with attitude.

I didn't have a need to go into detail. She wouldn't understand, and with my outcome with Travis, it paid off. My frame of mind shifted like the earth when there's an earthquake. Mine is for the good.

"Whatever! Just say that you missed me for those three days." I laughed.

"Anyway. I was calling to let you know that the dude that Michelle met at the club the other week is a winner. His name is Marco, I think—it's something 'different'. He cooked her dinner at this crib. It's somewhere off Ponce de Leon and Briarcliff. The house was laid out," squawked Sonya.

"Okay. It's only been a week, and anything can happen," I responded.

"So what! I'm trying to be hopeful that it'll workout. He's a man who has stability and is looking for the same. Not too often do you or Michelle run across that in Atlanta. She has a prospect, Erin has a man, and you have been going through a drought," she said in a snappy tone.

I understood Sonya's position, and for some time she has dearly wanted her girlfriends to be in committed relationships, like herself.

Sometimes she jumped the broom too soon. With the overwhelmed feeling I was experiencing, her negative comments couldn't pierce through me.

"There you go, talking like you know. For your information, I have a date tomorrow night," I taunted.

"What! With who? You forever keeping your business on the down low. Who is the brother and where did you meet him?" she asked with intrigue.

That wasn't supposed to happen, me opening my big mouth about Travis and I. I'm still in the early stages. But the Bishop always says that we should speak prophetically. I didn't want to let the cat out the bag that soon. Maybe I was in competition with my girls and didn't want the pity.

"Oh, now you want to know the who, what, when, where, and how? I met him at the bookstore and we talked for a little while. Everything clicked and he asked me out." I paid the cab fare with the phone cradled between my ear and shoulder.

"Humph. Were you with him this weekend and that's why you cut the phone lines?" she joked. "I can understand."

"No!"

"So what's his name? You acting like you don't want to share the info." Sonya sounded put off by my evasiveness.

"I'm trying to get to the train. His name is Travis and he's about thirty-three. No children and not sure if he's been married. I got to go, my train is here. I'll talk with you later."

"All right, I hope you have more energy tomorrow. If you head out like you are right now, dude may keep on going."

"Thank for the support, Sonya. You always know the perfect words," I said sarcastically.

I sat on the train in a daze of utter fulfillment. I still couldn't believe Travis asked me out, on an official date.

"Thank you, God," I whispered.

CHAPTER FIFTY-THREE

I couldn't get through the door before the phone began to ring. Not an inch of doubt that talks had begun amongst Sonya, Michelle, and Erin; on the other end of that ring was one of them.

Breathing slightly heavy, I answered, "Hello."

"Oh, you weren't going to tell me about your little date? Huh? I had to hear it from Sonya? I thought I was your girl," ranted Erin in a joking manner.

"Damn! I just told her and I just got home. What are you doing discussing me and my business anyway? Ya'll talk too much," with frustration in my voice.

Too much gossiping among the workers was getting old to me. Why was this such an issue for me? Could it be that I wasn't ready to let them in? I knew I wasn't prepared for the questions or up to the lying.

"What's wrong with you? I was playing! I would think you'd be in a good mood, since you have a hot date tomorrow," said Erin.

"The mood was good, but that was ruined. Why couldn't you let me call you and share the news with you? So what, Sonya ran her mouth. So sit and chill. It's so obvious that you all talk behind one another's back," in a solemn tone.

Erin was taken by my honesty and my feelings. I'm sure it wasn't her intent to jump on the gossiping wagon, but there are times we all, including myself, get sucked in. It's like being at show and tell, when your best friend blurts out what you brought and makes it into a joke. Why share? The excitement has been stolen.

Silence spoke louder than Erin. "I'm sorry, Maré. I don't know why I allowed my feelings to come before yours and this is your occasion. I didn't mean for it to come across in a selfish manner, but it did. I was joking."

"Well, I need to go; I just got into the house and need to prepare for tomorrow." I made my way to the kitchen.

"Enjoy your date tomorrow," she muffled in the phone.

I could tell Erin felt bad about what happened. She knows me better than any other person, and that when I express myself, I'm disappointed. To reassure her that I was okay wasn't an interest tonight.

Pouring myself a glass of white zinfandel, I looked out the kitchen window and saw my neighbors, the Taylors. They are a loving couple and every time I see them, they are either touching, hugging, or kissing.

Sitting in the dark, I sat at the nook and fantasized about Travis and I. We could have the same level of love in our relationship as the Taylors. Having his arms around me on any given night was where I wanted to be.

Sipping the wine sweetened the day's achievements, and a smile brushed across my face as I began to rethink my time with him.

"I can't believe I have a date with Travis—Travis, me and Travis! I have to find something to wear," I conversed with myself.

Cupping the thin-brimmed glass in my hands, I rested my elbows on the tabletop. As I took a sip of the exotic fruit-flavored wine, my cell phone rang. I placed the glass on the table to make my way to my purse, with a bit of perturb in my mood. I rummaged through the disorganized bag to see Travis's name on the display.

With delight in my voice, "Hello."

"Maré, I hope I haven't called at an inappropriate time," stated Travis.

Could there ever be a wrong time for him to call? I hoped he wasn't calling to cancel our dinner date. That's all I needed.

"No, I was just relaxing. What's going on?" Astonished by his call.

"I wanted to make dinner reservations and I was unsure what type of food you like. Then I thought we never really set a time. So-o-o, I'm calling to get the 4-1-1 on you," he said jokingly.

Laughing with him, I said, "I pretty much enjoy all foods. I enjoy Italian, American, seafood, a little of everything. I'm trying to stay away from Chinese and Japanese, since the discovery that many of the warehouses distributing their food aren't sanitary."

"Okay, how about a time?"

"I can possibly meet you there about seven-thirty," I said, contemplating if it was realistic.

"Don't even worry about meeting me anywhere. I'll pick you up and we will accompany each other to dinner," directed Travis.

At times I feel as small as a grain of sand, but Travis has made me feel like a 747; no way was I going to be missed.

"Are you sure that won't be going out of your way?"

"I'll be at your place at seven o'clock. Now, can a brother get directions?"

Travis and I laughed as we made it through my long-winded version on how to get to my house. I could tell that his pilot was lit, compared to earlier that day. For the first time, we felt like more than acquaintances who only met at the bookstore, and more like kindred spirits.

CHAPTER FIFTY-FOUR

The next day flew by faster than the speed of light, and even that was too slow for me. Anticipation filled me for my date with Travis. The freshness of him asking me to dinner still ran through my head.

My classroom was empty of students and April, as I gathered my purse. A pack of air released itself from my nostrils as the peace I encountered at the very moment brought chills to my flesh.

"Can it get any better than this?" I shuffled through my desk drawer.

Let me tell it: the moon, stars, and the Lord were working on me right then. I had gone so long being proper, unlike many of the sultry women in this city, and it hadn't gotten me anywhere; not where I needed to be. The saying must be true: "Patience is a virtue."

On the entire ride home, I mentally went through my wardrobe and nothing screamed out at me. I wanted to get home. There wasn't time to buy anything, only to make due.

I dropped my purse and bags in the foyer as I did quite often and sprinted up to the closet. Standing in the smaller-than-a-Yugo-sized closet, I turned my back to the casual clothing. I frantically rummaged through each item, starting from the front of the closet.

"Nope, that's not going to do it," I said, pushing the printed wrap skirt forward.

Nothing that I touched seemed good enough or sophisticated enough to mark my beauty on Travis's arm. Making it to the back of the closet, I found the perfect dress, for the perfect night. I had forgotten about it, being that I hadn't worn it since Sonya's wedding, the occasion for which I purchased it.

With sparkles flashing in my eyes, I removed my jeans and winter green T-shirt. I prepared my sauna illusion by allowing the shower to steam. I laid the dress across the bed, not a flaw to be found on its fabric. Time was still flying by; the time chimed in at ten minutes to six o'clock.

The pulsating water released tension in my back and warmed my heart. I rolled my neck so that the water could hit between my shoulder blades.

Thoroughly dry, I stepped out of the tub wrapped in a yellow towel and opened the door. Nothing but steam burst out of the bathroom as I pranced out.

"Hmm, what kind of fragrance should I put on?" I asked myself, as I massaged body oil into my skin.

I touched each and every part of my body with the unscented oil; I knew it would liven up my skin. The bath towel fell to the floor when I stood. I left it in its place to search for my bustier in the second drawer.

I remembered what the sales clerk said when I bought it, to lean forward and cup each breast into place. If I could wear one every day . . . It does wonders. I looked almost as perky as Patti LaBelle.

My eye caught the time and I had only forty minutes for the arrival of my man. I remained calm as I stepped into the dress and began to inch it up over my hips; not a tug or yank needed.

I stood in front of the full-length mirror as my hands caressed my body, making sure all was perfect. I couldn't blink; I was taken by the curves the dress accentuated.

A bridesmaid dress that wasn't a waste of money. Sonya made a fantastic choice, with the red. The sleek, fitted dress took hold of my body; the opened back dropped to a V at the small of my back. The shoulder straps blended with the loose, flowing fabric that brought attention to my B-cups and the hem draped the floor just a tad.

I couldn't believe it. I felt like Nefertiti waiting for my king to arrive. I wanted to emphasize my neckline; I placed my hair up, leaving a long piece to stroke my right cheek and hook my chin.

With ten minutes approaching seven o'clock, I picked up the last piece to the assemble: Polo Sport. I sprayed a mist into the air and walked through the soft, sweet scent. As I rule of thumb, I had to spray my pressure points: arm joints, behind the knees, neck, ears and a spritz between my breasts.

I had no clue where we were going, but it was better to be overdressed, than underdressed. The shoes I bought with this dress hadn't been worn since Sonya's wedding. I hoped the reunion would leave behind happier feet.

The open toes brought attention to my feet, and the strap crossing the bridge of my toes glistened with diamond-like stones. The two-inch heels lifted me beautifully and added more flair.

There it rang, the doorbell, and out of nowhere I felt confused, as if I wasn't prepared.

"Oh, my God, he's here! Calm down, girl." I grabbed my handbag and sheer shawl to dart down the stairs.

No matter how fast I wanted to move, the slim fitted dress wasn't made for dashing. With one hand on the rail and the other with purse at hand, I quickly made it down the stairs.

"Damn, all my junk is in the way," I moaned, somewhat kicking the bag and books with my foot.

I promptly caught my breath and regained my self-control, standing at the door with my right hand on the knob. Turning the bolt lock, my eyelids slowly closed to prepare myself for what was on the other side. The basic wooden door opened and there stood Travis, looking debonair . . .

"Maré, you look beautiful," he said, with a pleasing voice and expression.

"Thank you. And so do you. I'm pretty much ready. I need to grab my keys. Um, come in as I try to find them. Please excuse the mess." I stepped to the right to motion him in.

Ever the gentleman, Travis entered and closed the door. Searching through the living room, I had begun to become nervous. I had Travis in my home and I looked disorganized.

"This is a nice place you have here. Do you mind if I take a look at your living room?" he asked.

"Sure! Come on in." I found my keys between the sofa cushions, where they must have fallen.

"Is this some of your handy home improvement work?" he asked.

"Yeah, this is my doing."

"I'm impressed. Your craftsmanship looks professional," he complimented, as his head bobbed down and up.

"Thank you. I worked hard at getting this room just like it is. I got my keys." The clinking sound made it apparent.

With a smile on his face, he said, "Let's go then."

Travis rushed to my side to open the door to Kayla's black BWM and closed it once he knew I was safely in.

"Again, Maré, you look radiant." His eyes caressed me as he began to back out the driveway.

My mind couldn't stop spinning and I found it difficult to loosen up. I sat next to my man with butterflies, ladybugs, and love bugs invading my stomach.

CHAPTER FIFTY-FIVE

"Where are we headed to?" I asked, noticing he took I-20.

He looked over at me with a smirk. "Don't worry about it. I do hope that you like it."

The man smelled powerful and his gear was working right along with it. He had caught my attention at the door, but I wanted to keep myself in check.

When he had stood at the door, I noticed his warm, subtle, brown plaid suit; it embodied an old-fashioned quality, with a classic twist. His tie eloquently touched up the gear with tri-tones of blue, crème, and brown. Travis was a man with style, and setting off his suit with a tan, button-down dress shirt, made it apparent.

I only needed one look to have an entire portrait of him in my soul. Like many times before, I just wanted to stare at him and breathe in his physical and spirit-filled air. I hoped my visible reaction didn't come off too laid-back.

"Who is this playing? I like it," I asked.

"It's a brother named King Britt out of Philadelphia, who's a DJ. Um, actually the group is called Sylk130, which includes his accompanying vocalist, lyricists, and MCs. His music is some of the purest blend of hip-hop, house, nu-jazz, funk, and what have you, that makes it simple, yet extraordinary," stressed Travis.

"I don't think I have ever heard of him. Has he been out for a minute?"

Travis preceded to exit at Courtland Avenue. "Of course not. With these cookie-cut radio stations, and each one thinks they are somewhat different than the other. They play the same old prepaid artists. If it's clean, it's not played."

I could see Travis raring to debate and politick tonight. The flame in his eyes had begun to spread. He felt strongly about the lack of versatility of music displayed in the mainstream.

"That's what's selling in the culture—negativity. Who wants to be uplifted and moved? God knows, not our people. There's so much music out there that we're missing." I became dissatisfied along him.

"Internet radio is the drum major of educating people on all the genres of music. It's allowing many unknown artists to become identified. If it's left up to FM and AM . . ."

I had become submerged into our conversation and I hadn't paid attention to my surroundings. Travis looked over with a smile and the car came to a complete stop. I wasn't sure if it was the car or if it had it been me, as his glance most definitely stopped me.

"Here we are, Madame. Dailey's," Travis announced, reaching to turn off his radio.

Quickly, two valets made it to each of our doors almost simultaneously. A short, pale man assisted me out of the car with a welcoming smile. The night of downtown Atlanta whispered to me. I could feel it touch me as cars drove past and drivers looked at me.

Travis took my hand from the lingering attention of the valet. Without hesitation, he placed my hand into the fold of his right arm. The light, gentle breeze slid my shawl off my right shoulder.

"Wow, this looks beautiful," I stated, filled with bewilderment.

Towering over me, his head tilted slightly towards me. "You're going to enjoy yourself. Good food and entertainment."

"How about good company?" I asked, crooking my neck.

"Nah, that's what I'm looking forward to."

I wished for a night never-ending, the compliments, the touching, and the exuberant feeling I had. Carefully, we made it up the red brick staircase to the restaurant, making sure not to step on my dress.

"Good evening. Do you have a reservation?" asked the maitre d'.

"Yes, Atkins, seven-thirty."

The balding man skimmed through his list, just as a large party trampled in behind us. It was a beautiful restaurant and the people who dined there exhibited success.

"Yes, sir. I have you here, Mr. Atkins."

"Please, follow me this way," directed the waitress.

The décor was something I had never seen. I observed it as we made our way to the table. Horse carousels were sporadically placed throughout the room.

It felt unbelievable to be in an upscale place like this, and with Travis. Our conversation in the car had helped loosen me up.

"Maré, this is what I've needed. Thank you for coming out this evening," Travis said with sincerity in voice, once we sat.

"No! Thank you for asking."

The boyish-looking waitress made it back to our table to inquire on drinks. I made it simple. I ordered water with lemon; Travis ordered a drink I hadn't heard of before. For the first time, he and I experienced an awkward moment. I wasn't sure if it was the beauty we were feeling or just quietness.

"So, I take it that you haven't been here before by your expressions." He took a swig of his drink.

I gathered that whatever he was drinking looked to be a kind of brandy. The short-stemmed glass and the dark color of the liquor gave me the tip off.

"You got me. No I haven't. This is a unique restaurant, especially with these chalkboard menus. It has elegance and simplicity in one. It took creativity to put this together." I continued to marvel at the restaurant.

At that moment, I sensed Travis in another place for the first time, ever in my presence. I wasn't on his mind or a part of his thoughts. Had I said something to lose that connection?

CHAPTER FIFTY-SIX

Browsing the menu, my attention targeted the prices and it couldn't be budged. The entrées were averaging twenty-five dollars. I felt timid about indulging in the expensive dinner.

"Maré, would you like to order an appetizer?" he asked, rubbing his chin.

I felt startled, and I guess still overwhelmed. "Ah, I think I'm okay."

"Please order whatever you like and don't feel boxed in. Whatever you want, order it. Okay?"

Those words felt warming to my soul. I had been waiting for a man to take care of my basic needs, wants, and desires. Within a few hours, Travis had exceeded my expectations for the evening.

"Thanks, I'll just focus on the main course," I said, acknowledging his thoughtfulness.

Placing his menu away from him, "So what's going on with the research you were working on?" he asked.

His eyes were my telescope into determination, persistence, and love; it hurt for me to be deceitful to him about my accomplishments. Travis's temperament was the flip side of yesterday. He seemed to be trying to get out of the swing of what life had pushed onto him.

I took my attention from the menu. "It's hasn't been a top priority with the school year kicking off. I guess I've allowed myself to be lazy."

"It's up to you. I heard a bishop here in Atlanta who stated, 'Do not allow a moment of hopelessness to rob your joy, peace, and purpose'. You have to keep on pushing. It's not going to be easy."

"I haven't put it out the way, only to the side," pleading my 'case'.

"That's what you cannot afford to do . . ."

"Good evening. My name is Leslie and I will be your waitress this evening. Are we ready to order, or do you need a few more minutes?"

"We are ready whenever she is," Travis said.

Coincidentally, I ordered the least expensive meal while Travis went for what he said was his favorite. For seventeen dollars, the herb chicken, rice pilaf, and green beans better satisfy my hunger and feed me tomorrow.

I enjoyed seeing my people taking pleasure in the finer things in life, with hopes no one was wearing a mask. I felt that I was real and that people got what they saw.

The restaurant was far from empty, and far from being silent. The patrons consisted of the make-up of Atlanta: young, old, black, white, Latin, and who knows, rich and poor. It inspired me to be around a different sector of people.

A typical white tablecloth dressed each table and brass center-pieces brought contrast to the burgundy carpet and chairs. A single-stemmed daisy on each table added an effortless touch to the room.

"Don't think you're going to get off that easy," smirked Travis, continuing our conversation. "Stay on it and never give up on your hopes and dreams."

I agreed with him. "I won't, believe me. I won't."

"I'm not going to lecture you. You've seen people sweating and bleeding to get money for someone else's company. Could you imag-ine what this world would be like if people stopped doing overtime for others and put in the overtime to build their own?" said Travis, filled with more questions. He noticed our food.

The waitress placed each of our plates in front of us and the food looked scrumptious; I may have just been starving. The steam from Travis's salmon wasn't a joke. I picked up my silverware, pre-paring to grub.

"Maré, please allow me to say grace," he said in a deep, authori-tative tone. He stretched over the table for my hand.

I placed the fork down and took a hold of his sturdy hand. Travis's head bowed; his voice seized the noise around us.

". . . and Father, please protect us this evening. We thank you for providing all our needs. In Jesus' name, Amen," he prayed, as he squeezed my hand.

"Amen. Thank you."

"You're going to enjoy that dish; it's one of my favorites," he gloated, cutting into his salmon.

"It's looks and smells good. If I don't, then I'll put the blame on you," quietly laughing.

Both of us had our mouths occupied by succulent food and happiness in our eyes. No one had a complaint. At least, so far I did-n't.

"Travis!" said a southern twang.

Quickly we both searched for the person who called out his name. I hadn't a clue who I'd be looking for. It could've been anyone in the restaurant.

"Sara! How have you been? I haven't seen you since you left the *AJC*," said Travis, filled with surprise. He wiped his mouth.

He and the short, blond-haired woman embraced candidly. It was a pleasant surprise, and most definitely for me.

"Yeah. It's been, what? At the time you had become engaged. Is this the woman who stole your heart?" she asked, glancing down at me.

His facial color dissipated along with a portion of his smile. "Ah no, this is a friend of mine. Maré, this is Sara. She used to work with me eons ago at the *AJC*."

I extended my right hand. "Nice to meet you."

Sara became slightly flushed in the face. "I apologize! Are you still with the *AJC*?"

"Yes, I've moved up to editor of my own socially conscious column," he said with gleam and a smile.

"Whoa! That is fantastic, Travis. You always had that edge. I apologize if I disturbed your dinner, but I couldn't walk out of here and not say hello." She reached for another hug.

"It was good to see you, Sara. Hopefully, it won't be such a long time before we run into each other again," said Travis, returning to his chair.

Silence again. I knew what it could've been; the misidentifying of me as his wife. I didn't want to deal with that. It was over and done with; it was my time to shine.

CHAPTER FIFTY-SEVEN

"Travis, the meal was fabulous. So was the evening and the company," I raved, adjusting my seatbelt.

Travis pulled onto Andrew Young International Boulevard. "You're welcome. I enjoyed myself, too."

The dynamics of the evening had become lost after the interruption by Sara. It put Travis in a different place, one he was unable to get out of; he seemed to try, to no avail.

"Travis, is everything okay? You've been kind of quiet," I queried, barely leaning forward to see his eyes.

"I'm fine, I just have a lot on my mind. Thank you for asking," he replied, looking straight ahead.

It began to hurt to see Travis not being his happy and activist self. I didn't want an injured doe. I wanted a buck.

The bright lights on I-20 lit up the inside of the car and I noticed the time, eleven o'clock. A late weeknight for me. The solemn mood got to me and I had to do something to save it.

"Travis, I was thinking that maybe you can educate people on different genres and artists on your show," I said, desiring a connection.

He looked over at me, puckered his lips, and twisted them to the left, "Yeah, that sounds good. Maré, I haven't been honest with you."

At a loss, I asked, "What do you mean?"

He yielded to merge onto Flat Shoals Parkway. "I've been going through a lot, and it's been life changing. I wanted to be strong by this time, but I'm tired."

Tears began to trickle from his right eye. No matter what followed, I wasn't prepared to respond.

"I feel so alone, and there are so many unanswered questions that I have to face every day. Why did this happen to me? I wanted to ask Jesus why, but I didn't . . ." he confessed, refusing to look at me.

My blood pressure rose with anticipation of what he may say. "I'm here if you need me to be. I'm here to talk or just listen," I said, trembling through each word.

It felt like a roller coaster ride, waiting to reach the top and drop to an unknown depth. I was headed into unidentified territory that I couldn't control or set a course to.

He pulled into my driveway and looked into me. "My wife was killed!"

"What are you talking about?" I asked, with disbelief in my tone.

"Someone killed my wife. I refuse to believe that she would kill herself," blurted Travis as he rubbed his right thumb underneath his left eye.

"Travis, I'm so sorry. Let's go inside, is that okay?"

The trembles that were in my words had spread to my body. I became filled with fear from the words that rushed from Travis's mouth. I shook like it was forty-one degrees outside and as if I stood in it without enough clothes. Yet we now sat in the comfort of my warm house, on the sofa.

"I don't mean to burden you with my problems."

I rushed to my feet. "Please don't feel like that. Can I get you something, maybe tea or wine?" I asked.

"Wine would be fine," he requested, placing his handkerchief into his back pants pocket.

Where was I going with this? The best I could do was to console him and listen. Most important, show him my feminine supportive side. I could recall him saying his wife didn't do it well.

I handed him the short glass. "May I ask what happened?"

"I got back from Chicago to find my wife in the family room, bleeding," he said, holding back tears. "I just went into shock, you know? She was looking forward to seeing her family. I wanted her to visit them while I was gone so she wouldn't be alone."

I was at a loss for words. "I'm so sorry, Travis." I could feel my heart throbbing in my chest. "That's something I wouldn't want you to experience, no one."

"It's something I couldn't have wished on my worst enemy." His voice filled with anguish, and he tossed down the wine. "There wasn't a reason for her to die. Our relationship was fine." He placed his left hand over his face to hide his crying eyes.

I placed my arms around him. "I'm here for you."

"The autopsy is quote-unquote 'consistent with a suicide'. There was an odd level of chemicals in her lungs that they were unable to explain. They said it was cleaning agents that she used in the kitchen," he rambled. He pulled away. "Are you okay? Your heart is beating fast." Travis looked at my chest.

"I'm fine. It does that sometimes when I drink alcohol." It felt like the Y2K panic of all the countries taking placing in my body, wondering if I was about to be shut down.

Again, I had failed to think how Travis would feel about the traumatic situation; the pain and heartache never entered my mind. I would have never seen myself as being a selfish soul, but looking into the suffering eyes of Travis, it shamed me.

"I don't know. There weren't any signs of forced entry and nothing was stolen."

Standing, I asked, "Would you like some more wine?"

"If you don't mind." He handed me his empty glass.

Placing the glasses on the kitchen counter, I took my freed left hand and put it against my chest. The pounding was rapid and strong. I wanted to control it, so I took in deep breaths to slow it down. I didn't have much time; I needed to return to Travis.

"Thank you," said Travis, taking the drink from my hand. "You know what hurt me the most?"

"No." I replied, sipping the wine.

"I was a suspect in my wife's death. They wanted to pin it on me. The black man." He took another gulp of his drink.

A tear fell from my eye and sadness controlled the mood. Where was I going to go now? My love for this man was still the same, and what I'd done wasn't in vain.

"It's getting pretty late, Travis, and I don't think you should be driving home. You're going to stay here tonight."

Reaching out his arm, he said, "Thank you for being here. I didn't want to spend another night alone. I needed this night, Maré. You're my angel that made it happen."

I held him in my arms. "Travis, I'm happy that I was able to help you."

The embrace and the drinks increased my libido. His arms were strong and muscular, something I had longed to feel around my waist, while his large hands cupped my back.

My chin rested on his upper chest and I closed my eyes. I smelled his spirit and touched his soul.

CHAPTER FIFTY-EIGHT

The sun peeped over the pine trees in an orange sherbet hue. It was going on seven-thirty, the time I should've been at work.

"Good morning, Catherine. This is Maré. I won't be coming in today," I said in a soft voice.

"Okay, would you like to notate any specific reason?" she asked, preparing to take notes.

"Yeah, a friend of mine had a family member die and they needed consoling late last night."

"Sorry to hear that, Maré. I'll make a note of that and we'll see you tomorrow. Oh, you forgot to stop by and sign off on those policy forms."

Mr. Graham doesn't like call-ins no matter what the reason may be; hopefully, my explanation will give me some lead way. Me not following through on signing those forms wouldn't help matters for the good.

Travis looked serene cramped on the sofa. I wished he hadn't fallen asleep, so he could have slept in the guestroom. I could see that he was emotionally drained, something I could relate to, so he slept where he lay.

"Travis, Travis—Travis," I said softly. "It's time to get up." I rocked his shoulder.

"Ugh-Ugh," he moaned, stretching his legs over the sofa's arm. "Good morning. What time is it?"

I sat on the edge of the sofa. "It's a quarter to eight. I hope I didn't wake you too late. I didn't wakeup, not too long ago," I said.

"This is fine. I'll probably go in later today or call in," he grumbled, rubbing his eyes.

I couldn't recall the last time a man slept in my house until the break of dawn. I knew this one I wouldn't forget. Being together this morning was my dream come true. Hell, the entire evening had been a fairytale, but this one had no ending.

"I've already made my phone call," I bragged with a smile filled with joy. "Can I get you something? I do want to let you know there isn't any coffee in this house. I don't do coffee."

Travis made it to the upright position. "No, thank you. You have extended your hospitality far enough. It amazes me when the Lord knows what you need and when you'll receive it."

"I can say Amen on that," I concurred, barely giggling.

"Yesterday morning, I was in a different mode of thinking and spirit. This morning, I'm at a higher level. I needed to get out of that house and spend time with someone who wasn't overly sympathetic to my loss."

"I'm glad that your spirit has been lifted. I'm sure there'll be some tough days to come, and if you need me, I'm here," I said, noticing his full lips.

"I don't know how I can ever repay you. I'm going to head home and get into bed. Somewhere where I can toss and turn," he said jokingly.

"Don't even go there. I have a guestroom, but Mr. Grizzly was unmovable last night," I said, joshing back quickly. "You must be alert, with the morning jokes."

Travis put his self together. He looked as handsome as he had last night, except now he had a twelve o'clock shadow to go along with twelve four hour goatee. He tightened his tie and laced his shoes.

"Thank you again for being here for me. Thinking enough about me to stop by and check in on me. People ask what makes a friend, I would have to say you," he said, stroking my back.

In the foyer, we held onto each other to say see you later; the hug had a hint of intimacy. Travis pressed my head against his chest with his hand, and my hands caressed his lower back.

Pleasantly kissing my forehead as he stepped away, Travis said, "Enjoy your day and I'll talk to you later."

I lay on the sofa and breathed in his scent, which had seeped into the fabric. It gave me aromatherapy and spiritual cleansing; I didn't want it to end.

I heard a bang at the door. I wondered if Travis had forgotten something. It seemed like hours had passed. I jumped to my feet to rush to the door. I opened the door to find myself bomb-rushed by the DeKalb County Police.

An officer wearing bifocal glasses forcefully pressed me up against the wall. Behind him stood a suited white man with a huge forehead.

"Ms. Alexander, you're under arrest for the murder of Kayla Atkins," he spurted as he began to read me my Miranda Rights. "You need to come clean, to save us time. And it could save yourself some extra time."

I began to hyperventilate with the unexpected turn of events. What was I to say or not to say, not to incriminate myself? What evidence did they have to link me to the crime? What was the evidence?

The sofa that comforted Travis now comforted me, as I sat handcuffed with my head between my legs. They knew I was petrified—if not by the hyperventilation, then by the golf-ball sized tears.

Sitting on my curio trunk, the big forehead man whispered, "I can help you, if you help me."

My chest cavity felt like it was going to implode. I stretched my eyes as far as I could without adjusting my body. I could only see a corner of the man's forehead.

"I don't know what you're talking about," wheezing through each word.

"You got what I want and I can get you what you need. Medical attention," he taunted. "Check the bedroom and closets, we'll come up with something," he yelled.

I sat upright. "You don't have a search warrant and I want you out of my house. Please! Why are you doing this?"

He pointed behind me. "You have to ask him," he said.

Barely getting enough air, I turned around to see the one in charge of the mayhem. Our eyes met, and my breathing completely stopped.

Why?" I said with my last breath.

"You killed my wife and you're going down. I gave you many opportunities last night to clear yourself. Before I walked out that door, your chance was there, but you wanted to act like everything I said didn't pertain to you," he said. His eyes now contained the fiery inferno I had determined to get back.

"No, Travis! No!" I wheezed.

"We got your prints from the basketball. Now all we need to do is pair them up," added the big forehead man.

My eyes were heavy from the lack of oxygen to my brain, so I decided not to fight anymore. I passed out. I found myself back at Travis's house, killing Kayla. It all seemed so real.

"You have to go." I stepped forward, with the knife in my hand.

I pulled her away from the leather chair a little and wedged myself between her and the chair. I had one shot to get it right. I propped her head against my face, then I put the knife to her neck.

"Damn it, you're about to mess this up," chastising myself. I took the knife with my left hand.

I closed my eyes and sliced through her esophagus. I closed the gap between her and the chair. I placed the knife in her left hand, raised her hand to her neck and allowed it to freefall.

I heard the commotion of the police in my house. I lay numb from head to toe and heart to soul.

"She is going to suffer like Kayla!" ranted Travis.

"Ring—Ring."

Everyone's attention redirected to the phone. They were astonished to hear it ring.

CHAPTER FIFTY-NINE

I pulled myself from the drool spot on the sofa, rubbed my pillow smashed hair, and jumped to my feet to answer the phone. As I walked, my mind raced with the surreal images. I found it hard to catch my breath.

Feeling light headed, I said, "Hello."

"What are you doing home? I was calling to leave a message for you to call me. I wanted to see how the date went. It must've gone better than good, being that you didn't make it to work this morning," probed Michelle.

"It went well. Can I call you back? I was in a deep sleep and I jumped up too fast," I replied, feeling the perspiration on the back of my neck.

I hung up and not only felt dazed, but my heart ricocheted off my ribcage.

As my head fell backwards on the sofa, I mumbled, "I thought I was gone."

The dream seemed so real that my body experienced every physical reaction within the dream. No matter how hard I tried to slow the pace of my heart, it drove on its own accord.

I had no control over my body's functions. It was evident when a tear trickled from my left eye. I was uncertain as to why it appeared. It could've been that I was concerned about my body, or that the dream showed me reality.

I detached myself from the drama that took place on the other side, until Travis showed it to me last night. His pain. Dealing with my struggles was enough for me to handle and now I had the panoramic view.

Going through something like this frequently could cause lasting wear and tear on me physically, mentally, and spiritually. I felt cornered like a cat by a Rottweiler. There weren't any options but to bear the pain.

"God, I need help. I can't take these flashes of fear and paranoia in my life," I begged through a set of light tears. "What am I going to do?"

No matter how hard I pumped myself to be strong, something

came up to pull me back down. I'd heard it many times before: our inner-voice is our worst enemy; it's more negative and doubtful than people.

Deep inside, I knew in order to survive I would need some psychological attention—by doing a Tony Soprano.

It was like BellSouth. The phone continued to ring off the hook. "Hello."

"Did I disturb you?" he asked.

I wiped my eyes. "Ah, no. I was just sitting here."

"I decided to call in and enjoy the day. I really don't have anything to do and I don't want to be alone. I was wondering if you would like to have lunch with me?" asked Travis.

Who would've thought that he would want to be with me rather than be alone? Everything was coming together easier than what my inner-voice said.

"Food sounds pretty good right now," I said, laughing aloud. "Let's meet up, I don't want you to have drive way over here. We know there aren't any places to eat over here."

"Maré, I don't have a problem with that. Men should take the lead in all they do, but the flip side is knowing when to follow. So I'll follow today," declared Travis. "Any place in particular?"

"Hum, good question. Let's say Macaroni Grill by Perimeter Mall. How does that sound?"

"I feel you on that selection. We'll meet there at twelve-thirty?" he suggested.

Back on my feet, I had to find something that coordinated with the picture I painted the night before of elegance, class, and style. I knew I couldn't be overdone. It would appear as if I was trying too hard, though that's the truth.

I hadn't fully recuperated from the dream, still shocked by how real it seemed. To ever have Travis know what I had done would be the end of life for me.

He and I pulled up at the same time. This time he drove his SUV. Travis didn't think I noticed him because of the different vehicle. I began to walk towards his truck to greet him and I caught myself. I stopped to dig into my purse, acting as if to search for something. I returned to my car.

Once I turned around to head to the entrance, Travis made his way towards me. "Is everything okay?" he asked, placing his hand on the small of my back.

I stepped onto the walkway. "Yeah, I left my cell phone in the car."

I chose Macaroni Grill because I knew I could afford it and for the upscale reputation it presented. My girls and I know, don't ever suggest a restaurant that you can't afford. I'd heard stories where men played the 'I left my wallet at home' game. Then they look at you to pay the bill and you don't have two lemons to squeeze together.

Too many women want a free ride and the vehicle they are hitch-hiking on is just as unreliable as they are.

"On my way home I turned the radio on and heard this man speaking to a caller about her finances. This woman at one point and time had nine credit cards. Can you believe that?" asked Travis, astounded. He slid back to allow the waiter to place his plate. "She proudly said that she got it down to five."

"Nine credit cards! You know she has nothing but debt. People think credit cards are the answers to their money problems. I don't even have a department credit card. Give me the basics." I began twirling my angel hair pasta in my spoon.

"The advisor said something that I hope many people heard and understood. People go into debt trying to impress others. I can't remember word for word, but he said that a man will spend fifteen-thousand dollars on a car to impress someone for two minutes."

"That's some expressive impressing," I said.

"And that's exactly what the advisor said. People are out here leasing cars or constantly buying new ones and never owning. It saddens me to see people putting their value into things and not into themselves," he said in a preaching tone.

The restaurant became packed, but our waiter was very attentive, even with a full section. He refilled our glasses and returned to the table in a timely fashion to see if we needed anything.

"Low self-esteem is what a large percentage of the population has. These people are raising children who are seeing what mommy and daddy are and thinking that's how life is supposed to be. Now they are living an empty life," I added, stabbing into the bread.

"Keep it real. That's why I enjoy your company; you are very grounded. I run into too many superficial people. Those who got money are much worse than those who are trying to perpetrate as if they have it," said Travis, laughing at his statement.

The soft-spoken waiter brought the check. I pulled out my wallet to pay for my meal. Of course I desired Travis to pay, but I didn't want to not offer or make the effort to pay.

"Put that away!" he demanded, reaching across the table. "I will take care of it. Your choice of lunch was very convenient for me. I live up the street."

"Really!" I said. But I could have made a bad mistake, by not asking him where he lived before I selected the restaurant and location.

Travis held the door as we exited and the crowd was still coming in droves. Not a cloud in the sky. The air was filled with a constant breeze.

"You have to stop by one day," Travis suggested, allowing others to pass him by.

"Maré?" said a questionable tone.

Both Travis and I cut our eye contact to turn to see a brother looking into my face, with an expression of doubt.

"Hey! How is it going, Ezekiel?" I asked, reaching to hug him.

"I thought it was you, but I wasn't sure. I had hoped it would be you. I didn't want to embarrass myself. How is it going, my brother?" he asked, acknowledging Travis.

"Travis, this is Ezekiel, my girl's boyfriend. He has a nice spot in downtown Decatur, with spoken word and jazz," I introduced, touching Travis's elbow.

"That sounds all right. What's the name of it?" asked Travis.

"Café Sacrifice. I need to get everyone back down there to have a good time. I'll have Erin get that going. I'm sorry, but I better go, I'm here to pick up my lunch." Ezekiel rushed, again shaking Travis's hand. "I'm still waiting on you to do your thing," he said to me

The first sighting with Travis wasn't expected to happen so soon. I forgot that Ezekiel lived near here. I knew he would go tell Erin he saw me.

CHAPTER SIXTY

"The life I have come to love, I want to bottle it up," I whispered to myself.

The fall season had made its presence known with cooler temperatures. No matter if it rained, snowed, or sleeted, I found people to look at outside my classroom window.

The more time Travis and I spent together, the more I fell in love with him. My love for him was a birthmark on my heart that could never be erased or replaced.

I waited for his arrival; we were heading to Ezekiel's café to hang out with the entire crew. After weeks of begging and minds filled with intrigue, I agreed that I'd introduce the man of the hour to everyone.

This would be the first time for all of us to be together with men; our first couples' gathering. It felt exciting to be in a place where my life was filled with content and balance. Now that Travis had a presence in my life, I began to put real effort into opening my own school.

His syndicated show started in Chicago, and from what they could see, the ratings looked great. It was a possibility he would work on Washington, D.C. next. It paid to know the man in charge of the show; he brought me a recording of the broadcast each week.

With Mr. Graham having his eye on me, I made sure I stayed on track at work. No need to get whatever I could get anymore. I had the entirety, whenever I wanted it.

"Hello," I said, answering my cell phone and walking towards the window.

"Are you ready? I'm a block away on Luckie Street," said Travis.

"I'll be at the front of the school." I reached for my black leather coat.

The school was empty except for a few overachievers who tended to make life hard for their students. Fridays were anticipated just as much by the teachers as the kids.

I felt a little nervous about the night; I didn't want anyone to invade Travis's privacy with a lot of questions. Most importantly, I didn't want Travis to reveal anything—like exactly when we really met.

Travis pulled up right as I zipped up my coat. He could see me standing at the glass doors.

"It's good to see you," said Travis, leaning to kiss my forehead as I got into the car.

"I'm happy to see you, too," I replied with a schoolgirl grin.

Travis did a U-turn and I noticed Eugene standing at the doors, with broom at hand. He and I still had bitterness between us. I still thought he told Mr. Graham about me leaving early that day. I waved to him with a taunting smile. He didn't move and we kept on driving.

"This place is off the chain," marveled Travis when we arrived.

"Yeah, that's how it was the first time I came. A line for days. I'm glad we don't have to wait in that line," I said, walking towards the bouncer. "Hi. My name was left here at the door by Ezekiel."

"Let me checkout the VIP list," said the steroid looking man. "What's your name?"

"Maré Alexander."

It went smooth as a freshly painted fingernail. The ambiance was on fire. Soon, as we walked through the door, the jazz band's melodic notes pulled us into the café.

"This is Atlanta's best kept secret!" Travis said, stunned by the establishment. "Is that your friend over there, waving?"

I could feel all the eyes on us, wanting to see Travis. When Sonya stood to get a better view, I knew my feelings were right. Travis and I were tonight's focus. I wanted to meet the man Michelle had been seeing. My situation had more excitement, I guess.

"What's up, everyone?" I greeted, leaning over to hug Erin. "Everyone, this is Travis, as if you don't already know. Travis, this is Erin, Michelle, Sonya, Adrian, who is Sonya's husband; I'm sorry, I don't know Michelle's friend's name."

"What's up? I'm Marco," said the dreaded brother.

"Um, this is who you've been hiding," teased Sonya.

"Whatever. No need for that tonight. Please!" I looked around the place. "Erin, where is Ezekiel?" I continued.

"Somewhere around here, working himself to death. He'll be back this way soon," she said, looking through the café.

Erin's eyes remained on Travis and I for a second longer, even with the announcement of the poet coming to the stage. The band paused as the applause roared inside the café.

"Good evening, my people. I would like to welcome you to my world, my heart, and my soul. Welcome to Aya's," she said.

Emotions
Yesterday my heart & soul could not breathe
Because they were filled with emotions of you
I took deep breaths every 15 minutes,
to slow down the beating of my heart
The way I felt was something new
Maybe it was a fear of losing you
I am saddened each time you walk out my door
You are the one God brought to me
I am for sure
Tears fill my eyes and I don't know why
You have entered a part of me that no other
has before
These emotions have me thinking
of you all day
But when I see you or
when I hear your voice
My heart and soul seemly breathe again with ease

Silence sat among the café, then everyone recognized the poet by enthusiastically clapping. It felt like she took that piece straight out of my book of poems.

"Travis, have you read any of your girl's poetry?" asked Sonya.

"No, I haven't been honored to see that side of her, yet," he replied, glancing at me with a smile.

I wasn't sure why Erin was so quiet tonight. Normally, she's the one I have to give the "please, no more questions look." I didn't feel at ease with her silence.

"Yo, Travis, what type of work are you in? Not to be forward, but a brother was laid-off and I'm trying to get in where I can fit," asked Marco.

"I work at the *AJC*. What I can do is check on what we have and I'll let Maré know. We have to look out for each other. Don't ever get above ourselves and not throw the rope back," proclaimed Travis loudly.

"Good looking out. I would really appreciate that," Marco said, reaching across the table to give Travis a pound.

"How are my people doing? It's been crazy tonight," panted Ezekiel, leaning to give Erin a peck on the lips. "What's up? Travis, right?"

"Yeah. This is a very nice place here, without a doubt. You have Atlanta's best kept secret."

"Thanks. I hate to hit and run, but I gotta work."

"Travis, how is it a man like you is still single?" asked Michelle.

It presented a possible sinkhole that could take me. With Erin in the cut doing nothing but listening, someone may put two and two together. Travis's answers to the many questions that were about to come his way would be detrimental, the attention set upon him to see why he was single, as if he couldn't be. As I thought of the question, it made me feel unworthy of this man's love.

Interjecting myself into the conversation, "What are you trying to say, Michelle? A sister can't charm a man like him?" with a smile.

"Just wondering where he's been hiding. You were lucky to have found him," said Erin, breaking her silence.

"It's been a blessing to have her in my life. As to being single, life brings us situations," stated Travis diplomatically, as he squeezed my hand.

"So, what happened to your last girlfriend?" asked Sonya.

"Damn, ya'll acting like NYPD up in here. Leave the brother alone and let him enjoy the night," Adrian said with irritation in his voice. "Don't let these nosy women bother you."

Adrian helped me more than he could've ever known. Travis was a good trooper about it all and appeared unbothered. He and I had a good friendship.

"Thanks. I thought I was being interrogated," Travis laughed.

"You know? If we did as much research in other things like buying homes, investing, education, and politics," advocated Adrian.

"I'm feeling you on that. Stop jumping into decisions without thinking and researching," agreed Travis.

He found his center, politicking on topics that matter. Everyone became engaged in the conversation and Erin added her two cents, here and there. It became a joyous evening.

"Travis, you are a cool brother. Something about you seems familiar," pondered Adrian.

"Yeah, I know what you're saying. What is it, the name?" said Erin sarcastically.

I had the meeting of my two worlds, the one I had all along and the one I created with Travis. A success story, if I said so myself. I had the love and the friends.

As always, Travis drove me home, and quite often he slept over. I wanted him to stay the night. I yearned for him like a forest fire seeking its next shrubbery, tree, or piece of grass. Nothing or no one could stop it from wildly spreading.

"I enjoyed myself with your friends. I'm happy to see that

they're filled with thought-provoking ideas, like you," complimented Travis, taking off his shoes.

"I hope my girls' personal questions didn't bother you," I said, turning on the television.

"It wasn't too bad. Adrian put it in check. He's very philosophical," he replied, making his way towards me, on the sofa. "I've been wanting to kiss you for some time now." He placed his full lips onto mine.

Quivers went through my body and chill bumps ejected from my skin. His kiss felt gentle and his lips were like a perfectly ripe strawberry, soft, sweet, and firm. I had an out of body experience. It had nothing to do with the spirit; it was all about the physical.

His hands caressed my breasts and I moaned as a tear slipped from the corner of my eye, as my body exploded from each kiss and each touch.

"Maré, I respect you," he said softly, looking into my eyes. "I want to hold you tonight."

I grabbed his hand. "I want you to hold me."

Leading Travis to my room was more than enough for me. We continued where we left off on the sofa. The kisses he gave were passionate. I became lost in the moment as my eyes remained shut.

His hands made their way under my blouse to my bra clasp. Every move he made flowed easily, like the night had our names on it. The silhouettes of our bodies were barely visible in the pitch black bedroom. Travis leaned over me and began to unbutton my blouse. Each button he undid, the more I wanted him.

My upper body was naked. He touched my body, like an art sculptor, aware of each curve and each indent. Travis made me his work of art.

I had yet to feel the depth of his body. I lifted myself by grabbing hold of Travis's shoulders. My hands made their way underneath his polo style shirt and I inched it up slowly as I kissed his neck.

Travis assisted me by removing the shirt once I got it over his upper chest. The shirt landed on the floor, I heard it. My eyes were focused on his chest and its fullness. His arms were hard as tires. From embracing himself on the bed, I could feel every groove. My lips caressed the well-defined left chest muscle.

"Ring—Ring."

"Is that the phone?" moaned Travis.

I tossed his heavy arm off of me to reach for it.

"Hello!" I said, filled with intent.

"I know what you did!" said the faint voice. "I know what you did!"

The phone slid from my hand and onto the floor as my heart began to beat to the tenth power.

CHAPTER SIXTY-ONE

"Maré! Who is it?" asked Travis.

I couldn't move, nor speak. It had become a true nightmare and I wasn't ready for it.

The call shook me. "I-I-It was someone playing a perverse game on the phone."

"Are you okay?" Travis asked, reaching to stroke my hair. "They must've said something really inappropriate, to have you this shaken."

"It's okay. I was taken by surprise." My back remained towards him.

"Maré, come here and let me hold you. I'm right here and everything is going to be all right."

Travis took me into his arms and I placed my head on his chest. I had the security of his strong arms wrapped around me; they couldn't keep me safe. The world outside was coming back to get me.

I couldn't find sleep if it sat on one of my eyelids, unlike Travis. He found it and stole it. I picked up his heavy arm that bolted me to his chest and placed it onto his leg. Careful not to awaken him, I slowly rolled out of bed.

The sun began to make its way up as it thieved a look through the blinds. I really didn't care about the time of the day; I crept down the stairs.

"What's going on?" I asked myself, sitting on the sofa.

I sat there in my nightshirt and pajama pants, rocking back and forth as my fingers ran over my face. I needed to think, but my head became clouded by the voice. I couldn't get any other image into my head.

My fingers propped up my head with my chin. The cordless phone lay across the room in the big blue chair. It struck fear inside my . . .

"Caller ID. I can check to see who it was," I whispered, hesitating to get up.

I remained in my position as my fingers massaged the back of my neck. Uncertainty made me unmovable. What if they blocked their number? What if it was a joke? I lived a "what if" life; the phone lay less than five feet away.

I stood over the chair and leaned over to pick up the phone. My eyes read each button like I hadn't seen them before. My thumb clicked the arrow to display my last call.

Without my being aware, my eyes were closed and they weren't planning to bear witness to the number on the LCD display. With the phone in my right hand, I dropped my arms to full extension and my head dropped, too. My eyes were still shut. The phone made its way back up to my chest and I opened my eyes. I read the name.

"How? Why?" I questioned, dropping it to the chair cushion.

I fell into a whirlwind, with no way out. No room for a tear or emotions. At that moment and time, all I could think of: how and why. I stood there gazing at the phone. An expression couldn't be found on my face.

There were two thumps on the ceiling, which would be Travis making his way out of bed.

"Maré, are you down there?" shouted Travis.

"Yeah!" I grabbed the remote control.

"I hope you got my breakfast ready. You know how I like my eggs cooked," he said, scratching his head at the last step.

"You're at the wrong place," I joked, trying to play along.

"Good morning." He kissed me on my forehead.

Travis still had his shirt off. I could see his muscular physique; I captured it perfect last night with my touches. The rounded shoulders and the six-pack stomach made a beautiful presentation for the morning. It was apparent, the attention he gave to his body.

"How did you sleep last night?" I asked.

"Very well, thank you. Are you feeling better, since the rude phone call?"

"I'm doing just fine." I changed the channel.

"I'm not sure what would've taken place last night, but I think that call helped us out. I enjoyed every moment with you and I don't want to do anything to hurt you," he shared, licking his full lips.

"What do you mean?"

"I don't know if I'm ready for that step yet. Physically I am, emotionally, no. You mean too much to me—too much."

Travis and I stared into each other's eyes with reassurance of the respect he had for me. Through the gunfire on the television, he held me. I comfortably placed my right check on his bare chest.

"Ring—Ring"

"Do you want me to get that?" asked Travis.

"I got it." I stood.

"Ring—Ring"

"Let me know if it's that same jerk from last night."

"Hello," I said, noticing that it wasn't the jerk from last night.

"Is Miss Alexander available?"

"No, thank you, I'm not interested," I said, rushing the telemarketer off the phone.

"Ma'am, we have a great vacation deal available in your—"

I ended the phone call abruptly. I couldn't believe where I stood and how everything turned from a high to, within one night, a low.

CHAPTER SIXTY-TWO

Travis duped me into riding with him to his house. The ride had the scent of uneasy overtones, which all escaped from me. For the first time, my mind wasn't on Travis and me. My eyes peered straight ahead as if I could see thirty miles down the road.

"I thought about what you said some weeks ago and I have decided to bring positive hip-hop to the show. What's pumped out every day on the dial aren't lyricists, and that's what we need to be represented every day on the airwaves," said Travis.

I didn't feel like riding on the activism train. It took energy, something I couldn't spare. I should've declined his invitation, but I knew getting out of the house would be good for me.

"Yeah? Have you come up with a format?" I asked, with a speck of interest revealed on my face.

Travis took his eyes from the road. "Not yet. We'll get it together. Listen to this cut of Mos Def; it's filled with knowledge. He's a lyricist. Listen to what he's saying. True hip-hop is that rapper who is a teacher, an activist, a movement, and another source for enlightenment."

"It hurts to see how hip-hop has become money hungry. The craft is lost. Those who don't have the true lyrical gift are the ones who make it into the mainstream," I replied, closing with a tear inducing yawn.

"We have to work to it get back. We can't give up because sex, crime, guns, and the street life 'sells'. I'm going to do my part. Maybe once a month I'll feature a socially conscience rapper on the show. How does that sound? Lock in Mos Def, The Roots, Talib Kweli, PE, Wyclef, and maybe Pharohe Monch," said Travis, filled with hype.

"That sounds good. Promote the date and time of the show, to get as many people as possible tuned in."

"Are you okay?"

Travis had noticed my lack of enthusiasm during the ride. He turned his head, dropped it and his eyes tried to find mine. I hadn't noticed the effort he put into seeing how I felt. I did notice the tow truck changing lanes like a compact car, with little concern of those around it.

"I'm peachy keen," I said, flashing a soft smile.

"Just checking. You've been quiet today. I would like to think that you feel comfortable enough to discuss anything with me. I want to help you."

I understood Travis's concern and I found it appealing. He knew me well enough to notice my disposition had changed. He made his statement; there was no need to press me on the issue.

The small talk continued; he turned onto his street. I detected the neighborhood full of children. We both saw the little one wobbling down the road on his scooter. Travis began to laugh and so did I.

"That thing is too big for him," he stated, turning into the driveway.

"He had it though," I said, still laughing. "If it wasn't for you, he'd still be wobbling."

The house looked immaculate, from the sunroom to the kitchen. I stopped to take a seat at the breakfast bar. Travis continued around the bar towards the refrigerator.

"I'll grab a few bottles of water. It's time to get to work."

"Huh? What are you talking about?"

"You didn't think you were coming over here to relax?" he asked, with a smirk on his face.

"I don't know about you, but yes I did, and yes I am," I exclaimed.

"Well get yourself together while I run upstairs to change my shirt." He placed the bottled water on the counter.

I sat in the sun lit kitchen, only inches away from where Kayla and I struggled. It scared me to look back at the spot where she laid. My eyes remained on the tulips outside the kitchen window.

The quiet kitchen became filled with the noise of my memories. My forearms rested on the cool Corian countertop. I allowed my head to turn left.

Her body had once lain motionless on the hardwood floors and my cap sat next to her leg. An ill feeling began to pressure its way into my spirit.

"Maré. What are you looking at, so intensely on the floor?"

"Nothing. Just thinking."

"You got a lot on your mind. You stared into that one spot for a long period of time," continued Travis, dropping to one knee near the spot to tie his shoe.

I sensed an unrested feeling in the kitchen. I'm not sure if I could bear being alone in that house. Right now, I was making myself sustain, with Travis near.

Was Kayla really gone? Was I losing my sanity? The call last night had brought doubt and fear.

CHAPTER SIXTY-THREE

Unbeknownst to me, I had volunteered to help Travis clean out his garage. Why did he think I'd enjoy that chore? To be honest, if I didn't have a lot on my mind, I would clean whatever he directed me to, to be at his side.

"Travis, what did you drag me into?" I asked, with one hand on my hip.

"Aw, come on. Help a brother out," he begged, folding me into his huge chest.

I felt loved at that moment. Travis hugged me back into the times when Gran drowned me in her arms. We were one; I felt his stomach muscles move as he laughed. In the doorway of the garage, he moved me with a tender sway and his chin made its way onto the top of my head. I laughed, soon allowing his comforting to capture the mercies I had began to mislay.

"Travis, you know you're wrong, for bringing me over here under false pretenses."

"What are you talking about? I don't recall giving a reason for the ride to my place," he proclaimed, spinning me around.

I looked into his smile. "You think you're funny. Let's get to this, so you can make me a meal."

Glancing over the garage, I noted it wasn't an absolute mess. Maybe he didn't want to be here alone. Travis had been working on getting his life together and I think with me in his world, it made it attainable.

"I want to get everything out of here so I can pressure wash the ground. With my lovely assistant, maybe she'll also aid in the treatment process," he hinted, with an, "I hope she doesn't kill me" grin.

The temperature had to be abnormally high today, or all the moving of the large items made it feel that way. I helped roll out his tool cabinet; it had to weigh a ton.

"This is inhuman," I whined, wiping my sweaty forehead with the back of my hand. "I would like to think even indigent servants in Third World countries get water."

"We left the water on the kitchen counter. It's probably warm now. Go in and grab the others out of the fridge." He noticed a blue Chevrolet sedan pulling up.

Travis and I both stopped and watched the two people exit the vehicle. Walking the long stretch of driveway, the approaching woman put me back into the Bermuda Triangle. It was the detective I had seen on the news some weeks ago.

"Good afternoon, Mr. Atkins. I hope I didn't catch you at an inconvenient time?" she asked.

"Not really. Doing a little cleaning."

"This is my partner, Ed Mason, who has been helping me on your case." She peered to see me, standing behind Travis.

"My apologies, Detective Crews and Detective Mason. This is my friend, Maré," said Travis, removing me from his shadow.

"It's Investigator Mason. I haven't made it to detective yet," said the slender-built, dark-haired, and thick eye browed man.

"Hello," I said, quickly waving.

Detective Crews's attention remained on me for several moments longer. She multitasked; pulled out her notepad and glared at me. Investigator Mason followed her lead, reaching into this coat pocket.

"Maré, I'll be back with you in a moment. I need to speak with the detective briefly." Travis took several steps away from the garage.

I fumbled around in the garage, nowhere in earshot of the conversation. I stood there reading their facial expressions and body gestures for clues. I continued to remove the items, going unnoticed.

Both the detective and investigator had a look of "ah ha" upon their faces. It ate away at my insides, wanting to know what was being said and if I needed to run as fast as I could.

The investigator had a cute James Dean sort of style going on. The cleft above his top lip made him look rugged. He stood with Detective Crews, concentrating on every word that flowed from Travis's tongue.

My production had dropped to half and I became more eager to know what they said. It came to an end. Everyone gave handshakes and cordial smiles.

I hustled back to work, seeing that nothing ended on a down note. Tired, hungry, and filled with "what's happening," I pulled on a tarp. Out of nowhere, tools and junk crashed to the ground. The noise made a monstrous sound, sending Travis's attention towards the ruckus.

I beat him before he made it into the garage. "I'm okay."

"I think this belongs to you," said the detective.

My reflexes were quicker than I had thought when I caught the ball tossed to me. I'm not sure why she made the fast pass to me, rather than to Travis. However, I tossed the ball to Travis.

"This isn't my ball," he bellowed.

CHAPTER SIXTY-FOUR

You would've thought Detective Crews had the hearing of a cat, how she jerked around to the loud statement of Travis.

I looked at the ball and panic took over. The damn ball came back to haunt me, right in my face. I didn't want to be anywhere near it or the conversation. I knew it would seem very suspicious to walk away. Right?

Crews and Mason quickly high-stepped back towards the garage. Detective Crews didn't let her size allow her to miss a step. She glanced back at her partner to make sure that he followed her strides.

"What is it, Mr. Atkins?" she queried.

"This isn't my basketball," repeated Travis.

"What makes you believe this doesn't belong to you?" probed the investigator.

"This is a Wilson brand and I only purchase Spalding." He gripped the ball with both hands. "This ball is brand new or barely used. My ball is worn and it's far from having a orange color."

"Excuse me, can you show me exactly where you were before the loud commotion?" asked Detective Crews, directing her question to me.

My feet were planted to the ground. Deafness came upon my ears. The laughing of the children across the street, the passing cars, and the overhead airplane were no more.

Schools of thought scattered in my mind; I wanted to know if I was facilitating in the investigation of my crime. Would my position give her a clue to lock me up? I just wanted space to escape, if needed.

"Um, yeah." I shifted my body. "I was right back here in this area. Then I tugged on the blue thing. That's when everything came crashing down."

"Did you see anything suspicious, Ma'am?" questioned Mason.

"No, nothing," I mumbled, crossing my arms.

"You seem a little uncomfortable, are you okay?" asked Detective Crews.

"I'm fine. Just wanting to help as much as I can."

The two continued to search the garage with hopes of coming up with new evidence. Travis and I had interrupted the scene, so they couldn't determine the relevant information.

"Like I said, I want this investigation to continue until my wife's murderer is found."

"Sir, per your request, our investigation is geared in search of a killer and disregarding the suicide findings," said Mason, unsympathetically.

Detective Crews's eyebrows folded inward, her top lip darted upward. She couldn't hide her expression at her partner's statement.

"What I can do is take the ball to have it dusted for fingerprints. I want to be honest with you, there's a high possibility nothing will be found," stated Detective Crews.

"Any particular reason?" asked Travis.

"The surface of the ball is rubber, with little to no smooth surface. Unless there are prints on the logo section, we don't have anything. Second, we all touched it and that in itself could have ruined possible evidence," educated Mason.

"I am not concerning myself with 'could haves', I want this to be investigated," demanded Travis.

"Please, Mr. Atkins, we want to make you aware of the circumstances when it comes to dusting for fingerprints," said the detective, reflecting Travis's temper. "We'll take this and have it dusted."

"Ma'am, we're going to need to have your prints," said Investigator Mason.

That threw me into a miniature shell shock. I didn't want to turn myself into a sitting duck and that was what I had become.

"Okay. How does this help?" I asked.

Mason continued, "Being that Detective Crews, Travis, and yourself touched the ball, we need to exclude those prints and look for a fourth pair."

The day started on a spectrum that I would never have expected and continued on that current. From last night's phone call, to the police. I wondered if my day could get any worse.

CHAPTER SIXTY-FIVE

The visit from the police put Travis into a foul mood and filled me with paranoia as to what was taking place with the investigation.

We never completed the task of pressure washing the garage. Once they left, we placed everything back into the garage and headed inside the house for a meal. The entire time, Travis didn't say one word.

"Travis, are you okay?" I asked, placing my glass onto the counter.

His head hung low and his finger and thumb rubbed his eyes. I didn't know if he heard me or tuned me out. It would be my first time going unheard in his presence. Placing my emotions and fear to the side became toll-taking on me, but I wanted to know what the detectives said.

"Travis, I'm here. Whatever you need, I'm here."

Acknowledging my words, he said, "Please hug me. That's what I need."

"Hold on to me and I won't ever let you go," I said in a gentle tone, squeezing his midsection.

"I'm so angry right now!" Travis bellowed, pushing away. "The police have not found anything new since Kayla's death."

"Why did they stop by today?"

"Thinking about it, for no damn reason. Detective Crews wanted to keep me briefed on the progress of the case. Hell, they could've called, instead of wasting gas and energy." Travis spoke with force as he paced the kitchen floor.

"Travis, you have to think positive." That statement could've been the death of me. I knew I was thinking positive . . . that the police were positive that they weren't close to nailing a suspect. Me.

"Positive! I'm positive that Monday I will have my own investigator on this. Then I'll have the *AJC* do a reprint on my story, with a new reward. Right now the ten thousand dollars isn't working," he said, filled with rage.

Information fell from his mouth and I didn't know how to catch it. The entire story had been in the *AJC*. Now he wanted to push even harder. I needed my own space and I needed to get out of that house. My cup overflowed too much for me to console Travis.

Travis gathered himself together well enough to drive me home. The entire ride I thought of reality, my phone call, and how Travis tortured himself with the thoughts of his wife.

The radio's low volume made it impossible to hear the music clearly. The only audible sounds were the passing cars and the roaring engine.

"Travis, I'm sorry," I said apologetically, leaning to kiss him.

"Why are you apologizing? There isn't a need for that. Please don't start with that, please. You've been the only person who hasn't given me a pity party and that's why I enjoy your company." He placed the SUV into park.

"I'm sorry that you're going through this and I chose to come home."

"Tonight I need some time alone. I need to realize that being alone isn't a bad thing. I don't have to be sad when I am."

"I'm proud of you. Call me when you make it home."

Travis made sure I made it into the house. Little did he know that I had to deal with another ghost that haunted me. I didn't have a refuge anymore. My home had been invaded.

"I gotta make this call." I stood at the sliding glass door. "I don't know where this is going to go, but I know I'm not ready."

I hadn't prepared myself for the call. I used Travis to escape my reality. Seeing the police brought many things into perspective that needed reflection. There were a few scenarios that could occur.

"I'm tired—tired," I said, filled with an unexpected tear. "I want it to end. They found the ball." I pouted hard. "I have to handle my business."

What I'd always used as my comforter found its way to my lips. The trip to my lips seemed long, but the wine felt good to me. In the quiet house, I sat drinking, not for the taste of it—for the courage. I wanted to know what my caller had to say. I needed help hearing it.

I became angered. How dare this person have the audacity to call me and to disrespect my home? I carried the wine bottle in one hand and my glass in the other. Three glasses later, I found myself searching for the phone.

My lack of rest had to be the reason the wine had taken such a quick affect on me.

"I'm going to take care of this right now," I slurred, dialing with the Caller ID feature.

"Hello."

"What's up? I'm calling you back." I continued to slur through my words.

"Have you been drinking?"

"Why does it matter, huh?"

"You may want to sleep that off Missy. Meet me at the Savoy tonight."

"What!?!"

"Find yourself some sleep and get down to Roswell Road and Peachtree, no later than ten o'clock. I'm giving you enough time to nap and prepare yourself."

Uncertainty became the name of the game. I had the questions and everyone else had the answers. What I thought I knew was fiction.

The other line beeped, but I didn't have the oomph to answer Travis's call.

"Why do we have to go through all these hoops?" Again I fumbled through my few words.

The caller said nothing. I heard dead silence and then, "If you would like to a make call, please hang up and try your call again."

CHAPTER SIXTY-SIX

I passed out from exhaustion and the wine. An Army tank could've crashed through my front door and I wouldn't have moved. I knew I was tired, but not that tired. Picking myself up from the feathered pillow, I didn't recall walking up the stairs to get into bed.

"Man, I slept hard." I could taste the stale wine in my mouth.

My feet dangled from the bed as I sat on the edge, both of my arms bracing my drained body and mind. Even in the upright position, I felt as if I was sleeping; my eyes remained shut and my head sloped low.

Catching a thought, I said, "Damn, I need to get up."

A chill ran through my body. I didn't know if it was authentic or a spirit speaking to me. Through all I'd done, shame became the leader of my character. To kneel, to ask for Gran's help, wouldn't release itself from me. In my heart, I said a little prayer for God's help, but I knew I wasn't worthy to speak it aloud.

"Let me throw on something and get down to Buckhead. It's already eight thirty-seven," I moaned, stepping onto the floor.

I made my way into a warm shower, to clean away the hot day and hopefully some of the tension. As always, I soaked up as much of the warm water into my pores as I could. The sound of the running water soothed my mind.

It wasn't a night on the town, so I threw on a pair of jeans and a button down, big collar, cream linen shirt. Because of the humidity, I pulled my hair up into a clip and allowed the ends of my hair to fly.

"Out of all the places to meet up, it has to be in busy Buckhead on a Saturday night? This is out of control," I complained, adjusting the radio volume as I drove to my destination.

Travis lent me one of his Mos Def CDs because he wanted me to listen to it. I'd had the CD for some days now and I had yet to give it my attention. Not sure if it would get it tonight.

On low hum I heard the hook of a song:

"Tomorrow may never come . . ."

I reached over to turn it up and caught a snippet of the flow, and what he said tuned me in.

> *". . . For you or me*
> *Life is not promised*
> *Tomorrow may never show up*
> *For you or me*
> *Life is not promised . . ."*

The beat moved me and I tuned in on the words. I drove up I-20 mesmerized by the song as if it spoke directly to me. I knew I had to hold onto the feelings I had for Travis; the days and nights we'd had together. Nothing or no one would take away my world.

The concern of being arrested left me the more I replayed the song. Music has the power to speak to you and it pulled me in, told me to be strong.

As expected, traffic had the streets locked down to a crippling pace. The lights on Peachtree Road lit the night. Buckhead has the magnetism to draw the partygoers. There had been many a night when I had partaken in the mayhem. This wasn't one of them.

"This is getting out of hand." I noticed the non-moving cars. "The light has turned green twice and I've yet to move!"

On beautiful warm nights, the scene reminds me of spring break in Daytona Beach. Everyone trying to get as many numbers as possible and making sure they pump their radio systems as loud as they could possible go to draw attention.

"It's about time," I said impatiently, making it onto Roswell Road.

At the stop sign, a group of young ladies crossed the street in front of me. Pure shock struck me to see one of the women in a pair of hot shorts, to the point I could see her butt cheeks. She struggled to walk in her high heels that were strung up to her knees. Had she been alone, it would've been easy to mistake her as a seller.

As usual, the parking fees were mad. A lot attendant, wanting twenty dollars, had snagged the bank parking lot. That's the number one reason my friends and I stopped frequenting the area: the astronomical parking prices.

"How much to park up in here?" I asked, as I pulled into another lot.

"Ten dollars," said the preppie male lot attendant.

That was the best deal I was going to get all night. Without haste, I pulled into one of the spots to make my claim.

The night air ignited me with energy. I could see the illuminated Savoy sign. As I got closer, I felt empty of emotion. Somehow, eagerness presented itself the closer I got.

With the clear sky and the atmosphere, it surprised me to see the patio empty. I stopped at the entrance to see the bar hadn't filled up.

"Hello, can I see your ID please?" asked the woman at the door.

"Ah, yeah. How much is the cover?"

"It's ladies night, so no cover all night." She handed me back my license.

The Savoy is a quaint spot; nothing too huge, just enough. With the right crowd, the vibe could set the night right. I noticed three people standing at the bar. The cone-shaped lights dispensing from the ceiling brought attention to the person on the far end of the bar.

Sitting on the chrome barstool, the person asked, "Do you want to talk here or in the back room?"

I leaned on the black counter. "It doesn't matter."

"Let's head to the back. There're better seats in there."

We made our way to the back room. It, too, had a bar, but I hadn't come to drink. The room sat empty, except the bartender. We had a choice of any seat we wanted, the leather sofa or the black leather chairs.

"What's going on with you, Erin?" I asked with intrigue, making myself comfortable on the sofa.

"No, don't come in here acting, Maré. It's known, what you did!" She placed her drink on the table.

"What are you talking about? I haven't tried to holla at Ezekiel, if that's what you think." I wanted to play on her insecurities.

Music filled the empty room and the bartender continued to prepare his bar, as if he expected to have a full house.

"I don't have all night with you. I got somewhere to be, so let's get this over with."

"Erin, tell me then. You call me in the AM with the Darth Vader voice," I said, becoming edgy to her temperament.

"Travis. I know all about him and what you did."

"And what exactly is that?"

I sat there with my closest friend and she may have put together her own puzzle, of Travis and me. It escaped me as to why I lacked the fear of what she could know.

"You are tied to the death of that man's wife. I'm not sure if you two plotted it or what. I remember when you came into Taboo talking about him. Yeah, you thought no one heard you, but I did."

CHAPTER SIXTY-SEVEN

I sat up straighter and felt the need for a drink. Where Erin could take this had become more enlightening to me. I blocked out everything and focused on her voice and lips.

"Then you started acting funny. You going long periods of time without calling," she said, taking a sip of her drink.

"I'm not sure what that has to do with anything."

"Oh, I'm not finished. It bothered me, but, hey, who knew what was going on with you? It ties up so smoothly, Missy. Remember when we were at the Shark Bar? Do you?" She shouted loud enough to grab the attention of the bartender.

"Yeah," hesitating to answer.

"Well, you kept your attention on some brother at the bar. Hey, again I didn't know nothing." Erin took a large swig of her drink.

"Erin, we've been friends for, what? Like fifteen years, and you can think the worst of me?" My eyes drooped with sadness.

"Don't give me that. I'm not done. Still nothing added up. We sat there in Club Nocturnal discussing the death of a woman and you got all crazy on Michelle. You did a good job making it her fault. The next day, I read the *AJC*. It gave the names of the victim and her surviving husband. He gave an interview, being that he's an *AJC* employee," she stated, giving a smug look.

Several people trickled into the back room and stopped at the bar. Their laughter disturbed my focus, but not enough to restore my pigmentation. I felt like an albino. I knew she had connected some serious dots. Now what was her plan?

"Erin, I had nothing to do with what you're insinuating," in a plea-filled voice.

"Yes, you do. You put the period to it when you brought him to the café that night. Yeah, that's right. I was like, damn that's the same guy from the Shark Bar and he has the same name of the dude Maré met at the bookstore, some months back."

I could see hurt and anger in her eyes; she didn't know me. I didn't want to hurt her, and for her to put this together put a dagger in my soul.

"Erin, come on! You can't believe something like that. You know me too well to think I could. You have crushed me into two, to hear all of this."

"Let's put it like this. I'm going to the police and let them decide." Erin grabbed her purse and jumped to her feet.

"Erin!" I shouted.

Erin marched out the back room in a fashion that drew attention. I jumped up in hot pursuit. The bartender and the few patrons gave me a weird look. No doubt, they thought we were lovers. How she stormed out and how I shouted her name, we looked like a couple in a squabble.

We were outside in front of the bar before I caught up with her. I knew I needed to calm her down and bring rational closure to her idea of calling the cops.

I stood in her face. "You're trippin'. How can you go to the police on your 'girl'? Oh, you supposed to be Jessica Fletcher and your investigation is true? Why aren't you even asking me?"

"There isn't a need to ask you anything, when everything is right in my face. Maré, I love you, but I can't live with this on my shoulders," she said in a quivering voice, with tears in her eyes. "I have to go, I'm meeting somebody. First thing in the morning, I'm contacting the police!"

"You never were a friend of mine," I shouted, as she walked off. "A true friend wouldn't assume the worst."

Erin made an unexpected stop. "You think this isn't killing me? It is taking the life out of me—every bit."

Erin turned me into a vigilante on the streets of Buckhead. I walked beside her, continuing to plead with her, but she refused to hear me. My medium-sized brown leather purse slipped from my shoulder to my hand.

My arm extended parallel to my body, with purse in hand. Erin was one step ahead of me and refused to acknowledge me. The traffic on the strip had not lost its congestion. She treaded closer to the curb the more I spoke.

The more she ignored me, the more vigilant I felt. Before I knew it, I swung my purse in between her fast strides. Erin's feet became tangled and she lost her footing into the oncoming traffic.

As she fell backwards into the street, she reached for me and my reflexes made me reach for her. The screeching of tires and the impact of metal on metal sounded like a movie theater, filled with surround sound. It was too late, as a Dodge Durango made the first contact of the many vehicles.

Witnessing the tragedy, I went through a form of rigor mortis. The muscles stiffened in my face, hands, and then my feet. The circulation of my blood ceased and I collapsed to the pavement.

The catastrophic turn of events brought the street to a halt. Erin lay out in the street and I was sprawled out on the sidewalk, nearly unconscious. Bystanders provided assistance and called the police.

The sirens blared as they transported me to a hospital. They performed CPR on me, due to my faint heartbeat. It was the first time the entire ordeal affected me to this extreme. In the midst of the transport, my cell phone rang.

"Hello," answered the balding paramedic. "Yes, this is Ms. Alexander's number. We're in the process of taking her to Northside Hospital. I'm not inclined to say. We'll be there shortly."

I awakened later in a bright-lit room, with tubes and IVs stuck in me. My head pounded like a bass drummer determined to find the downbeat. I couldn't lift an inch of my body, not even a finger to scratch my cheek.

"Hello," greeted the smiling, fair skinned nurse. "You gave us a scare. You should have a friend coming to see you soon."

She checked my vitals and made notations on my chart and left the room. I didn't have the capacity to speak. To even think brought pain to my body. A friend coming to see me. Who could it be? Who did she consider a friend?

My eyes faded into a peaceful rest. The beeping of the medical machines placed me into the REM of sleep. I heard a rush of voices and they dispelled before I could lift my eyelids.

"Maré—Maré," whispered a voice.

I felt the touch of a hand as they took hold of mine. I mustered up the strength to see who had come to my side.

"Travis!" I murmured lethargically.

"Shhh, don't say a word," he said in a soft tone, holding my hand. "I'm here and I'm not going anywhere, so just rest. I'm just glad I called your cell when I did. You should never have to be alone."

Tears gushed from my eyes. The reason for my tears couldn't be found. Could they be for what I had done to Erin; for what I'd become; or for keeping my tracks clean? It may have been a combination of them all. Whatever they meant, it felt good to cry it out as Travis wiped my tears away.

Simplicity —be true to yourself . . .

C.F. Jackson

• •

Qty. _____

Price $12.95 U.S.

Subtotal _$_____

Postage/Handling _$_____
($2.95 for 1 book, $1.00 for each additional)

Total Payable: _$_____

Method of Payment

Please do not send cash

☐ Check

☐ Money Order

To order, complete this form and send it along with a check or money order for the above, payable to C.F. Jackson: Post Office Box 920622, Norcross, GA 30010-0622

Name

Address

City and State

Zip/Postal Code

Apartment/ Unit

Phone

Signature

To order online, please visit the following website:

www.cfjackson.us